Maureen,
Happy Fall
2018! Enjoy
reading
little

MW00330815

Kimberly

KIMBERLY DANIELS

EVERNIGHT PUBLISHING ®

www.evernightpublishing.com

Copyright© 2018

Kimberly Daniels

Editor: Audrey Bobak

Cover Artist: Jay Aheer

ISBN: 978-1-77339-666-8

KIMBERLY DANIELS

DEDICATION

To Emily and Natalie. Always remain dreamers, because reality is never as much fun!

ACKNOWLEDGEMENTS

To my husband and two daughters who had to put up with my bad moods from sleepless nights and the many hours away from them, while I locked myself away in my own creative world. Every single word I wrote was and always will be for you.

To Jess Mullen, my former grade partner, beta reader, proofreader, reviewer, and most importantly friend. Words will never be enough for your dedication, support, and advice. Your belief in my story made me believe in myself as a writer. And for that, I owe you my life.

To Evernight Publishing, for giving this story a chance. Your continual support throughout the process has been both professional and friendly, more than I could ask for in a publisher-author relationship.

To my editor, Audrey Bobak at Evernight Publishing, for the most thorough and honest evaluation I could ever imagine. Your critique of my story set it far above what I could ever imagine and for that I truly see you as my partner in this.

To the talented Jay Aheer from Evernight Publishing, who was able to lift my story from its pages through your amazing cover design. When it comes to your work, the only word that comes to mind is "Wow!"

To Sandra Pesso from Evernight Publishing, your promotional and marketing advice guided me through the process with such ease and confidence.

To Nazarea Andrews from Inkslinger, for your organization and guidance through the marketing of this book.

To XPresso Book Tours, for your help and support with the cover release of Lost Until You.

To my beta readers and bloggers, especially those who read it in its infancy four years ago. Your feedback only pushed me to make it the best story it could possibly be.

To all the wonderful and hard-working bloggers and reviewers for encouraging people to read it.

And last and most certainly not least, to my readers who gave a debut author a chance and fell in love with the story. I look forward to sharing so much more with you as this series continues. Thank you for allowing yourselves to get lost in this story. I love you all!

LOST UNTIL YOU

Finding You, 1

Kimberly Daniels

Copyright © 2018

Prologue

Reclining in the chair, I sit frozen, staring intently at the continuous swirls engraved on the ceiling panels that surround the large fluorescent lights. I picture him grasping my hand and kissing the top of my head, assuring me that everything will be okay. He used to always make me feel safe and cherished, like I am the only person that exists in his world.

Rolling my head toward the sound of the nurse's voice, I become even more aware of the loneliness that's crept its way into my life with no sign of leaving. After clearing her throat and repeating my name for what is probably a fourth time, the nurse says, "Miss Singer … Camryn … do you understand?"

I force a slight nod and stare as the nurse exits the room with a smile that radiates pity. With my breaths shortening and lungs constricting, I dash out of the medical building to avoid the impending panic attack.

Outside in the parking lot, I can see him—just waiting. As soon as his aqua-colored eyes meet mine, he begins to walk toward me. I spin around and dart away, only to feel him closing in. Just then, his arms wrap around me and his hands knead at my swollen belly as if he is trying to rip my baby away from me—the baby he never wanted. As I fight to wrestle out of his grasp, I fall to the ground and everything goes black…

"You can't have him!" I yell out as my body jolts awake.

My little boy, who is snuggled up against me, begins to squirm, mumbling out some incoherent words. I hold my breath, hoping he'll find his way back to a sound sleep. I can't bear for him to see the terror that has haunted my nights for the last five years—the fears that began the same day he entered my life.

Once he stills, I pull the stiff sheets back up to his neck and lightly brush the hair from his face. His chest moves up and down with slow, even breaths, and a bit of slobber dribbles down from the corner of his mouth. I lean over and gently kiss the top of his head, relieved that I've somehow kept this nightmare hidden from him.

After climbing out of the bed, I tiptoe across the thin carpet toward the bathroom, in need of a cold splash of water to my face. Maybe it will erase the images, somehow diminish the vision of one day losing my son to the man who abandoned us. But who am I kidding? Tomorrow we'll be home, back to the place that takes everything.

Chapter One
Break Away

I look in the rearview mirror at my half-asleep five-year-old whose normally spiked-up hair is falling over his face in a zillion different directions. Even groggy, he's still such a beautiful boy with sun-kissed skin and oversized teeth that lead a path to his dimples when he smiles. Over the last five years, his looks have reflected our California lifestyle. Through his messy bedhead I can still see those big, beautiful aqua-colored eyes that I can never say no to and would soften me in an instant.

"Right after we cross this bridge, angel, we'll be home-sweet-home."

I give him a cheerful grin in the rearview mirror, trying to cover up my own fears as we approach my hometown, Sea City Island. The shops on the street are starting to show life with neon-colored bathing suits hugging mannequins in store windows and wrought-iron patio furniture covered by canvas umbrellas lining the sidewalks. I stop at an intersection and wave across a group of surfers. They stroll across the street with their wetsuits half-zipped and towing their boards against their hips. Growing up with a mom who coached the sport, I was always told when that very first splash of cold water hits you, relief just streams through your body.

As the last one acknowledges me with a wave, my mind wanders to the many surfers I grew up with while living here. One in particular—Cole Stevens—seems to always find his way back to my mind. I've never forgotten him in the five years I've been away, yet I never really knew him. We only had one encounter in high school, but that one time changed my life. I quietly sigh, thinking that he's probably found his own relief, living that carefree surfer lifestyle somewhere.

After a car horn blares, startling me from my daydream, I start moving toward my destination again. The storefronts disappear and more homes line the streets as we approach the south end of the island. I am overwhelmed by an empty feeling that first appeared five years ago when I made the decision to move across the country to forget my past.

"Do you cross-your-heart promise we'll be there soon?" asks Gavin with a tinge of frustration. "I'm *so* hungry I'm gonna eat my arm."

"I cross-my-heart, pinky swear, and Scout's Honor that we'll be there soon!" I stick my pinky finger into the air, and Gavin claps his hands, applauding my answer.

Although I was forced to grow up much faster than other girls my age, I can never picture my world without Gavin, even though his entrance into it was uncertain and surprising on many levels. When I left here years ago, I was completely broken, but I had Gavin to loosely hold those pieces together. And somehow I've managed to give him the family that he needs and deserves.

"What was that question you asked again … I forget?" I glance back at Gavin with a confused look on my face.

"Aww, Mommy! I said… *Are we there yet?*"

"Close your eyes, count to ten, and we're there!"

Gavin squeezes his eyes closed and starts counting slowly. "One, two, three, four…"

Driving down the beach block doesn't have the same familiarity and warmth it once held since most of the original cape cods and bungalows have been knocked down and replaced by huge monstrosities. These homes are like fishbowls, wrapped in windows with no blinds or curtains. Each house boasts contemporary furniture, fancy chandeliers, and modern décor, and they reek of wealth and coldness, as they probably haven't seen a living person since the previous summer season.

As I pull into the small driveway of my mom's now modest, side-by-side, white duplex, that feeling of loss sets in full force. I never thought I'd return to my childhood home, the one my deadbeat dad had bought. When he decided to run off with one of the ER nurses from the hospital where he was a surgeon, the beach house was the only thing he left us. I think it was only because my mom had been the one to convince him to buy it when her parents died. It had my mom's aged touch all over it, and I doubt that his twenty-something home-wrecker wanted anything to do with it. Besides, she roped my father into buying her a mansion on the beach at the north end, farthest from us.

"All right, buddy … open your eyes!"

"Wow, this is Me-Mom's house? It's so big and there's a shower outside!" Gavin's excitement brings tears to my eyes.

Obviously, this move away from the only home Gavin ever knew is going to be much harder on me. Five-year-olds amaze me at the way they adapt to any situation, and Gavin has had so much more to accept than the average five-year-old.

"We both lived here until you were born. Me-Mom wanted to be near her favorite little man, even if it meant she'd have to surf in the Pacific!"

Gavin giggles, probably remembering the many days my mom would take him surfing and constantly complain that nothing beat the waves on the Atlantic coastline.

The quick change from laughter to cries startles me, as I can see tears streaming down his face. "Mommy, who's gonna teach me to surf here? Me-Mom can't come down from heaven for that."

With a huge lump in my throat, I am left speechless. This is the first time that Gavin has referred to my mom as being gone since her death two months ago. He had watched her suffer for a year as she lost her third bout with breast cancer. But Gavin never showed his sadness in front of her. He would constantly stay by her side coloring, building Legos, and playing Wii with her. However, sometimes, during the night I would hear Gavin pray and ask God to make his Me-Mom better. Even though her decline was affecting Gavin, I didn't want to take away any precious seconds he had left with her. There was no doubt that his presence made her fight for those last two gut-wrenching months of her life.

Trying to calm my broken boy, I turn around to him and say, "Me-Mom has taught practically every person on this island how to surf, so I don't think we're gonna have a problem finding someone to teach you." I watch his tears subside and add, "Besides, I happen to know that Aunt Lila and Uncle Carter are pretty good at the surfing thing too!"

The mention of these two brightens Gavin up in an instant. Lila's been my best friend since we were born, and with me never having a sibling of my own, she fits the role of sister quite well. We were born in the same hospital two days apart, and we were told that we reached out to each other in our nursery cribs. From that day forward, we were inseparable. This was especially true when Lila gave up everything and moved to California with me five years ago. I begged her to stay here and experience all the freedoms of life after high school, but Lila insisted that her dreams would be better served in California with my baby and me. She would always say, "Who better to learn the art of beauty from than celebrity stylists themselves?" So as Lila became a top-notch hair stylist, she helped me raise Gavin, take care of my mom when she became sick again a year and a half ago, and even met her fiancé, Carter, during the time we spent in California.

"Mommy, Uncle Carter's gonna be so surprised when I show him what Me-Mom taught me. I just know it."

I grin and nod at my boy's pride in his surfing abilities.

Carter was an amateur surfer who was going pro until he collided with an underwater jetty and tore ligaments in both ankles. He went on to teach surf lessons and now owns numerous surf shops on the West Coast. He fell in love with Lila during her very first lesson with him, especially when he figured out that Lila didn't even need them since my mom taught her when she was a child. Not surprisingly, Lila didn't have to twist his arm to move back East since he could expand his surf shop empire to the eastern shores.

I turn my body toward Gavin in the back seat. "Well, before Aunt Lila and Uncle Carter get here with the truck, you wanna run in and see your brand-new house ... maybe check out your new bedroom?"

Grinning from ear to ear, highlighting those perfect dimples, Gavin jumps out of his car seat and recites his favorite movie line, "To infinity and beyond!"

We race each other around the side of our house and over our rock-covered yard. I let Gavin get two steps in front of me as we climb the four wooden stairs that lead to our lower porch and front door.

Jumping up and down, he gleefuly yells, "I won, I won ... champion of the universe!"

"Next time, I'll getcha, buddy!" I lean down squeezing his cheeks, and plant a kiss right on his nose.

"No way, Mommy!"

Unlocking the door and entering into the next era of our life together is bittersweet for me. The smell of salty air mixed with fresh paint embraces me as I creep into the tiled hallway. The house still exudes the sense of comfort that my mom achieved with her palette of warm colors and rustic décor displayed throughout. All of my memorable childhood moments still linger in the air, assuring me that Gavin will be able to create his very own. But we will be living them without my mom, who was the most positive force in both of our lives.

Gavin screeches loudly when we walk in, "Mommy! Our house is upside down! My bedroom fell down!"

"Gav, the house is supposed to be like this. The bedrooms are downstairs, and the rest is up there." I point toward the stairwell.

"Oh. That's so cool!" he exclaims while jumping up and down.

"Hmmmm, let me think ... which bedroom is yours? Maybe it's that one with pink walls, your favorite color!"

"Eww, Mommy, no! Pink is for girls!"

"Well, Gav, that means there are only two more chances to find your bedroom. Which door will it be?"

"I think it's this one, right in the middle." Gavin throws the door open, gasping as he jumps up and down. "It's the best room I've ever seen! I'm never leaving this place ... *ever*!"

I stare in awe at what my mom had done to Gavin's room. Trying to fight the tears that begin to stream down my face, I gaze at everything in the room that represents him. The walls are painted dark blue with various framed pictures of surfers riding huge waves. My mom gave in to Gavin's constant begging for a bunk bed with one that has surfboards as the head and footboards. The other wall has a small flat-screen television with two gaming chairs placed in front of it. Next to the closet is a small desk and hutch that houses shells we collected in California, surfboard wax, favorite books, and framed pictures of Gavin with his family and friends. She even framed a picture of his very first surfing lesson with her. However, my eyes refuse to budge from one picture: it's of me sitting on Gavin's father's lap in a lifeguard stand. As much as my mom disagreed with Todd, she always tried to keep him a part of Gavin's life. She believed that he should know where he came from and that he was created through love, even though his father chose not to be a part of his life. Her understanding always amazed me, even though she lived through the pain that both my father and Todd brought to our lives.

"Mommy, did ya see this? Me-Mom bought me my own surfboard!" Gavin yells from his closet where he found the shiny, new surfboard leaning against the wall.

"No way she was letting you come here without a brand-new, shiny board, you lucky duck!"

My son's excitement and the idea that my mom managed to still spoil him brings a smile to my lips and a sense of relief that I haven't felt since our trek across the country began last week. As I leave Gavin in his surfer's palace, I explore the rest of the house, discovering all the little surprises left by my mom. Walking up the steep stairwell that opens to the living area of the house, I examine the gallery of pictures that began in my childhood and lead up to Gavin's fifth birthday two months ago, right before her death. I knew that my mom would return each summer to visit old friends and keep the house up and running, but I had no idea the extent to which she was making the house Gavin's and mine. I wipe another tear from my cheek and continue up the stairs, walking directly into the open kitchen decorated with shells and pictures of beach scenes. Off to the right of the island counter is a spacious family room that has a flat screen above the stone fireplace and a sectional couch with my mom's favorite blanket that is monogrammed with Asian symbols for strength, tranquility, and peace draped over the corner. Within a windowed nook is a wooden toy box filled with Gavin's favorites. Sliding glass doors lead outside to a large deck that has a breathtaking view of an old wooden pier jutting out into the vast Atlantic Ocean. I take a few minutes to appreciate the beauty our home has to offer. Yet beauty of the familiar scenery only helps the painful memories of past reemerge.

When I walk back in, Gavin has already discovered his toy bin and is knee-deep in all of the brand-new toys my mom had stuffed in it. As he looks up at me with a grin that travels from one ear to the other, I tuck my loss deep within me where I hope Gavin will never find it. I know it's time to cut the safety net I have weaved for us the last five years. Gavin is exactly where he needs to be because my mom's spirit is still very much alive here, and she always believed coming back to where we had lost everything will help us find what we need.

Chapter Two
Home

"Gav, there's someone here. Betcha can't guess who it is!" Yelling to Gavin inside the house, I stand on our front porch, watching Carter pretend to know how to back the U-Haul into the small space next to my four-door Accord.

All I can hear is Lila's high-pitched voice. "Carter! Your ass is mine if you hit Cam's car!"

"If that's a promise, babe, then maybe Camryn wouldn't mind a little dent in her trunk. There's plenty of room in the back of the U-Haul, if ya know what I mean!"

"You're crazy if you think I'm getting naked with you in a box truck! You know I'm a tractor-trailer kind of girl!"

Just shaking my head at the playful banter between them, I watch as the truck is finally parked. Carter jumps out first. His looks scream "California Coast" with messy, blond, spiked hair, naturally dark-toned skin, and crystal-blue eyes. He covered his long torso with a graphic t-shirt that hugs his thin frame, and his board shorts, a staple item in his wardrobe, accents his muscular legs. He's the epitome of a laid-back "surfer dude," and nothing ever fazes him. I never once heard him raise his voice to Lila, and that alone is an accomplishment. He opens up the passenger door and lifts Lila over his shoulder, swinging her around in circles and teasingly smacking her ass.

"Carter James Benson, put me down right now!" I imagine that the squeals from Lila are all you can hear for blocks. "Sex ban in effect if you don't stop!"

Hearing Lila's threat, Carter places her down quickly and proceeds to grab her hips and drags them into him. "You'd never punish me like that, sweet lips. You love my tongue, among other things, a little too much. At least that's what I heard you scream last night!"

As I cough loudly after Carter's explicit bedroom talk, they both turn quickly to see me standing on the front porch, staring wide-eyed at them.

"Could you bring it down to G-rated when you're at my house? Little ears live with me." Not waiting for me to get an answer, Gavin flies out from behind and runs straight for Lila and Carter.

"Uncle Carter, Aunt Lila, Me-Mom bought me a surfboard! Now I can catch waves with you!" Gavin jumps into a surfer stance, rocking back and forth, pretending to ride a wave.

Carter, obviously being the one who made the board for Gavin, acts surprised about this gift from my mom. "No way, dude! You gotta show me it."

He scoops up Gavin in his arms, and they run into the house toward Gavin's room.

Lila makes her way up to the porch and gives me a long hug. Without her saying a word, I know Lila's asking how I'm handling my return to the origin of my heartbreak. I just squeeze her tighter, silently assuring her that I'll be okay. Stepping back and looking at my best friend, I can't help but notice how opposite we are physically, yet mentally and emotionally we are perfectly synced.

Lila is model tall and thin with an exceptionally large but surprisingly natural chest. Her blonde hair that accents her yellowish-green eyes is cut in an asymmetrical bob that's longer in the front around her face. Currently, she has a few red highlights strategically placed to frame her face, but those change almost daily. A vision of beauty, and I always thought she would land in the spotlight, but she preferred to work behind the scenes, making others beautiful. In California, she worked as a private stylist who would go to the homes of celebrities. Within the last year, she had moved her career to a more public setting as head stylist on movie sets. She wasn't doing the work but rather telling other stylists how to do it. I never imagined she would want to leave the lifestyle of the rich and famous, but when I told her I was moving home, she jumped at the chance to escape the hustle and bustle of Los Angeles to open her own salon and spa in our hometown.

I pull out of our embrace and place my arm around Lila's shoulder. "Let's go in. I'll show you what my mom did with the place."

"No doubt in my mind that Milena made it perfect and will be haunting you on a daily basis to make sure you don't screw it up."

I laugh, realizing that Lila is exactly right. My mom had a plan for everything and if you knew her, you did not dare interfere. It was my mom's world, and we just lived in it. I'd missed that world each day since she died, and I knew in this house we could still have a slice of it.

When we walk upstairs, Gavin and Carter are playing Avengers in the family room. Carter, wearing Hulk hands and mask, is running around the family room with Gavin, a mini Captain America. Lila and I giggle as we watch Gavin pretend to slay the couch pillows, with Carter assisting him as he tackles them to the ground. I guess boys never really grow out of this stage in life, but I am grateful Gavin has Carter. Only women had surrounded my baby boy for his first few years of life, and having a strong male presence around opens Gavin up to a different side of thinking. I know I will especially need Carter's male guidance as Gavin enters his teenage years, a prospect that frightens the hell out of me.

"You'll never beat Captain America!" Gavin hollers as he jumps up and down on the pillows.

"The Hulk and Captain America win!" Carter raises his hands in the air, claiming victory.

"Uncle Carter, can we play again? I can be Hulk this time!"

I interrupt their pretend fun. "Uh, Captain America and Hulk, you better unpack the truck or I'm going Wolverine on both of you!" With that announcement, Carter and Gavin move at lightning speed.

The four of us spend the afternoon settling into the house and reminiscing about growing up in Sea City, which makes Carter seriously consider our sanity. Lila and I tell him about scaring tourists off the beach with fake reports of shark attacks, inviting people we hated to secret bonfire parties on the bay beach and then calling the cops on them, and the many nights sneaking out for the lifeguard parties and drunk biking home. Despite the grief this place has brought to my life, I would never trade in those crazy moments we experienced together just to erase the pain of abandonment from my father and Todd.

After eating dinner, Gavin curls up on the couch and fell asleep, still exhausted from our cross-country trip. Carter and Lila are getting ready to leave and unpack their portion of the truck at their own house. They decided to buy closer to town since both of their businesses were located there. Even though it's just a three-minute ride from the south end to town, it feels like they would be living light-years away. While in California, Lila lived with us until her relationship got serious with Carter, and then they rented a place right next door.

"How'd you get Gavin surf lessons so quickly?"

Lila asks me.

I give her a telling smirk. "Well, now how do you think?"

She tilts her head back laughing. "Milena has struck again! I should've known that she'd never let you choose. "

"Yeah, she left some messages for me on the corkboard in the kitchen: surf instructor, school for Gavin, my job—you know, the basics. I think she'll be haunting me for quite a while."

Carter, looking a bit spooked, interjects, "But you gotta love Milena. She's my kind of woman ... gets what she wants!"

Shaking my head at Carter, I push him out the door. "Lila, take him home and christen your new house or something!"

Lila grabs Carter's shirt and drags him out the door.

"Hell yeah, Cam! You have always been my favorite of Lila's friends. Thanks for helping a brother out!

"She's my only friend, genius. Let's get your horny ass home!" Lila throws her hand up for a quick wave as she pulls her man to the truck.

I wave from the porch, watching the U-Haul disappear down the dark beach road, knowing that my two greatest friends will never feel the same loss as me as long as they are together. I'm not envious of what they have. I'm just grateful they've made room for Gavin and me in their lives. But I know I'll need to find my own satisfaction in life, and my mom seemed so sure that whatever it is that I need can only be found here.

I close my eyes tightly and whisper, "Mom, maybe you could give me some hints along the way. I need the strength to move on without you here and not feel so … alone."

I sigh, knowing that loneliness awaits me behind my front door. Although grateful for the strong feeling of my mom's presence with us, I still feel broken without her. My life seems defined by losing those I love, and others who I thought loved me. That never-ending fear of loss continues to taunt me in my sleep as I watch Gavin being taken from me over and over again. Those nightmares will return tonight, of that I am sure. But how intense will they be now that I am back to the place that holds the one person who validates my fears? There's always a niggling thought in the back of my head, that even though Todd didn't want anything to do with Gavin when I got pregnant, he could change his mind as soon as Todd sees him for the first time.

Chapter Three
You Had Me from Hello

Beep, Beep, Beep, Beep, Beep

The horrid sound of six AM enters my heavenly, king-sized bed. The excess of pillows is perfect for beaming directly at the evil machine spewing that horrendous noise. Sleep finally found me in the early hours of morning. I spent most of my first night home reliving the recurring nightmare that has haunted me for five years—the one of Todd chasing me in the parking lot, trying to take away my unborn baby. However, last night Todd didn't just catch me but rather took Gavin from me and brought him to the first man in my life who left me high and dry—my father. I woke up in a cold sweat when I saw my father running away with my baby in his arms, and was unable to reach him. After that, I spent the night in and out of Gavin's room, watching him sleep safely in his bed.

Losing Gavin would be something I could never handle, and that's the reason I didn't demand anything from Todd or his family. Moving across the country helped to solidify that distance between us, and after a few years, I felt confident that Todd would never come looking for him.

With my head still wrapped under my duvet-covered down comforter, I hear a faint pitter-patter of feet down the tile hallway coming straight into my room. "Mommy, wake up. It's time to surf!" Gavin is practically crowing across my room.

I peek out from under the dark abyss of blankets to see a bright-eyed boy with a serious case of bedhead, smiling so wide I can see all of his teeth.

"All right, all right. I'm getting up. Get your surfboard, and…" I pause, staring at my boy who is already wearing his new wet suit.

"All ready, Mommy! Your turn!" Gavin giggles.

Never wanting to disappoint him, I groggily stumble out of bed and turn the shower on cold, hoping for a quick wake-up call. Once life finally finds my body again, I put my bikini on underneath a pair of ripped jean shorts and throw a tight tank over the bathing suit top. I let my hair hang down my back in soft waves and apply a little bit of waterproof eyeliner and mascara to my dark eyes to hide the evidence of my sleepless night.

I want to spend as much time as I can with Gavin before I start my job, which of course my mom set up for me. It's a nursing position at Shore Memorial Hospital, the place she worked while living here. She was there for so long that she practically owned the place, and even being away for five years, it seemed that she still had clout, as she continually placed people in positions there. I was no exception, as she left a number on the corkboard to call. After my phone call with the head nurse, I found out my mom secured me a maternity floor position that required only three twelve-hour shifts per week. That ensured that I would have plenty of time with Gavin, and I wouldn't be putting Lila or Carter out too much with babysitting. However, knowing those two, they would be occupying more of Gavin's time than I needed from them.

Staring at my beautiful blue-eyed boy slurping his milk from his Cheerios, I start to ramble out instructions to him.

"Gav, you know that you need to pay attention to your instructor at all times, never paddle away when you're not supposed to, and don't try anything too fancy."

In the midst of my nagging, Gavin looks into his bowl, rolls his eyes, and huffs. "I know, Mommy.

'Member? I did this before."

"Hey, mister, lose the 'tude." I stare wide-eyed at my five-year-old.

With slumped shoulders and a pouty face, he mumbles, "Sorry, Mommy."

I nod and reach my hand out to him. "All right, big boy, let's head out. I'm sure Me-Mom got you the best instructor in New Jersey."

Hand-in-hand, we walk down the steps of our back deck onto the cool, soft sand of the morning. To get to the beach, we only have a short walk. The south end beaches remain quiet even as we approach the upcoming Memorial Day weekend. As we shuffle through the sand, I watch Gavin take in all the sights and sounds of what feels like our own private beach, especially compared to those in California, where people swarmed at all hours of the day. We stop to watch a shoreline fisherman reel in a small dogfish and then a feisty seagull try to pry it from the hook. That received a serious belly laugh from Gavin, which, in turn, gives me the giggles. We run and splash each other with the brisk ocean water that tumbles quietly onto the shoreline. Just as I turn around to pelt Gavin with a very large, curly mass of seaweed, my body slams into something very hard, causing me to fall backward into the wet, cold sand.

As Gavin roars with laughter, I look up to a long, muscular arm reaching out to help me. As the hand of the stranger reaches mine, I am pulled up with ease to unbelievable, sky-blue eyes outlined by endless lashes that seem to curl over the tops of his eyelids. The alluring squint of his eyes captures me the instant we make contact with each other. The definition of his cheekbones rising with his smile highlights his perfectly straight teeth. His lower lip is slightly fuller than his upper lip, creating the most perfect bow shape. My gaze travels up to the messy spike of his sandy-blond hair, tempting my hands to run through it. I have to take a step back to get my bearings.

I squint behind my sunglasses, inspecting this guy who looks so very familiar but I can't seem to place, and I stutter, "I… I'm sorry. I didn't mean to walk right into you. Just having some fun with my son and wasn't paying attention to where I was going and…" *Stop rambling, Camryn.* "Well, I'm just sorry." My words sputter out of me at an uncontrollable speed.

Shaking his head, he leans in and says, "No problem at all. I saw you walking this way." He gives me a quick wink and backs up a bit. Extending his hand to me, he says, "Cole Stevens."

With a slight gasp, my gaze jumps back and forth between his extended hand to his eyes while the recognition sets in. As I'm face-to-face with the one guy from my past who still finds his way into my thoughts, my head is spinning, my mind flooded with a thousand questions. Is it really him? Does he remember me? Could he possibly know what he once did for me? With my heart pounding through my chest, I attempt to construct a greeting back. "You mean the Cole Stevens who once saved my teenage life?" or maybe, "We only spoke to each other once, but do you know you're the one person who made me feel normal again?" Realizing those would make me sound certifiably insane, I come up with, "Umm … the Cole who's supposed to be Gavin Singer's surf instructor?"

With a knowing grin, he answers, "Yeah, that's me. So I assume that little man behind you, who's laughing uncontrolably at your inability to walk backward, is Gavin?"

Blushing in embarrassment, I nod to him and stutter out, "Uhhh … yes … this is Gavin … um, my son."

I quickly bend down to Gavin's level and say to him, "Buddy, this is your new surf coach, Cole. Can you say hi?"

"Hi." Gavin flashes a timid wave to his new coach and ducks behind my body.

Bringing my attention back to the godlike man towering over me, I can't help but notice a large tattoo peeking out of his shirt, taunting me to rip off his sleeve to get a closer look. Getting a glimpse of the rest of his body is tempting, as there is no mistaking the muscular definition of his chest and abs, hugged by a very form-fitting wet suit.

Cole bends down and extends his hand to Gavin, speaking in a kid-friendly tone. "Hey, dude! You ready to catch some waves today?"

Forgetting his previously shy greeting, Gavin starts jumping up and down and furiously claps his hands together. "Hell yeah!"

My eyes widen, and my mouth drops. "Gavin Michael Singer ... I did not teach you to talk like that! Don't ever say that again, or you'll be in big trouble."

"But, Mommy ... Aunt Lila says bad words. And I told her I would say it to you if she gave me five dollars. Now, I'm rich!"

Between Gavin's howls of laughter and Cole's insanely sexy smirk, it is impossible to convey my anger at my five-year-old's ability to hustle his own mom. Turning away from them, shaking my head, I move my way up to the soft, dry sand to spread my blanket out.

Just as Cole's lesson with Gavin begins, I remove my jean shorts and tank top and make myself comfortable on my blanket. I position myself so I have full view of Gavin with his stomach on his surfboard and his short arms feverishly moving in a circular motion as they dip in and out of the water. My attention wanders over to Cole, who is holding the board still while Gavin is practicing how to paddle. I stare in awe at how his upper back muscles lead down to a slender waist, giving way to the most perfectly shaped ass I've ever seen. He's definitely bulked up over the years. Although his long legs are immersed in the calm waves of the ocean, I know from growing up with a mom who trained in the sport that Cole most likely has amazing, toned legs that bulge muscles in places that I didn't know even existed.

Just as I'm gawking at this beautiful male specimen, I feel two eyes searing into me, knowing at that moment I am caught. Quickly bringing my eyes up to his, I see Cole grinning at me lazily, his expression lustful. Flushing red, I grab my oversized sunglasses and lie back on my towel. I will have to scold my leering eyes later or just get used to wearing dark-tinted sunglasses at all times around him.

Noticing the many different surf instructors populating the beach, I begin to reminisce about my mom when I feel cold drips falling onto my sun-soaked back. "Mommy, Mommy! Cole taught me how to stand up on my board! And I did it by myself! Can you believe it?"

"It was amazing, Gav!" I find myself fibbing to my son since I was actually zoning during his monumental move. "You're gonna go pro soon and leave me all alone." I stick my bottom lip out, pretending to pout.

Gavin reaches his arm across my shoulders and comforts me. "Mommy, I'd never leave you alone. You're the only girl that's not gross!"

Just as Gavin pretends to spit at the thought of other girls, a shirtless Cole comes and sits down in the sand next to me, his smooth, taut chest drawing my eyes in his direction again. I work my way up his body and stop to study the tattoo, which is now in plain sight. It's the image of a broken heart with a pink rose woven through the cracks and crevices. Because it's not the typical tribal band or koi fish that surfers usually sport on their bodies, I figure it has significant meaning and it isn't just an eighteen-year-old's drunken whim, like the star Lila had sketched on her toe. Examining the way his muscles bulge where the ink meets his skin, I wonder what, or who, it represents, and why he chose that particular image. Snapping myself out of the this new staring habit, I realize I will really have to train my eyes to stay put above his shoulders, or maybe just gouging them out of my head will be an easier solution to my newfound problem.

Cole, smirking at me gawking again, says, "You know, he's really good for his age. He has no fear of the ocean or being on the board."

I look over at Gavin, who is now busy digging for crabs in the wet sand, with a proud smile. "He had a great teacher before you. I think he learned to stand on a board before he took his first steps." I start to well up at the thought of my mom.

"Well, Milena was, no doubt, the best out there." Cole nods to me just as my mouth falls open.

"You knew ... how'd you know my mom?"

With his sparkling eyes glistening at me, he matter-of-factly states, "I only learned to surf from the best. Plus, she landed me this summer gig a few years back."

I nervously laugh and say, "Should've known my mom would set Gavin up with one of her own."

Cole winks at me, stands up, and runs down to Gavin, grabbing him and pretending to throw him in the ocean. Gavin laughs with glee, and I just stare at Cole, forgetting how small of a town this is.

Gavin and I spend the morning on the beach making sand pancakes, digging New Jersey's deepest hole, and playing an exhausting game of paddle ball where the rubber ball keeps rolling by me each time he hit it. In between his surf lessons, Cole would join us to help dig or chase our ball. Gavin is more than thrilled to invite him into our beach fun, and I'm impressed how comfortably Cole interacts with my five-year-old.

Later, I begin to focus on Cole, thinking about what he's been doing for the last five years, wondering if he has found some peace since the turmoil he faced in high school. I catch him peeking over at me many times, causing my heart to skip a beat, but, luckily, my dark sunglasses hide any acknowledgement of his gazes.

Breaking me from my thoughts, I hear, "Mommy, can we play football, puhlease?" Before he waits for my answer, Gavin looks over to Cole. "You want to play too, Cole? Mommy's pretty good … for a girl."

Laughing at Gavin's comment, Cole replies, "Of course I want to play with you and your mommy." He looks in my direction with a seductive glance.

Before Cole can notice my flushed cheeks, I grab the ball out of Gavin's hands and run straight toward the water with them chasing close behind. Cole and I throw the ball to Gavin and then run up and tackle him in the water. He giggles so hard that he needs help to stand up. Right as I'm about to reach around Gavin and tackle him into the water again, I feel two strong arms grab my waist and drag me down first. I land with my legs tangled in Cole's feet and my eyes stare into his, which are sparkling from the reflection of the water. He leans in close and stops right before he reaches my lips.

"Let me take you out to dinner." His demand sounds more like a question.

My mouth slightly opens, and my breathing becomes quick with his close proximity to me.

"Umm... Sorry, I shouldn't." I shrug, looking directly at Gavin.

He pulls my chin up to his face so that I stare directly into those spellbinding eyes, leans into me, and huskily whispers, "Don't worry, it's not a one-time offer." He smirks and backs away.

My mouth parts to respond, but speech fails me. It feels like my cheeks are on fire, but I can't seem to turn away from his searing stare. What startles me even more is that I don't want to take my eyes off him. I want to freeze time so I can revel in the closeness of our bodies.

Gavin grabs the floating football and reaches his hand to me to help me out of the water.

"Mommy, that was so funny! Cole tackled you like a real football player!" He laughs and then goes over to Cole to give him a high five.

"Gavin! You little traitor!"

I run over and grab him, tackling him into the water. Cole follows and pulls me down again right next to Gavin, but this time I hook my leg around his knee and bring him down with me. We all are laughing uncontrollably when we hear the few people on the beach clapping at our spectacle. Gavin stands up and takes a bow for the crowd, which gains him a few louder cheers and whistles. In the midst of my laughter, I look over to Cole and lip, "Thank you." He nods to me and grabs my hand to help me back to my feet. It's the first time I feel a bit of weight lift since my mom passed.

I look over at my smiley, wet son and say, "All right, Gav, time to go home. Aunt Lila and Uncle Carter are coming over for dinner, and you need a bath, smelly boy."

"Awww, Mommy, can Cole come too? Pretty puhlease?"

Startled by Gavin's quick connection to him, I stutter, "Um … Gav … um … I'm sure Cole already has plans."

I quickly turn toward Cole and shrug, slightly embarrassed by my son's forwardness. But Cole has a huge smile plastered on his face.

"Gavin, I'd love to join you and your mom for dinner tonight." He turns to me and continues, "I'm also pretty good with dessert." He winks and gives me the most seductive half-smirk that makes me want to jump his bones right there.

While Gavin is already doing a football-end-zone victory dance, celebrating Cole's coming to dinner, my mind scolds my mouth for not shutting the plan down immediately. The idea that this can technically be classified as a date is very unsettling.

"Dessert sounds great. Thanks. Then I guess it's a date … err, I mean dinner."

Cole grins, clearly amused by my flustered response.

Trying to avoid any more unintentional invitations, I start to pack up our beach items. "Gav, let's get home. You know what would happen if we leave Aunt Lila and Uncle Carter in the kitchen for too long?"

"Yeah, our house would burn down!" he exclaims cheerfully.

I tuck my arm around him and start leading him away. I turn to Cole with gratitude for making my son's day. "Thanks for coming. I'm sorry if he put you on the spot. However, now he may never leave you alone."

Cole's eyes sparkle. "No worries, Camryn. I want to come."

Feeling my cheeks flush for yet another time

today, I begin to walk back toward our house, grasping the beach toys in my hand. I remind myself to wear extra toner tonight to hide any more instances of red cheeks. Cole grabs Gavin's surfboard and reaches for his hand, and the three of us walk together.

When we reach the pathway that connects our duplex to the beach, I turn to Cole. "You didn't have to come with us this far. Hope you're not too out of your way."

A wide grin appears on his face. "Nope, I'm exactly where I need to be."

I give him a confused look as he hands Gavin his board and whispers something into his ear that causes my son's mouth to drop in surprise. Cole sprints toward the stairs of the wooden deck that is connected to ours, climbs them and then slides open the glass doors. He turns around and gives us a quick wave.

"See you both in a bit. Don't forget, I'll bring dessert." With that, he flashes what must be his sexiest smile.

I stand frozen with my mouth wide open. *Oh my God, he's my neighbor!*

Gavin is jumping up down chanting, "Cole lives here, Cole lives here!"

I watch my ecstatic son dance and just shake my head in disbelief. This could be very interesting. At that moment, I peer up to the sky and wonder if my mom somehow knew what Cole Stevens had once done for me.

Chapter Four
Crashing Down

It sounds like my cabinets are smashing to the floor as I frantically tear through the kitchen. Gavin's head twists back and forth, watching me search for pots and dishes and gather ingredients to prepare for our company. I'm relieved Carter is planning to grill because I think I could burn the house down in this instance. I eye the bottle of wine on the counter and pour myself a glass to get my nerves in check, and then slump on the couch with Gavin to watch *Batman Begins*. Maybe a little Christian Bale will help me forget the impending desire to vomit that is welling inside my stomach.

Gavin inspects me with confused eyes.

"Mommy, what's wrong?" Looking down at my hand, he continues, "You're drinking mommy juice again."

My eyes focus on my half-empty glass of Pinot Grigio and back to him. "Gav, I always drink wine." I shimmy closer to him. "What's your worry, buddy?"

Gavin looks down to his hands, and he starts to massage his knuckles over and over—a nervous tendency of his. When his eyes meet mine, I notice fear in his normally sparkly blue eyes.

"Gav, what is it, sweetie? It's okay. You know you can tell me anything."

Tears start to form, and his body begins to tremble. "Mommy, after Me-Mom died, you and Aunt Lila drank a lot of that stuff and then you would cry. It was scary."

With vivid memories of that horrid day flooding my mind, I yank Gavin in close to me, patting his faux hawk. I want to assure him that I'm okay, that I'm only acting like a crazed lunatic because I haven't been with a man, let alone been at the same dinner table with man, aside from Carter, in years. However he's too young to understand this and all he sees is his mom on the verge of a breakdown. At that second, I feel so selfish because I never stopped to consider how my vulnerable five-year-old was coping with our loss. I reach over and pull him to me. This is the very reason why I uprooted my entire life after Todd left in the first place. I have to protect my baby.

With tears dripping into Gavin's hair, I console him, "Oh, angel, I'll always keep you safe." I pull his face up to meet mine and continue, "You never have to be scared when you're with me."

He hugs me tighter and nods his head in understanding. "I love you, Mommy!"

"Well, I love you the mostest."

I embrace my son as we watch Batman fight evil in Gotham City. Gavin is my first priority, and whatever feelings Cole stirred up in me have to be extinguished until I know Gavin can handle it.

Just as the Batman symbol flashes across our television screen, I peek up to see a very concerned Lila and Carter watching me clutch my red-faced little boy. Lila orders me downstairs to my bedroom, and Carter tries to cheer up Gavin with their secret handshake. It manages to get a small giggle out of him, and I am grateful for their timing.

Lila sits me down on my vanity chair and starts brushing through my long hair and blotting my eyes with cold cream. She speaks to me through the reflection in the mirror.

"All right, Cams, spill it. Why the breakdown with Gavvy? Does it have anything to do with the heart-stopping guy you texted me about earlier?"

I stare and nod at her reflection in the mirror.

"Gav thinks when I drink wine it makes me cry, and he saw me drinking a glass and got upset."

"And let me guess … you were also acting like a crazy woman because hot-bod surf instructor slash neighbor is coming over?" She leans in closer, making me feel like I'm under interrogation.

With my gaze sinking to the floor, I mumble out, "He's not just Gav's surf instructor and our new neighbor." I watch Lila's feet inch closer to me and I can feel her eyes searing right through me, waiting for my latest reveal. Hesitantly, I whisper, "It's him, Li. The one from that day I stormed out of the cafeteria." I slowly lift my eyes to her, embarrassed by this connection I've felt since that day in high school. "It's Cole Stevens and I'm literally freaking out about it."

Lila's eyes widen and she blurts out, "Cam, what's there to freak out about? I'd say this is your second chance, and it was pretty much hand-delivered right to you."

I shake my head. "Oh Li… I'm such a mess. I'm seriously losing it. I mean, we met guys in California and not one of them affected me like this. If anything, they turned me off."

I dated a handful of times during the first few years we were away but never allowed myself to form any kind of bond with any guy. A couple of times, I gave into my needs and slept with them, but it was always the type of sex where I found myself doing my grocery list as I was going through the motions—detached and unemotional. And when my mom became sick again, all of the dating and mind-numbing sex ended all together.

Lila walks around the chair to face me. "Cam, you're allowed to find guys attractive. Hell, you can fuck them if you want," Lila blurts while she applies more makeup to my face . "And maybe this blast from your past is your way to that."

"Do you know who you're talking to, Li? You know, the one who has absolutely no experience with this. While I mastered the art of diapering, other girls our age were mastering the art of bed hopping." I playfully joke about my own lack of skill with men.

"All I'm trying to say is just because you have Gav and life dealt you a bad hand with the past men in your life, doesn't mean you have to become some born-again virgin." Lila sweeps a makeup brush across my face to cover my any more blotchiness.

Turning more serious, I add, "Li, it's not just me anymore, and I don't ever want him to know what it feels like to not be wanted." I grab the wrist that is brushing toner across my cheeks. "I don't ever want him to feel broken."

"You running away from every man that shows the slightest bit of interest isn't gonna stop life from disappointing him. You're an amazing mom who is adored by your son. That will get him through anything. Besides, Carter and I will beat the shit out of anyone who tries to hurt that kid!"

I wrap my arms around my best friend while her honesty sinks into my racing thoughts. She's lived through all my lows with me, which used to be daily right after Todd walked out. They all began to skim through my mind, as if I'm viewing a slideshow of my past. I see the day we got wasted from tequila and smashed every bottle from my father's overly-priced Scotch stash after he left with his floozy. Then there's the day she picked me up off the ground of the parking lot where Todd left me pregnant and alone. I remember her exaggerated breathing noises in the labor room when it took me twenty hours to bring Gavin into the world. And I could never forget the endless hours she spent helping me sponge-bathe and spoon-feed my mom during those last months of her life.

Trying to lighten the mood in the way that only Lila knows best, she interrupts my sentimental trip down memory lane. "Besides, you're too sexy a bitch to waste on never sleeping with a guy again!"

With an unattractive snort, I examine myself in the mirror. "Without you, my ass would never look this hot!"

I'm amazed how quickly Lila turned me into something presentable. The puffy eyes and blotchy skin are no longer evident. She gave my eyes a smoky look that brings some spark back into them, even though everlasting loss would always be there if someone looked hard enough. Lila straightened my hair so it falls in the middle of my back with my long front layer parted to the side and tucked behind my ear. She picked out some cropped skinny jeans and paired them with a floaty halter-top.

I throw on a pair of wedge sandals and link my arm through my best friend's elbow as we head back upstairs together. Peeking out the door, I see Gavin swinging his light saber like Luke Skywalker and am once again thankful that Carter is able to turn Gavin back into my smiley, playful boy. As Lila and I walk through the sliding glass door, I nearly bump into her as she stops in her tracks.

"Holy shit, Cam! I think referring to him as Hot-Bod is an understatement?" Lila is talking so that I can only hear her, but she is looking straight at the person Gavin is dueling. "That boy is some fine eye candy if I say so myself."

I roll my eyes and cough out a small laugh. "You seriously have issues."

Lila speaks out of the side of her mouth so she

won't have to take her eyes off Cole. "Uhh … maybe. But he's come a long way since he was the tall and lanky surf team captain, who dated some whacked-out blonde bitch, and would beat the shit out of … well everyone."

My eyes lock with Cole's just as a green light saber juts into his gut, and he quickly turns his attention back to Gavin as he sinks to his knees, pretending to die a painful death. While Gavin is celebrating his victory over "Darth Vader," Carter yells over to me.

"Cam, if you told me you invited my landlord to dinner, I would've brought my rent check!"

My mouth drops open while Cole and Carter just look at each other and start laughing. When I'm finally able to formulate sounds together, I look at Carter and ask, "What do you mean? You two already know each other?"

Cole explains, "I own some real estate here, and it just so happens I own the place where Carter's got his shop. We met when he signed the lease papers, but your mom set everything up from day one."

"So you're my neighbor, a surf coach, and a business owner? Any other surprises you want to reveal tonight?"

"Don't worry, I have a few more tucked away." He winks at me and I feel the heat emulate through my cheeks.

I struggle to form a cohesive thought, let alone string together any sensible words. No amount of toner could have been able to hide the crimson blanketing my entire face. Cole has sex appeal written all over him, and I am falling prey to it. My thoughts begin to wander underneath his low-hanging jeans and fitted black V-neck that hugs his chest and arms in all the right places.

Shaking my head of dirty thoughts, I look to Carter, then to Lila, who is still gawking. "Well, I guess, then, there's no need for introductions."

Just then, I hear Lila clear her throat as she approaches Cole and throws her arm out. "I'm Lila … Cam's bestie, Carter's hottie, and Gavin's auntie." She proudly smiles as she sees Cole's amused expression.

He reaches for her hand and replies, "I'm Cole … Gavin's instructor, Carter's landlord, and Camryn's … well, ask me that in a few weeks, and I'm sure I'll have an answer." His charming grin appears as he eyes my reaction to him.

Oh shit, I'm in trouble. He is obviously going to make himself very difficult to resist, especially witnessing the blush of my very uncooperative cheeks.

The nerves that had taken over my body earlier settle as Cole and Carter man the grill, and Lila and I prepare the rest of the meal in the kitchen. Our Thursday and Sunday night family dinners became a tradition that my mom started when I was young, and they continued when we moved to California. She was insistent that Gavin grow up with at least two nights a week of "a crowded kitchen, loud conversation, and the occasional food fight." I promised myself that I would continue family dinners until the day Gavin moved out, and even then, I might consider forcing him to come home for them.

Lila stands watching through the back window with a sense of awe in her expression. "You know, Cam, looks like he adores him."

"Gavin warmed up to him in minutes. I was nervous about it at first."

Lila turns toward me and yanks me next to her.

"I'm not talking about Gavin. I'm talking about Cole … just look."

We watch through the window, spotting the ball in the net, as Cole holds Gavin in his arms like a proud father hoisting his son up after scoring the winning soccer goal. Gavin has one arm wrapped tightly around Cole's neck and the other arm fist-pumping the air in celebration. Cole is staring up at him with a genuine smile across his face, and Gavin is gazing back in awe. Frightened and inspired by their instant bond, my mind begins to wander back to thoughts of my father and Todd. The connections, the disappointments, and the despair all rush back to me, reminding me that each tore a piece of my heart out and took it with them the day they decided to leave.

Lila grabs hold of my waist, probably sensing my need to sit down. Once she situates me on the couch, she grabs my face to hers.

"Cam, not everyone leaves." Loosening her grip on my cheeks, she adds, "You have to let people in. Don't shut everyone out because you're … afraid."

I flop back on the couch, as if I'd just finished a marathon and my body can't hold itself up anymore. "You don't think I know this? That I want nothing more for him than to one day have a dad who wants us, who adores us?" I feel my anger rising with each word.

"Then you need to start letting people in. It's the only way you'll ever know if someone can be that to you. Claim your second chance, girlfriend."

Lila pulls me in and strokes my hair while I lean against her. I know she is right, that fear will always hinder me, but it also strengthens me. It keeps Gavin safe, it holds our family together, and it gives me a reason to fight. Losing Gavin in my nightmares each night is just a reminder of what could be at stake if I give in to my fears.

"Li, I wish it was that easy, but I have to consider how my actions will affect Gavin. He's never seen me with a man. And then I ask myself, why the hell would

Cole be interested, anyway? I'm carrying around some major baggage."

Wiping my eyes and taking a few deep breaths, I stand up and start to put serving dishes on the table. Lila must sense that I need "normal" tonight, and she won't press the issue any further. Instead, she yells for the boys to come in for dinner. I watch them saunter through the door and feel the warmth settle in as we gather around my mom's table to continue a tradition that she began. At that moment, loud conversation in the crowded kitchen fills the house. Gavin works the room throughout dinner with his plethora of knock-knock jokes. Having heard them thousands of times, I study our new dinner guest as he brightens with every joke that rolls out of Gavin's mouth.

Aside from Carter, all of the other men that I've met would avoid Gavin. I would often mention him while on dates as a scare tactic. Rarely would I be invited on a second date. Being a young mother was an instant turnoff, judging by most men my age, but it didn't seem that way with Cole.

When Gavin's comedy hour ends, we resume our party on the deck. While we devour Cole's mouthwatering strawberry shortcake, Lila decides it's the perfect time for my mom's third rule of family dinners, the occasional food fight. Scooping up a spoonful of whipped cream, she flings it directly at Carter, striking him right in the eye. Carter snatches his plate and smashes his leftover cake in Lila's face, which causes Gavin to launch two cream-soaked strawberries in my direction. Within seconds, whipped cream, strawberries, and vanilla cake are soaring across the deck. I'm sure our laughter can be heard miles away as we mutilate the rest of our dessert. Just as I duck behind Gavin's basketball net, I feel a strong arm hook around my waist and a plate of whipped cream collide with my face.

I yelp, "Cole! You're mine!"

I leap toward the table to grab leftover cake, pelting it at him and smearing it on his face and in his short hair. While everyone erupts in laughter, Cole holds my arm up to crown me victor.

Pulling me into his chest, he whispers, "I'll be yours anytime."

"If I can smear you in whipped cream and cake all the time, then I just may take your offer," I retort, rolling out of his grasp, somewhat mortified by the sexual image I just planted in his head.

Carter and Lila decide to call it a night when they realize the only dessert left is caked on all of us. With Cole's offer to help me with the cleanup, Carter yanks Lila out the door, promising to "lick her clean" when they get home. Trying to push aside that mental image, I bid them a quick farewell and make plans to see them for the grand openings of their respective shops this weekend.

I embrace my son and ask, "So, how was your first family dinner here? Was it everything you thought it would be?"

Practically tackling me to the floor, he shrieks, "Best. Night. Ever!"

He sprints to Cole and jumps up in his arms. "That was so cool! Mommy got you bad!"

Cole tosses his head back in amusement. "You ain't kidding, little guy!" He captures my gaze. "She definitely did."

I linger, caught in his gaze for a few moments, contemplating what could be if I get over my haunting fears and give in to my desires. I envision ball games, amusement parks, picnics, lovemaking, romance, arguments, and making up. Could Cole even be the one who could make those visions a reality?

Leaping out of my daydream, I gently command my son, "Gav, time for bed. You have an early surf lesson tomorrow before the block party at Uncle Carter's and Aunt Lila's stores."

"Aww, Mommy! Do I have to? Can Cole read me a story first?" Gavin begs.

I quickly glance at Cole who leans down to Gavin with a contented smile.

"I'd love to … uh … if it's okay with your mom."

I surrender to my pleading boy and give the okay. Besides, it will give me time to scrub the aftermath of our food fight. As they disappear downstairs, I start the search for cleaning supplies. Starled as my fingers grasp an envelope in the mop bucket, I pull it out and rip it open, recognizing my mom's handwriting on it.

> *Dear Camryn,*
> *I hope you're retrieving this for the sole purpose of cleaning up the result of a family dinner food fight. If not, then put it back right now because Mrs. Hegarty has been cleaning the house for five years on Tuesday mornings. This night is just the beginning of your journey to feeling whole again. Thank you for keeping family dinners a part of Gavin's life, but remember to "grow" them. Your path led you home for a reason. Keep your head up and your heart open.*
> *Love to you and our precious boy,*
> *Mom*

With my hands trembling and my eyes watery, I choke back the tears. I wish I could talk to her one more time and share my secrets and fears, so she can make sense of everything for me. This emptiness is swallowing me whole, pushing me deeper into my loneliness.

Suddenly, I am startled by the urgency of Cole's voice. "Camryn, what's wrong? Are you all right?"

I quickly pull myself together. "It's fine. I'm fine."

The warmth of his body close to mine and the manly musk smell penetrating from his skin is intoxicating. This insanely sexy man somehow causes flutters deep within my stomach, which only intensifies as each minute passes. An unexplainable desire is urging me to open up to him, just like he once did to me. However, the rational side of me pushes it back down and reminds me that I don't really know him and I doubt he even remembers that day.

He hesitantly nods at me, probably seeing that I am the farthest thing from fine. "Gavin wants to say goodnight." He reaches for my hand and leads me downstairs to my son.

Staring at our linked hands, I wrestle between the yearning to open my heart to let him in and the fear of falling for him, a man who could possess the power to one day break me. I tuck my pain away when I see Gavin waiting for his goodnight hug and kiss.

Leaning over, I kiss his forehead and recite, "A kiss for your mind, so nightmares stay far behind, a kiss for your nose, to keep away monsters' smelly toes, and a kiss on the heart for tomorrow's bright start."

Gavin giggles at our bedtime rhyme, and then says in his sleepy, lisping voice, "Night, night. I love you, Mommy."

"I love you mostest, angel. Sweet dreams."

Gavin then reaches out to Cole. "Do you know any goodnight rhymes?"

Cole reaches for Gavin's tiny hand and holds it in his. "Hmmm … let me think, buddy." Cole leans in closer to Gavin and whispers, "How about this one?

Goodnight, sleep tight, don't let the bed bugs bite, and I'll see you in the morning light."

Gavin giggles. "That's a good one … right, Mommy?"

"It's perfect. Now go to sleep, surfer boy." I eye Cole while we spread blankets over Gavin, wondering if he is real. Besides Carter, I've never met a man who can love outside of himself and who can give so freely to someone else. Most guys see Gavin as a nuisance, a whiny little kid that gets in the way, a cock-block, as the few guys I dated referred to him. Guys didn't even waste their time on me since most other twenty-three-year-olds were easy lays with no children attached. However, Cole is different. It's as if he's done this before, like he's experienced how a small person can capture your heart and define your whole existence.

After putting Gavin to bed, I grab Cole a beer and pour myself some wine as we continue our night on the deck. The vacant beach block makes it feel like we are the only two people who exist in the world. With Cole, I have an odd sense of comfort when I am around him, like we are old friends meeting up again for the first time in years.

"Thanks for everything today. I haven't seen Gav that happy since my mom died. We've both been going through a really difficult time without her." I reach down to my pocket where I stuffed my mom's letter.

"You know, your mom got me outta some bad shit growing up here. Without her, I'd probably be cleaning the streets or sitting behind bars."

"Really?" I eye him up and down. "You don't seem like the jailbird type."

Cole stares out toward the beach and lets out a breath like he is recalling a difficult memory. "It was over a girl. Your mom always warned me about her, but I didn't listen. You know how the story goes … met in high school, she said she loved me, then I caught her with someone in my grandmom's bed."

I gasp. "Tell me you're kidding! Your grandmom's bed?"

"My grandmom raised me after my mom died, so having people in the house was normal, especially since my grandmom spent most of her time on her boat. I trained at the beach every morning before school, so the house was open. That day, your mom and the rest of the coaches gave us off, so I figured I'd catch some sleep. When I found them, I did what I did best. I pulled him out on to the deck and beat the shit outta him. Your mom happened to be walking down the alley behind my house and stopped me before I knocked him past unconscious." Cole shudders at the memory of hurting someone that severely. "The prick was from a family of lawyers, and he was going to sue, but your mom handled it. Don't know how, but the problem disappeared."

Shocked by his confession, I lean over and rest my hand on his arms that are tightly wrapped around his waist. His muscles relax at my touch, but I still can sense his pain.

"What happened with you and her?"

At that instant, Cole freezes, as if the life was just sucked out of him. I give his arm a slight squeeze, and he snaps back to reality. "It was her ploy to make me jealous enough to spend more time with her. It worked until…" His voice lowers to almost a whisper. "Well, the relationship just couldn't work."

At that moment, I catch a glimpse of the darkness living deep within his eyes, the same grief that was penetrating his soul that day he followed me out of the cafeteria. I know that darkness well because I have the same living in me. I recall those fated words that punctured me, "Get rid of it… I'll never want it." Words that left a wound that would never heal closed. Words that Todd Connelly, the man who held my heart through high school, spoke to me right before he threw away our life together. He left me to raise Gavin on my own so his precious Villanova Law School dream wasn't shattered.

I brush my hand down his arm and reach for his hand. Our eyes meet and, at that moment, Cole reveals the loss he feels to me with no more words spoken. He is broken like me, and just like that, the wall I had built around me—around Gavin—crumbles to the ground.

Chapter Five
My Fight

The sounds of squawking seagulls and incessant knocking on my door wakes me in the morning. Cole had stayed until the early hours of dawn, just listening to me ramble on about my past troubles. I thought it was fair to share some of my secrets, as he had with me. There was no doubt that by the fourth glass of wine I had exposed all of my deep-seated heartbreak. I have never bared my soul like this to anyone but Lila and my mom, so I saw this as a breakthrough, or maybe just a step in the right direction. Our night finally ended with a soft touch of our lips before we parted ways, which left me wanting more.

Having been unable to sleep due to the memory of the gentle kiss that still lingered on my lips, I fumble out of bed and trudge down the hallway, peeking into Gavin's room to assure myself he was safe in his bed. Sometimes the reccurring nightmares play games with my head, so occasional reality checks calm me. Satisfied with the sight of him tucked snuggly in his bed, I proceed to answer the front door to a charming grin and bright eyes glistening against the low sun in the early morning sky.

Cole holds up two paper bags as he announces, "Breakfast!"

His glance rakes up and down my body, inspecting my "just rolled out of bed look" that consists of sleep shorts with a fitted tank top.

"Or we can take these to your room and make it breakfast in bed?"

Amused by his suggestion, I playfully punch him in his rock-solid abs. "Keep your dirty thoughts to yourself, Mr. Stevens." I lift to my toes and grab the bags out of his hands. "Or I may just have to take the goods and run!"

One side of his lips tilts upward and he shrugs. "Can't promise you that I won't have dirty thoughts, especially if you answer the door like this everyday."

With my body tingling from the oh-so-sexy look in his face, I start to ache with desire. I want him at this moment, and I probably would take him at the front door if I could. Just as I focus my gaze on his mouth and our heads began to tilt, we jump apart at the sound of a little voice.

"Mornin', Mommy. Mornin', Cole. Ready to go surfing?"

Cole quickly leans down to high-five Gavin. "Sure thing, little man!" Cole leads Gavin toward the stairs. "But first thing's first ... we make some breakfast!"

Watching my giggling son travel up the stairs, I sigh at this yearning to know Cole, but Gavin can't know that. I never want him to get his hopes up just to possibly have them smashed. I wander to my room and think about my son's needs, reminding myself that they far outweigh my own desires.

After getting dressed for the beach, I peek in the kitchen to find Gavin standing on a chair in front of the stove and Cole behind him, helping him scramble the eggs. In a strange way, they favor each other, both with endearing eyes, revealing smiles, and a wardrobe consisting of board shorts and Rip Curl t-shirts. Watching them interact so naturally together makes me realize I don't want to run away from the posibilities of being with someone. Maybe it's time to jump right in, and take that chance. Maybe I'm ready for this ... maybe.

I take a seat at the table, and Gavin trots over to

me with a huge smile plastered on his face. "Mommy, you're gonna love this. It's so yummy! Cole showed me how to cook!"

I pull him in for a hug. "Gav, if you made it, I'll love it."

Turning toward Cole with a sly smile, I add, "And maybe I'll get to see more of your surf coach's other hidden talents!" Heat creeps onto my cheeks from my forwardness as I silently pray that I don't sound like a complete idiot. Damn, I should've paid more attention to Lila in the clubs back in LA.

Gavin runs to get my plate, not catching on to my flirtatious comment, but Cole nearly chokes on his orange juice. My heart pounding, I decide to play something with Cole that is completely out of character for me. I look at him and motion a "one" with my finger and point to myself, then I do a "zero" and point to him. A sexy smile creeps across his face as he lips to me, "Game on," and at that moment I know there is no turning back. The gates that locked my heart for so many years are unlocked and I am ready to walk right through them.

Cole spends breakfast trying to convince Gavin why Spiderman's powers are far superior to those of Batman while I strategize my next flirty move. Cole glances at me and grins, which sends my nerves into overdrive. I curse him under my breath because this will require no effort on his part. I have absolutely no skills when it comes to guys, whereas Cole oozes with sensuality.

While I clean up from breakfast, Cole and Gavin wax their boards on the deck. Gavin's lesson is first, then we are all going to town to help set up for Memorial Day Weekend. Both Lila's and Carter's shops will be having their official grand openings, and Cole and I offered to help them work their sidewalk sales throughout the weekend. There is already a lot of buzz around Carter's surf shop since he is a successful surfer from the West Coast, a pedigree that earns respect from any East Coast surfer. Carter can build a board that will make any surfer drool, so business is sure to boom.

Grabbing my beach bag and sunscreen, I venture outside to start our walk to the instruction beach. Gavin splashes in ankle-deep water, while a few steps behind, Cole and I walk together.

Watching as Gavin kicks water ahead of him then runs through it, I begin to think about the fond memories of my own childhood. I tell Cole how my father would get home from the hospital, throw me on his shoulders, and run as fast as he could to the beach. While I bounced and giggled above his shoulders, he would dive under the waves but keep me above like I was on top of the water.

I stop in my tracks and peer across the endless sea that was such a staple in my early years of life. "Sounds crazy, but my father made me believe that I could walk on water."

Cole moves into the space between our bodies.

"His loss that he's missing out on this." Cole fans his arm out across Gavin and me. "The way you are with him ... your dad would see that you really can walk on water."

I tilt my head and grin at him. "That means more to me than you'll ever know."

Cole leans in close to my face and whispers, "Anyway, I'd much rather see you wet than dry on top."

I jerk my head up and gasp at his instant switch from sentimental to erotic as he yells out, "Hell yeah! Score! You have no chance at this little game you started."

He taunts me as he does a quick victory dance

that ends with signaling a "one" with his finger to himself and then to me. I push his hand away and dash ahead of him, pretending to ignore him.

"Awww, Camryn, you set me up so well! I had to take it!"

Behind my back, I slip him my middle finger. Cole catches up to me and grabs it, saying, "You can anytime, anywhere, baby." He gives squeezes my finger and leans down to my ear. "And can you say two to one?"

Laughing, Cole sprints past me, indicating a "two" with his fingers as he holds them up in the air. I have to crack a smile, knowing that he's right—he'll have no problem with this game. He reaches Gavin and scoops him up, pretending to throw him into a wave.

With Cole swinging him back and forth, Gavin exclaims, "Do it, Cole! I double dare you!"

"You asked for it, buddy! Close your eyes and count to three."

"One, two, three..."

At that instant, a huge splash emerges as they both dive under the wave together. I gaze at the water as their heads pop up with Gavin's arms tightly wrapped around Cole's neck. Their laughter is infectious as it echoes across the vast ocean. Cole shifts Gavin to his shoulders, and he swims him to the beach on top of the water. Smiling at the connection Cole just formed between my childhood and Gavin's, I feel him start to take possession of my heart. The only thing I can do now is hope that he doesn't leave me shattered.

****

Carter is trying to construct a small canopy when we arrive in town that afternoon. All of the stores are setting up for the first wave of weekenders who are probably already sitting in hours of traffic, trying to be the first ones on the island to kick off the new summer season.

Catching sight of Cole walking with me, he looks relieved and yells, "Dude, you think I could get some help with this piece-of-shit tent thing?" He points toward the direction of Lila's salon. "Miss High-Maintenance over there thinks it will attract more customers."

Cole grabs the one leg of the overhang while I smack Carter on the back of his head. Leaning in, I threaten, "Use that language around my son again, and I will cut off your man-goods, got it?"

Shocked by my warning, Carter stands wide-eyed and replies, "Shit, Cam, I didn't think you had that in you. You've been hanging out with Li for too long." He walks behind me as he takes hold of the other side of the canopy.

I peek over to Cole, who is beaming at me. "I may just have to give you a point for how hot that was. Damn, girl … sweet and rough?"

I hold up two fingers to Cole as I grab the third leg of the tent, and Gavin pitches in with the fourth. Once the canopy is secure, I leave the boys to set up racks of wet suits and tables of wax and wax combs to sell during the sidewalk sale. As I make my way a block down to Lila's, I spot the sign outside of her salon and freeze as my eyes began to fill with tears blurring out the beautiful words in front of me.

Lila rushes over to me and tries to comfort me, saying, "Cam, I never would've done it if I knew it would hurt you. I'm so sorry…"

Pulling back, I interrupt her apology, "Li, never be sorry for this … it's the best thing you could ever do for me."

I reach for her hand, and we stand admiring the brand-new sign that reads *Milena's Retreat Spa and*

Salon from the sidewalk. It radiates elegance, with manicured bushes surrounding a stone exterior. In the huge window above the doors, a crystal chandelier hangs in the entranceway. Lila leads me inside to a large mahogany service desk topped with marble. Across from the desk hangs a black-framed picture of the back of a woman's head with long, flowing hair. I gasp when I recognize the image.

"That's my mom, isn't it? Before the cancer?"

Lila squeezes my hand and nods. "It was too beautiful to not use. It's the perfect tribute to the most amazing woman I ever knew."

Touched by her homage to my mom's legacy, I embrace Lila to reassure her that she could have done nothing better to keep my mom's memory alive in this town. This salon is perfect, from its namesake to its rich wood floor and black décor highlighted by zebra-striped accents.

Pulling myself together, I help Lila set up her hair and skincare products on a table outside. The boys join us just as we are finishing up. Lila nods to Carter, which I assume is the sign that I approve her acknowledgment of my mom in her salon. Cole approaches me with Gavin in his arms, reaching over for a group hug. As the three of us are huddled together, Cole brings his mouth to my ear and asks, "Carter told me when you left. How are you holding up?"

Fighting back tears, I nod my head into him. "I'm okay, perfect now. My mom needs to live on forever in this town. It was the place that meant the most to her. It's only right."

"Camryn Singer, you are pretty amazing. Milena would be proud."

"Thank you, Cole Stevens … you aren't so bad yourself," I say, nudging his elbow.

Opening weekend begins with a slow influx of people returning to the beach town, but by mid-evening, the streets are bustling again with the sights and sounds of the summer season. Gavin is gaining a lot of attention at the surf shop, so Carter is reluctant to give up the cuteness factor that was fueling his early weekend sales. Child-free, I spend most of the evening helping Lila build her clientele. She's able to secure steady bookings through the summer months, some even spilling into early fall. When the crowds slow down, her unavoidable cross-examination begins.

"So, I see you and sex-on-a-stick are making some progress? You want to tell me what's going on between you two, Cam?"

Shrugging my shoulders, I say, "Not really sure. We were up late talking last night, drank a lot, kissed, breakfast today, and…"

"Early morning convos, a goodnight kiss, breakfast, and working your BFFs' openings. And you're not sure? You hop on the crazy train this morning or something?"

I look away from her gaze and stare at the ground.

"Cam, he eye-fucks you every time he looks at you, and he adores Gavvy … so what's the problem?" She pulls my face back up to meet hers.

"I wanna try to … I don't know … see what happens between us. But I'm not sure I can be more than friends right now. Anyway, I think he's dealing with something … you know … from the past."

"We all have shit in the past. That's what it's there for. But I'm talking about the present, and just seeing the way he looks at you, I think he's already in the future."

"Li, it scares the living shit out of me. Besides,

what the hell does he want with me? I'm a total head case who runs when things get tough. And not to mention the fact that my five-year-old wouldn't make for very romantic dates."

"Lose the pity party, Cam. You're supposed to be scared shitless. That's what makes it real, that's what makes it last."

Just then, I see Cole making his way toward us with Gavin on his back. He gallops and bounces Gavin, then slows down, making Gavin throw his head back in a fit of laughter. I watch while replaying Lila's words in my head and know that Cole has a connection with Gavin that I can't explain. He already has my son's heart, and that means that he has the power to break it.

"Mommy, Aunt Lila, look at me. I'm a cowboy, just like Woody!" Gavin can hardly get his words out between laughing fits.

Lila yells back to Gavin, "Ride 'em, cowboy!"

That makes Gavin swing his pretend lasso while I clap and cheer for my baby boy. As they reach us, I attempt to forget about the conversation with Lila and see the perfect opportunity to move ahead in our flirty competition. In my best Southern drawl, I lean close to Cole and ask, "Howdy, sir, can lil' ol' me take a ride on you?"

I hold three fingers in his face and blow him a kiss with my lips. Clearly amused by my taunting, he says, "You're tougher than you look, woman. I might have to up my game."

Cole slips me a sexy wink and drops Gavin into Lila's arms. She waltzes away with him on the sidewalk and orders us to follow her to meet up with Carter and grab a slice of pizza. Cole innocently reaches out his hand for mine and asks, "Now will you and Gavin join me for dinner? It's still not a one-time offer."

I look over at Gavin, whose big, curious eyes are inspecting our every move and then to Cole, whose scorching gaze burns straight through to my heart. I slowly extend my hand to meet his, clasping tighter than normal to keep myself steady.

"We'd love to join you." I glance down to my fingers intertwined with his and know I am clinging on to much more than his hand, but rather taking hold of the possibilities, claiming my second chance. Drawing my eyes back to his, I add, "And it's not a one-time acceptance."

I peek over at Gavin, who is grinning from ear to ear, and give him a thumbs-up. He reciprocates with two of his own and whispers something into Lila's ear, causing her to break out in another waltz down the street. Gavin's laughter and Cole's fingers entwined with mine resurrect life from my cracked soul. At this moment, I will not allow my broken past to hinder my present, and for the first time in a long while, I am ready to take a chance.

Gavin, Cole, and I spend the rest of the weekend the same way as our walk to the pizza shop—together. With each passing minute, I gravitate closer to Cole who first showed up as a boy when I was lost, hanging onto my teenage dreams by a thread. Then, as a man, he walks into my life when I'm again grasping hold for dear life. But each minute also creates a fear that I've never experienced, despite all the loss I've faced. I've become more and more aware of what is at stake as Cole slowly takes pieces of my heart. Although he has the power to destroy the safety net I've built around Gavin that shields him from pain and loss, my heart refuses to stop falling for him.

After an exhausting weekend, family dinner on Sunday is low-key with the boys grilling burgers and dogs. Carter and Lila scoot out quickly after she complains about her lack of beauty sleep for the sixth time during dessert. Gavin is sprawled across the couch, sporting his Batman pajamas, waiting for Cole and me to start movie night, which he earned for his hard work at the surf shop all weekend. Cole and I are cuddled together on the couch watching *X-Men: First Class* with Gavin wrapped in a blanket, resting his legs on Cole's lap and me on the other side, leaning my head on his shoulder. Within the first ten minutes of the action film, my eyelids grow heavy and I give in to sleep, snuggled with Cole.

****

For me, the doctor's office is a place of pain, a place that makes me feel like I am dying inside. I always see what used to be, what should have been, while I lie on the examining table. Since the day he left, when I hear the heartbeat, it sounds more like a flat line, when I see the fingers and toes on the screen, they look like the claws of the devil, and when the doctor speaks of the approaching birthing date, it feels like the planning of a funeral. I know what waits outside the door for me. He'll be there, trying to take what is a part of me, the part he helped create.

Trudging out the door to my looming attack, I grasp my swollen belly to protect my unborn baby. I thrash in terror as he grabs me from behind and pushes me to the ground. I squeeze my eyes shut to avoid his violent glare, but he pries them open with ease. Gasping in horror, I stare into the eyes of the one who wants to take the only life left in me—Cole's eyes.

All I can feel are tears streaming down my cheeks and strong arms holding my convulsing body. Screaming in terror, I awake to the same pair of eyes that just terrified me in my sleep.

"Camryn, calm down ... breathe ... c'mon, just breathe ... please just breathe!" Cole is trying to bring me out of my nightmare.

Words are spilling out of my mouth, my half-awake self not able to grasp what my nightmare just revealed.

"You ... it was you. You tried to take ... you want to hurt us!"

Cole freezes at my accusations and then attempts to pull me in close to his chest. I jump back from him and trip, bumping the back of my head into the coffee table. He reaches down to help me up, but I crawl away from him, trying to get as far away as possible.

After my outburst, he tilts his head at me and attempts to soothe me. "Camryn, it was only a nightmare. No matter who I was, who you saw, it's not really me. It will never be me." He inches up closer and leans down to be at my level. "I'd never hurt you or Gavin. I'm not him."

At the sound of Gavin's name, I snap my head around, looking for him, hoping he didn't just witness the result of my nightmares.

"I tucked him in bed. He fell asleep a few hours ago."

Nodding in understanding, I slowly stand up and walk toward the stairs. My head is throbbing with pain from the blow it encountered a few minutes before. The terror of losing any part of my son envelopes me, and I know distance is what's needed. I speak to Cole without turning toward him.

"I don't know if I can do this. I have to keep Gavin safe. Please just ... go."

Without responding, I hear him moving toward the door. I look back and catch a glimpse of his profile. Within the reflection of the moonlight, I watch two stray tears stream down his face as he walks out with fists clenched. Once he leaves, I sink to the ground, pull my knees to my chest and cry for him, for me, for that goddamn dream that won't leave me alone.

My unsteady legs can get only get me as far as the couch, so I pull my mom's blanket over me, hoping to find some solace in her warmth. As I spread the Asian embroidered cover over my body, a small white envelope falls to the floor. My body stiffens at the sight of another message from my mom. Still reeling from her last note, I begin to tremble as I rip it open.

Dearest Camryn,

I regret that you are reading this note, as I know you never would have moved that blanket unless you needed comfort. The nightmares will continue to plague you if you make them your reality. Understand that they are distorted images of your fears but also a necessary part of your journey. Without them you would lose the "fight" in you, and that strength to keep fighting is what defines you. These sleepless nights are mere detours on your path, tests of strength that will make the "destination" worth your fight.

Love to you,
Mom

Clutching my mom's words close to my body, I collapse underneath her blanket, hoping to find that strength she is so sure I have. I let Cole in, and he is able to start deconstructing the walls, but when that darkness sets in, I build them up again. He gives me a glimpse of his own loss, and I push him away because of mine. From first glance, he's opened a door to possibilities, and I just slam it in his face. Regret is settling in as I ache for his arms around me again and his body pressed up against me. I struggle to push him out of my mind, to hide from the idea of us, but at that instant, I want nothing more than for Cole to be "my fight."

Chapter Six
Just Give Me a Reason

Bright sun filtering through the skylight brings me back to life after I finally went numb from replaying the night over and over in my head. Cole has been dominating my thoughts ever since our bodies slammed together on the beach only a few days ago. Now he is the very reason as to why I am running scared. And within an instant, I managed to shove the only person who broke through, away. The memory of tears trickling down his cheeks haunted me through the night and further shattered my already broken heart.

Staring at the wall that connects our homes, my mind drifts to the last few days we've spent together. His sensual tone rings through my ears, the feel of his fingers wrapped around mine sends shivers through my body, and the way our forms mold together while sleeping on the couch makes me crave more of him. I fantasize about knocking down the wall that connects our houses to explore every inch of his body. From the moment I asked him to leave last night, I was left in withdrawal, yearning for more of him.

Staggering off the couch toward the kitchen to wash down a few Advil to ease the pounding in my head, a memento from my blow with the coffee table, I glance at my phone to discover a text from Lila.

Cams, have Gav 4 surf lesson. Saw Asian blanket, def need to talk.

Fingering the buttons to return her text, I'm grateful Lila knows me so well. I need her no-bullshit advice to help me sort through my feelings. Of all the things I love about Lila, her bluntness is number one on my list.

Thanks for letting me sleep. May need more

than just a talk ;)

I push send, then trudge back to the couch to wrap myself in misery again, reading my mom's note over and over. How could she think I'm so strong? I've felt nothing but weak for the past five years. She would probably change her mind if she saw me slumped on the sofa, sinking into her comfort blanket, sulking over a guy. I could just see her red, manicured finger wagging in my face telling me, "Pull yourself together, Camryn. Men don't bring us down." But the thought of Cole not making eggs on my stove, discussing comic book characters with Gavin, waxing his board on my deck, or hinting at his erotic fantasies with me only drown me in my sea of regret.

I am rescued from my wallowing thoughts by Lila and Gavin when they scurry in from the beach. Gavin flies over to me with pouted lips and a scowl on his face. He broadcasts his obvious discontent by plopping on the couch with an exaggerated sigh.

"Gav, what's wrong? Not a good lesson?"

"No! Cole wasn't there. Some girl was my teacher, and she freakin' sucked!"

Reaching over, I pinch his cheeks to bring his face close to mine. "Lose the potty-words, or your Wii is gone. Got it, mister?" He nods his head and I loosen my grip, trying to process the news of Cole's absence. "Maybe he was sick. I'm sure he'll be back tomorrow."

Gavin stands up and crosses his arms over his chest. "No, he won't. This is your fault, Mommy!"

Startled by his accusation, I reach up and hold his elbows, trying to relax his tension. "What do you mean? How is it my fault?"

"I heard you yelling at him last night. You're a big meanie!" Gavin turns and storms downstairs to his room.

I flop against the back of the couch, bothered by Gavin's reaction. Lila inches up next to me and grabs my knee.

"Don't worry. He's five and will forget in like a minute."

"How'd he get so attached already? I tried my hardest to keep Cole from hurting him… I've failed."

"Cam, kids know the good people, and they're drawn toward them. Did you think that maybe Cole's not the one hurting him? I mean, look at you … you obviously pushed him away, and now you're molded to the blanket, and Gavin's pissed he's not around. So, really, who's doing the damage?"

I throw my face into the suede couch pillow that I've been clutching and let out a muffled scream. It is times like these when I wish my biggest decision is what outfit to wear out to the bars. It sounds so simple—the cropped skinny jeans or the long maxi dress? But instead I'm leaning on my best friend again, struggling to make a decision.

Gavin latched on to something that he was longing for, and Cole was ready and willing to give it to him. I let my son experience this and then selfishly took it away because I am scared of my own feelings and heartache.

Rolling over from my temper tantrum into the pillow, I give Lila a defeated glance. "I fucking suck at this. This crazy connection we have … I can't even explain it, but I know it started that day. Then I push him away because I can't handle getting hurt again, and I never want to feel the same way I did when Todd walked away in the parking lot that day. I'm one selfish bitch, aren't I?" I shake my head in my hands at this realization. "Li, I actually accused him of wanting to hurt Gavin. Am I mental?"

"Royally fucked-up runs in our family, honey. Gavin's the only one with a fighting chance." She pulls me up from the couch and pats my hair. "But it's not too late. Find him. Fight for him."

Lila's words ring in my head like the opening bell at a boxing match. Everyone is urging me to battle for the one thing that almost destroyed me, the thing that forced me to leave everything I ever knew, the thing I'm not sure even exists. At that moment I realize I'm fighting against myself, against the fears that I allow to define me. I want Cole to be with me to conquer those fears, to find myself again, to make me feel alive again. He gave me a small taste of what could be over the last few days, and I crave more of him. I long for the unknown with him, the areas of his body that are left unseen, the sensation of his hands on places he left untouched.

"Li, I never thought I'd come back here and want this so soon, but the second I saw him again, I had this unexplained yearning for him." I cradle my head in my hands. "But after last night, he may be gone."

"No way in hell he's walking away that easily. Besides, he spent the entire weekend with you and didn't even get laid once!"

Lila always knows how to lighten the mood, so I give her a playful punch in the arm and ask her to come help me talk to Gavin. I know if we tag team, there is no way my jovial boy can stay disheartened for too long. We decide to sneak attack him with his major weakness—the tickle bugs. After bombarding his room, we pin him down and go full force until he surrenders amidst out-of-breath pleas.

"Tickle bugs make you feel better?" I ask Gavin.

"Mmmm hmmm! Those tickle bugs are sneaky." Gavin reaches around my neck, pulling me in for an

Eskimo kiss.

Gavin keeps hold of me with one arm and pulls Lila into our hug with his other.

"I love you, Mommy and Aunt Lila."

"We both love you, too." We squeeze Gavin tighter against us. "Now, let's get dressed and packed. Time for your boys' night with Uncle Carter!"

This makes Gavin leap from his bed and fist pump the air. He grabs his rolling Avengers overnight bag and begins to rummage through his video games, tossing his favorites in.

Lila and I declare every Memorial Day a ladies' night out, or as she calls it, The Celebration of Vaginas. We began the tradition the day my dad left, which happened to be over Memorial Day weekend. It's evolved from sneaking whiskey in the garage when we were fourteen, to taking body shots off of bartenders— who clearly have spent entirely too much time in the gym—last year. Tonight we will start in our favorite seafood restaurant and then barhop along the Drive to places we haven't been to since our underage years. With the way I feel, our night out couldn't have landed on a better day.

I leave Lila to assist Gavin with packing while I step out on the front porch. The cool sea breeze tingles my bare arms, causing me to fold them closely to my chest. I peek over to Cole's driveway to see his Wrangler still missing, which sends a jolt of disappointment through my body. I know he will return, but whatever we started could be undone, making the knot in my stomach churn with an aching pain. I stare at the wooden swing hanging from his porch roof that is swaying with the slight breeze and picture us on it through the different stages of our lives. I see us stealing kisses from each other over Gavin's head while he sits between us cuddled in a fleece blanket, watching the first snowflakes of the season fall to the ground. Lila comes out to the porch and interrupts my longing thoughts.

"Lunchtime, girly! Then Carter will be here for Gavin."

I give her a confused look, wondering why Gavin is leaving so early.

"Oh yeah… forgot to tell you, we have a date at Milena's." Lila gives me a wink that I return with a wide smile, knowing why I love her more and more every day.

Lila and I bask in head-to-toe treatment at the salon to help edge out my angst and frustration with how I handled the situation with Cole. While I wait for my jumbo curlers to set, I work the front desk to give Amber, the receptionist, a break. Midday on a Monday usually attracts gray-haired women who are sprucing up their perms or housewives refilling their manicure for the week. So when I check in a girl close to my age who is awaiting highlights rather than a tightly-spun perm, I am a bit surprised, or maybe I just can't place where I know her from.

"Tara Chambers … three thirty?"

She nods at my confirmation.

"Gabby, your stylist, will be right with you. You may have a seat. Can I offer you anything?"

"No thanks. I'm fine," she snaps with a scowl on her face and no glance in my direction.

Gabby comes out and greets her and, as she takes her back to the coloring station, she starts complaining about a dire need for spring water and the lack of customer service. What a rude, lying bitch! I add a bolded "B" next to her name in the computer, knowing that Lila will understand the message when she checks through her client list. Maybe she can slip some hideous neon color into her highlights or accidentally bump

Gabby's arm while she is cutting her bob.

Pushing the bitchy customer to the back of my mind, I return to my best friend to finish beautifying our hair and makeup. Lila streaked purple highlights through her bouncy bob that curls out on the ends. Her makeup is bright and colorful like girls in cheesy eighties movies, but somehow she pulls it off in such a way that only adds to her exotic look. I am a bit more earth-toned, as my single-color hair falls down my back in loose curls and my eyes boast shades of tans and browns. Once we return to Lila and Carter's, we both decide to glam it up in form-fitting dresses, hers with a sweetheart neckline and mine with a deep scoop back.

Lila pushes a full shot glass in front of my face and holds hers up with her other hand. "To friendship, family, and vaginas!"

I raise my glass and throw it back, gagging when it travels to the back of my throat. "What the hell is this? Whiskey?"

"Jim Beam, biotch! We toast with only the kind that began this night nine years ago." Lila cackles as I recall polishing off a bottle of it between the two of us when we were fourteen. We ended up meeting some lifeguards that night after we stripped down and skinny-dipped in the ocean. Lila was felt up for the first time on top of the lifeguard stand while my make-out session ended with me puking my guts up on the guy's chest. Although I had a hangover that didn't go away for a week, I place that night in my top ten best of all time. Each year we try to top that first night, but we never come close.

"Sentimental or not, I'm upgrading tonight. Don't think I want to see this on a guy's chest later!" Howling in laughter, we make our way out of the house to celebrate our vaginas.

****

When we leave the restaurant and arrive at the first bar on the Drive, I'm three martinis in and feeling like my stilettos are floating across the sidewalk. As we enter the bar, a cloud of thick smoke and the stench of a sweaty armpit welcomes us, and if that isn't bad enough, my skinny heels struggle to loosen themselves from the years of caked-in grime that layers the checkerboard floor. Lila has already grabbed Jell-O shots from the waitress circulating the crowd, and I maneuver my way to the bar for two vodka tonics. Nineties cover songs are blasting from the stage that is next to the long bar in the center of the room. Grabbing my free hand, Lila leads us onto the dance floor and within minutes, guys are circling around us like vultures ready to attack their prey. By five songs in, we're on stage with the band, who are feeding us more Jell-O shots while we shout lyrics to the songs into their microphones.

The songs slowly drift into the previous decade, and I know that's our cue to leave. "Li, let's go!"

Nodding her head to me, she gives the lead singer a kiss on the cheek, and we sneak out the back exit that is exclusively for the use of the bands playing.

"They definitely went to school with us. You remember the twins, Brian and Ben Johnson? They hung out with all the metal heads?" Lila asks as we approach our next stop, Big Daddy's.

"Metal heads? Hmm, don't remember them."

"Cam, did that shitbag you dated ever let you out of his house?"

I grin at her affectionate nickname for Todd.

"He's just lucky my ass moved out to Cali with you. If not, his body would be floating in the ocean somewhere."

Laughing out loud at her comment, I shout,

"Yeah, well I'm outta the house now, so let's go make up for old times!"

Big Daddy's is much more sophisticated than the hole-in-the-wall we just left. It's a hotel, bar, and restaurant, and rather than housing deafening cover bands, it provides an atmosphere of swanky lounge music, which filters throughout various rooms of circular benches, high-top tables, and pillow-topped couches.

Lila reaches around my shoulder to speak into an ear that is still ringing from the band. "I'll grab the shots, you get the drinks."

Retrieving our drinks first, I snag us a booth next to a window that looks out over the moonlit ocean. A few minutes later, Lila approaches our table with a tray of shots, two extra guys, and excitement written all over her face. Her two guests are both tall and thin with very little muscle bulk protruding from their frames. One has short, spiked hair with tips that look like the bleach bottle had splashed up and landed only on certain parts. His friend looks very similar to him, like they could be brothers, but has long hair that is falling in all different directions from his hand traveling through it too much over the course of the evening.

I glare at Lila as the two guys squeeze next to me in the booth. Lila, oblivious to my discomfort, hands everyone a shot and raises her glass. We all join her and suck down the shots together. Feeling a little more sassy than normal, probably due to the large intake of alcohol all night, I blurt out, "I'm sorry, no offense, but who the fuck are you guys?"

Lila nearly spits out the sip of vodka tonic she has just taken. "Jesus, let's not scare them away with your profanity. This is Jace and Judd. They both work at Carter's shop." She looks at the guys and points in my direction. "This foul-mouthed girl is my best friend,

Camryn."

Feeling more comfortable knowing Lila knows the guys, I shake their hands to greet them. "Sorry, just thought she was bringing some randoms to our table."

For the next hour, Lila and I alternate rounds of drinks and shots, which sends Carter's employees into a drunken state that forces them to retire early. By the time they leave, we are in the giggle stage of drunkeness, finding humor in the most mundane things around us. With my bladder about to explode, I stand up to make my way to the bathroom, but instead, meet the eyes of the person who has occupied my thoughts all day. Cole is gazing right at me, taking in my whole body with one sweeping glance. I feel the heat penetrate from his eyes, which causes my body to warm and my blood to pump through my veins. No amount of alcohol could ever cause this reaction through my body. Just as I'm about to approach him, I see a familiar figure with newly-highlighted hair lean into his ear and whisper something. I reach behind to balance my body on the table, feeling like the wind was just knocked out of me. Lila grabs onto my hand after witnessing what I had just seen. I look to her and recite her client listing.

"Big, bolded B … Tara Chambers … three-thirty appointment … stylist Gabby … partial highlight, cut, and style."

"Cam, you have no idea what it's about. Don't jump to conclusions. Maybe there's a reason they're here together."

I look at the time on my cell phone and reply, "Twelve-thirty, at a bar, and missing all day … don't think I really have to jump to anything. It smacked me right in the face."

I try to focus on Lila's voice over my drunken thoughts. "Maybe she's his friend. I'm sure he has some of those."

"No way in hell that bitch has friends. No one would put up with her shit. There's only one thing a guy wants from that type of girl." I look back over to Cole and his companion, who is still leaning close and carrying on a conversation. However, his eyes are locked on me.

Just as Cole stands up from the bar and steps in my direction, I grab hold of Lila to stop my swaying and drag her out of the bar. Out of the corner of my eye, I see Cole stop dead in his tracks, watching my every move, his stare following me out the doors. I flag down a cab with urgency, and as soon as we slump into the seat, I unleash my tears as Lila, yet again, comforts my broken heart. Once home, she guides me to my bedroom, slips on my pajamas, and washes the makeup from my face. She lays in bed with me and strokes my hair until my eyelids grow heavy.

Right before I drift off, I feel her kiss my forehead and whisper, "At least we'll always have our vaginas."

Chapter Seven
Where You Are

The dark clouds casting a morbid glow in my bedroom seem to perfectly fit my mood. I decide to nurse my pounding headache and churning stomach as close to a comatose state as possible. If I keep my eyes closed, the real reason for my hangover will stay buried beneath my sheets. No amount of alcohol could ever cause this sickness. I felt it the instant I saw Cole with someone else last night. Jealousy is truly a bitch.

Tara haunted my dreams, showing up at the doctor's office, trying to take Gavin away. Everyone seems to find a way into this repetitive nightmare. Last night was no exception. I found myself awake in the early hours of morning, unable to stop my racing thoughts for a few hours. I tried to listen for Cole's Wrangler in the driveway or Tara's voice through the wall, but it never happened, and now I am left confused and crazy.

Flopping my arm behind me, I swat at nothing but balled-up sheets and misplaced pillows. I already heard Lila tiptoeing her way out my bedroom door earlier this morning. Before I flip my body over, I feel something crinkle beneath my fingertips. Grabbing it, I swing my hand around in front of my face and notice an envelope with a note from Lila that reads,

Instructed to give this to you in a dire time of need. Definitely think this may be that time. XOXO, Li

I hold it up in the air and debate whether I can handle the contents inside. With a deep breath, I inch my finger along the top seam, breaking it open at a slow pace. Through the folded paper, I can see the well-known handwriting seeping through. I straighten my back and brace myself to read what message my mom is trying to convey now.

Dearest Camryn,
I entrusted Lila to give you this particular piece
of advice at a crossroads in your journey. You need to
know that not all things are as they seem. No matter the
pain and loss you have endured in your past, I urge you
to move forward and to believe. Believe in explanations,
in reasons, in feelings, and do the one thing that is so
difficult to do—accept. Understand that life and love are
never seamless, and those small imperfections are what
give it character.
All my love,
Mom

My mom's presence is so strong that it's like she isn't gone. She knows my fear of rejection will be a hurdle that will hold me back from finding myself again, and her influence over this can only be felt through her written words. If nothing else, her latest advice urges me out of my hiding place and just to simply put one foot in front of the other.

After checking on Gavin with a text to Carter and chugging a bottle of spring water, I realize that staring at the wall between my house and Cole's makes me feel like one of those crazy stalkers on *The Jerry Springer Show*. If I remain like this for much longer, I'll probably start throwing chairs and curse words around the room. Needing a release and a break from my insanity, I know exactly where I can find refuge for a few hours. I throw on my workout clothes and running shoes and decide to take the beach route to my favorite spot.

With the thick clouds looming overhead and the holiday weekend over, the beach is virtually empty, aside from some kite surfers, who are taking advantage of the incoming storm breezes. As the distance from my house lengthens, I begin to feel more at ease and slow my pace. However, flashes of Tara whispering in Cole's ear occasionally brings me to a full-on sprint, so it doesn't take long to reach the inlet at the bottom of the island.

The rough current from the bay meeting the ocean slaps up against the rock jetties, creating a feeling that matches the turmoil in my heart. Lila and I would come here when we felt like our lives were spinning out of control. However, those times seem to define my life more so than hers. The inlet always makes me feel empowered, like the roughness of these waters emanate a sense of force from me. As I climb the rocks and find my spot next to the engraving that reads, *M.R.S. Ride on 4-Ever*, I recall my last visit here on the first day we returned home.

Carter, Lila, Gavin, and I trekked here ten blocks with my mom's ashes in hand. We etched her initials on the highest rock we could find and then spilled her ashes into the rough waters that skilled surfers would see as a pure joyride. I couldn't bear the thought of my mom in the crowded waters on the guarded beaches, so this sanctified place was the most proper burial place.

I tug at my mom's letter, which is folded in my hip-pack, and read it over and over again. Trying to relate her words of wisdom to my heavy heart, my eyes keep gravitating toward the word *accept*. She always wished that I could learn to accept my past and focus on what was ahead of me. It is a concept that I always struggle with, probably because my anger and fear have never allowed it. Just as my mind is trying to grasp the depth of my mom's advice, a familiar voice jolts my body to life.

"The best place on the island … no crowds, no guards … just you and the undisturbed water." Cole crouches down to take a seat next to me.

Shocked by his presence, I struggle with my words. "How did ... I mean, where ... why are you here?"

"Lila told me where to find you. I think we should talk." He reaches his arm out in front of him, extending his hand toward mine.

Noticing his trembling fingers, I ache to stop them and meet my hand to his, letting him guide me to sit down on the rocks next to him. Outlined by dark circles, his normally crystal-blue eyes are hazy, evident of a sleepless night. Light stubble begins at his cheekbones and covers his chin, casting a light shadow over his face. As he sits, his shoulders slumped against the rock behind us, he continues to stare at me, never allowing his eyes to leave mine.

Squeezing my hand tightly, he begins to speak, "I remember the first time I saw you in the cafeteria. You were sitting at the table closest to the doors, wearing a pink sweater that made your skin glow. You caught my eye immediately as I stood at the soda machine behind your table. I had just gotten off an in-school suspension for beating the shit out of one of the Murphy brothers and everyone at school was talking about it—talking about me. Everyone but you. The guy that had his arm around you was going on and on about how crazy I was, how toxic I was. But instead of agreeing with him, you pushed his arm off of you, stood up from the table and said, 'He's not crazy. Maybe he's misunderstood. Maybe someone that was supposed to love him broke him.' Then you stormed out of the cafeteria and..."

I place my hand over my mouth, gasp, and whisper back to him, finishing the story, "You followed me, stopped me in front of the lockers, and said, 'Thank you for not being them.'" Tears begin to fill my eyes as the memory resurfaces.

Cole lifts his thumb to my cheek, begins to softly stroke it, and continues, "I knew, at that moment, that you had something that no other girl would ever have—the ability to see me for who I really was, not the monster everyone made me out to be."

"I remember all the whispers and lies about you. I had never talked to you before that day but somehow I knew they weren't true and you were just hurting with no way to calm the anger. I never forgot that day. It was the first time since my dad left that I felt normal. I felt like someone was going through the same pain as me. I knew you were damaged, just like me."

He nods to me and says, "After that day, I had to know everything about you. So I asked around about you … made a point to see you everyday. But you never noticed anyone around you, except the guy who always had his arm around you. I was jealous of him. I wanted to be him … be the one who made you laugh, the one who held your gaze. It didn't matter though. By then you owned me, and I wanted you … I needed you."

I choke back the oncoming tears as he spills the contents of his heart to me.

"Before you walked away from me at the lockers, you turned around and said, 'Remember, it's okay to feel the anger, just don't live with it for too long.' That's when I knew everything I was feeling about my dad was okay. That I was going to be okay."

I take hold of his hands hands and ask, "Why didn't you tell me how you were feeling back then? Why didn't you try to talk to me again?"

"Oh, Camryn, it wasn't the right time. And you were in love. I saw that and figured I didn't have a chance. Besides I was fucked up … angry, bitter, and fighting everything that breathed. I was willing to wait for you … I'm still ready to wait for you." Cole clears his throat, trying to hide his shaky voice. "And when I saw you walking on the beach last week, I knew something had brought you back here … to me."

Unable to hold back the tears any longer, I give in and they begin to pour down my cheeks. Cole holds me as my emotions unleash. He has just professed what I've been searching for since I left here five years ago but was always too afraid to find. The anger from last night, the confusion from the past week, and the worries of the last five years disappear as he holds me. I am ready to give myself to him, to us, even with the uncertainty and the risks.

While in Cole's embrace, I confess, "After last night and seeing you out, I thought you gave up … that you didn't want to give us a chance anymore … that I was too broken for you. I couldn't bear seeing you with someone else."

He cups my face in his strong hands. "Camryn, what you saw last night was nothing. She … Tara … is just someone from my past, someone who needed to hear the truth from my mouth… the truth that there is no one but you and there will never be. I have my second chance and there's no way in hell I'm screwing that up. In some crazy way that I'll never be able to explain, I gave you a piece of my heart without you even knowing, and you took it with you when you left years ago. Now it's time to give you the rest of it … and have yours, if you'll give it to me."

I reach my hand to his face and drag my thumb over his scruffy cheeks. "I'm ready to give it to you … if you want it."

I wrap my arms around his neck as he pulls me into him. Tilting my head, our lips crash together, and a tingling sensation envelopes my body. I feel our tongues meet and explore every inch of our desire. Through his words, Cole has poured his heart out to me, and now in his kiss he confesses his needs.

Separating from our spellbinding kiss, Cole leans into me and professes, "Camryn Singer, I don't deserve you ... never have ... but I'll never disappoint you. That's a promise."

I pull his mouth back to mine and run my hands through his hair, weaving the ends through my fingers. Although lust is pumping through my veins, I set it aside, taking this moment to just enjoy his lips and feel the brush of his tongue against mine. We stay in each other's arms for a long while as we watch the waves ripple across the rocks and the seagulls touch down to peck the water for fish. I can feel our bodies finally surrender to a sense of calm. Although we still have so much to learn about each other and many more fears to face, we find a way to take that first step and will journey the rest of the way together.

Cole interrupts my thoughts as he shifts his body out of my arms. "As much as I wish you could stay in my arms like this, I think we need to get back. I'm sure Gavin will be home soon, and I owe him pizza and ice cream."

"How'd he rope you into that? Did Batman finally beat out Spiderman?"

Cole shrugs his shoulder and laughs. "Yeah right. Like that would ever happen. Actually, he bet on you ... said your heart would let me in."

I give him a playful smack in his ribs, and he pretends to hold his hand over them in pain. "You bet against me? You know, that's grounds for dismissal."

"If you would have seen the way you left the bar last night, even you'd bet against yourself."

I pause for a moment, thinking about how I had

rushed out of the bar, thinking the worst about Cole, "Good point … let's not keep the little prince waiting!"

We laugh and simultaneously reach for each other's hand. The beach that is so familiar and full of past heartache suddenly takes on a new life. Cole has given me a reason to look forward.

The walk home is spent talking about the normal things: work, surfing, summer plans. As we approach the end of our walk, three crazy people waving and yelling our names block the entrance to our houses. Gavin bolts toward us, jumps into Cole's arms, and reaches one arm out for me to pull me in for a group hug. The change in his demeanor from yesterday is astounding, and I know the sight of Cole and me together is part of that. Surely Carter also helped by pumping him with junk food all night at their sleepover. Lila and Carter join the hug seconds later, making me feel like I can call this home again.

We break apart from our embrace with Lila begging for the scoop, Carter complaining of hunger, and Gavin bragging about winning his bet with Cole. Before I can answer anyone, Cole puts his arm around me and looks at Gavin.

"Gavin, I want to make sure that you're okay with your Mommy and me spending a lot of time together."

Gavin looks from me to Cole and replies, "Does it mean you're gonna kiss each other a lot now? Because that's kinda gross."

"Well, I think you better get used to that." Cole leans over and whispers to him, "Because your mom's way too pretty not to kiss."

With a disgusted look, Gavin yells out, "Eww, gross!" He then reaches around Cole's neck again and says, "But it's okay if you and Mommy see each other.

Even if you have to kiss."

"Aww, thanks, buddy." Cole reaches his fist up to Gavin.

Gavin taps his fist back to Cole's and replies, "You're welcome, buddy."

Watching the two of them interact like this creates a feeling of contentment and satisfaction that is so new and refreshing. Everyone starts walking toward the back deck while I take one more look out toward the vast stretch of sand. This beach town holds the reason for my nightmares and heartache. But today, it represents the birth of my new life, one that includes Cole. However, looking toward the water's edge, my elation is quickly stripped from me as I stand staring into the aqua-colored eyes of my biggest fear.

Chapter Eight
Demons

The pounding of my heart and the unbearable weight of my legs takes over as panic lances through my body. Standing on the beach in front of me, Todd is as close as he was five years ago, only this time he isn't walking away from me. I can't pull my stare from him, maybe hoping he is a figment of my imagination, a consequence of my lack of sleep. However, I can feel his force and see his rage, just as I have every night, except now, I am wide awake.

My mind races through every possibility of why he is standing on the edge of my property. Todd ascends the beach in my direction, and while my head is telling me to run from him, my legs seem to be stripped of that ability. Anger blankets me, causing my fists to clench, as I realize that Todd still has the ability to affect me. Praying for the strength to face my nightmare, I watch him quickly turn away, scurry back down the beach, and then disappear from sight. As confusion settles in, a soothing voice brings me out of my shock.

"When you didn't follow us to the deck, I was afraid you might have changed your mind about me." Cole steps behind me and wraps his arms around so that they hook at my stomach.

Trying to catch the breath that has just left my body, I lean back into him and grab hold of his hands in front of me. "You're not getting rid of me that easily." I tilt my head backward and pull his down so I could meet his lips. "I told you I'm all yours, Mr. Stevens."

I kiss Cole with desperation in an attempt to erase the unsettled feeling Todd has just brought back into my life, or maybe I am just trying to mask the terror and uncertainty I am feeling. However, everything ceases to exist as I melt into our kiss, grateful for the few seconds Cole is able to erase Todd from my mind.

He interrupts the fire between our lips and whispers, "Call me Mr. Stevens again, and I promise you your back will be pressed against this sand and I'll be tasting more than these beautiful lips of yours." He places his index finger to my mouth.

Pulling his ear to my mouth in hopes that he won't see the worry evident on my face, I whisper back, "I'll definitely keep that in mind."

I slide my hand down his neck and then his arm to meet his hand. Urging him toward the house, I take one last look at the ocean, ensuring Todd is no longer there. I convince myself to keep the sighting a secret until I can find out why he's looking for me. The last thing I want is for Todd to find a way into Gavin's life and ruin any chance I have with Cole. I have to keep everyone protected, even if it means that I keep seeing Todd a secret. Yep, it is decided ... nobody needs to know.

Entering the house to Gavin setting the table and Lila and Carter arguing about how much cheese to put on top of lasagna, I am able to tuck away some of my anxiety. Once I observe the setup for family dinner, I shoot a glance to Lila.

"Li, I think we're a little early for family dinner. It's only Tuesday."

"No shit, Sherlock! This dinner's for you, Cole planned it."

Shock registers on my face as I peek up at Cole. He is wearing a boyish grin.

"For me? For what?"

"Well, I mentioned to Lila that we should give you a 'good luck on your first day of work' dinner, but..."

Lila interrupts Cole's explanation. "*Mentioned*! Ha! More like begged."

Cole continues, "Okay, Okay… I was a little persistent. But I think we have a lot more to celebrate now." Cole leans down and takes control of my mouth with his again.

Lila applauds our affection, as Carter yells, "Get a room!" and Gavin is pretending to stick his finger in his throat as he makes gagging noises. I smile into our kiss and ask Cole, "How'd I get so lucky to find you again on the beach last week?"

"I already told you that I've been waiting a long time for you. And you're wrong … I'm the lucky one."

As I blush at his compliment, I look over to Gavin. "You okay with dinner at home tonight, Gavs? I know you won a bet for pizza and ice cream."

"This is better, Mommy. It's a party for you and parties mean presents! Anyway, Cole said he can take me tomorrow."

I nod at him and throw my hands in the air. "Well then, tonight we party!"

Everyone cheers while anxiety begins to filter through my body. I can't shake the image of Todd's icy glare, his stiff upper body, and his determined march toward me. What can he possibly want, aside from my son? With that thought, the room begins to spin, and each breath takes more effort than my body can handle. I twist around as I plan my escape to fresh air and dash out the door. Running straight toward the deck railing, I lean over, my hand frantically grabbing at the fabric on the side of my pants where my inhaler would normally be if I had a pocket. I am in desperate need to find my breath or heave out the burning image of Todd.

Strong arms surround me and urge me from the side of the deck. I allow myself to collapse into the safety of Cole's embrace and plant my head against his chest, taking a heavy lungful against him. When my breathing begins to even, he questions me.

"How long have you suffered from panic attacks?"

I shudder at the term that reminds me of all my years of therapy. A few months after my dad left, the school had planned a Father Daughter Dance. Not having any brothers or uncles that lived close by, Lila's dad offered to take both of us. Sitting at my vanity while Lila did my hair for the dance, I thought about the looks and whispers I would get walking in there with Mr. Walters and Lila. I couldn't seem to catch my breath and eventually just collapsed to the floor. My mom forced me to a number of shrinks over the years, and they all tried to teach me "stress-reducing techniques" because "panic attacks were my body's attempt to release." Blah, blah, blah. When I became pregnant, I became more aware of the attacks and was able to stop most of them as they came on, so I convinced my mom that I didn't need the psycho-babble anymore.

"I guess it was a few months after my dad left, when I finally realized he was never coming back."

Cole continues to hold me, stroking my back, comforting me as I deal with it and maybe even reliving his own past through my attack.

Trying not to dampen the evening, I back away and smile. "I'm fine now. So just go in … let everyone know I'm good. I just need a minute … okay?"

Hesitating to walk back in, he leans down and kisses my forehead. "When the demons get too close, I want to be the one to get rid of them for you." He meets my eyes with his. "Promise me you won't fight them alone."

I shake my head and guilt swarms me as I realize

that I have already broken that promise. But nobody can know about Todd's return for Gavin's sake. This is one demon I have to face alone.

I manage to keep my terror at bay for the rest of the evening. Dinner is just as my mom would have liked it, with a crowded kitchen and loud conversation. After dinner, Lila brings out a cake in the shape of a needle that reads, "Happy Poking." While Gavin gets a kick out of it, I just roll my eyes at my best friend's interpretation of my job. We really can't be more opposite, but I would never have it any other way.

Gavin is so proud when he presents gifts to me. I let him sit on my lap and open each one. Lila and Carter bought me a new pair of designer scrubs with a card that reads, "No reason you can't look hot and sexy in polyester!" Gavin made me a card and gave me a wallet-sized photo of the two of us that is to be attached to the lanyard that holds my ID card. The last gift to open, wrapped in a small square box, is from Cole. Gavin opens the lid of the box, and my breath hitches at the familiar sight of a small silver medal with intricate angel wings engraved on it. On the back it reads, *Alone is impossible in a world full of angels.* My hand begins to tremble as I stare at the medal.

I look at Cole with wide eyes and have trouble finding my voice. "How … how'd … you get this?"

"Your mom gave it to me a few years ago … during a rough patch. Except for when I was surfing, it has never left the chain around my neck." He wraps his hand around mine that is holding my mom's medal. "I want you to have it now."

"I used to play dress-up with this when I was a little girl. When I didn't see it in her jewelry box, I thought she lost it."

He takes it from my hand and secures it around

my neck. "It's back where it belongs. It can be your comfort now."

I draw him into me and give him a slow, gentle kiss. Gavin jumps in between us and Cole holds him as we all admire my mom's medal.

Lila and Carter leave shortly after, as she insists that I need a good night's sleep since peoples' lives will be in my hands in twelve hours. Cole helps Gavin dress in his Batman pajamas and slippers. After we do the normal bedtime routine, Cole starts to gather his things to leave. A pang of disappointment hits me, knowing he isn't staying with me. Since we met, I've dreamed of waking up with him, among doing other things in my bed. I've already had a small taste of what he feels like when he was wrapped around me on the couch the other night. I can hear the teenage rebel in me screaming for him to stay, but that nagging mom voice wins out, reminding me of my son's innocence. Damn that goody-goody!

Cole reels me in, and his mouth meets mine with the same intensity as the very first time we kissed. I am sure the feeling of his lips on mine will never lose its passion. Everything about him defines sensual, and it drives me to want to explore every inch of his body every time we touch.

After I make him repeat his kiss three more times, he finally pulls away with a smirk on his face. "I'll get Gavin in the morning for lessons. He's gonna hang with me and my friend, Dusty. We're surfing all day."

"Uhhh yeah ... I know. He hasn't stopped talking about it since you told him." I laugh as I remember Gavin going on and on about hanging with his "surfing buddies."

"But for you, I'm available all night long." He winks, then walks across the deck to his door, leaving my body throbbing for him.

****

The water comes in and out and curls around my ankles, sending shivers up my spine. I watch as surfers glide across the waves, twisting their bodies back and forth for control. I envy their ability at that moment, since my stomach is too big to do even simple tasks. But I know that soon this being inside of me will be exposed to the world, finding the same solace in the beauty and tranquility of the beach.

I reach down to hold my growing belly but instead am filled with terror. I can't find my roundness. I can no longer feel the feet in my ribcage or the arms stretching down my abdomen. As I glare into aqua-colored eyes, I begin to scream, realizing he has stolen my baby from me.

As tears stream down my face and my body trembles in fear, I leap out of bed to check on Gavin. Seeing his chest slowly rise and fall brings me relief, as he is safe in his bed, unaffected by the horror that plagues me each night. Fearing the onslaught of another panic attack, I race upstairs to the back deck, and suck in the cool breeze coming off the ocean.

The small sliver of moon in the midnight sky gives way to the eeriness of pitch darkness. I light the citronella candle on the patio table to get my bearings and make my way to the railing, hoping the sound of crashing waves of the high tide would soothe the aftermath of my latest nightmare. While trying to sort out the details of my dream and figure out what each part symbolizes, I am surprised by a voice that I missed when he walked out my door a few hours ago.

"Sometimes the nightmares catch up, and you can't even figure out what's real anymore."

The sight of Cole illuminated by the dull light of

the candle makes my heart pump even faster. He is wearing gym shorts, low on his waist, exposing the "V" of his lower torso. I can't help but imagine what exists at the point of that "V," as my desire for him becomes almost unbearable. His muscles ripple down his tanned body, accentuated by hard lines that define every part of his expansive chest and stomach. His messy hair, falling in different directions, teases me to reach up and run my hands through it. I manage to gaze up at him and am met with the softest blue eyes, which hold both comfort and pain.

"Trying to remember a night without one … that's what doesn't seem real." My voice lowers, and I'm almost ashamed of what I'm about to say. "I sometimes wonder if they're just the consequences of the choices I've made … that I'm supposed to suffer in this world of what ifs."

Cole pulls my body into his and strokes up and down the sides of my form-fitted tank top.

"For me, I guess karma's a bitch when you've fucked up the way I have. But you didn't have a choice. You're not the reason for your pain. It was caused by others."

Appreciating his understanding of my life, I add, "Guess I'm just simple or maybe completely naïve, but all I'm looking for is that happy ending."

He nods and holds me tighter. I believe that he wants the same thing but for some reason doesn't think he deserves it.

I start to graze my hands over his arms, tracing his tattoo of a rose within a cracked heart with my fingers. My need for him is screaming over my rational side, which tells me to slow it down. But I want every part of his body over and over again, and if I don't get it, I might just explode. I have to let Cole know there is nothing more I crave right now than our bodies intertwined together as we discover what can make us moan and the places that will cause us to scream.

"Did I ever tell you how sexy you are, Mr. Stevens?" I whisper into Cole's ear.

Either Cole is stunned by my forwardness or planning a way to get me on my back like he promised before, because his stroking hands freeze on my waist. His comforting gaze transforms into a hunger that needs to be fed. I watch as a seductive smirk appears on his face. In a husky voice, he warns, "I think I already told you what I'd do to you if you called me that again?"

"Hmm… I think I might remember that. Maybe I'm just waiting for you to follow through." I hold his gaze and plant a soft kiss on his lips.

He tilts his head and cocks his eyebrow, suggesting that he is going to take my challenge. Sweeping my legs out from under me, Cole floats me over to the oversized lounge chair and gently places me down on my back. He slowly crawls up and kisses each part of me until he reaches my lips.

While he teases every inch of my body, my hands are weaving through his hair, feeling the short silky strands beneath my fingers. Every time his lips touch my skin, I tug at his hair and a moan would rise in his throat.

I pull his mouth to mine and savor the taste of him. My hands leave his hair and run down the lines of his carved chest, tracing around his nipples. Feeling the hairs rise from his skin, I travel further south over the ridges of his stomach muscles and then slowly slide my hands under the waistband of his shorts. I let them teeter there and tease him to arousal.

"God, Cam, you're gonna kill me." He runs his tongue down my neck and over the exposed part of my stomach, cupping his hand over my core. He murmurs in between contact. "I. Need. This. Right. Now."

With a sigh, I beg, "Please, Cole … take it … take me."

Using my plea as his invitation, Cole lifts my tank top over my head and wiggles my shorts off. His breath hitches when he sees I have nothing on underneath, and his eyes swallow up my naked body.

"You're so beautiful." Cole runs his tongue between my breasts, over my stomach, ending at my inner thighs. He stays there and alternates between licking and nibbling as my body throbs with need.

My hands tug at his shoulders, trying to urge his body to move on top of me.

He creeps up my body like an animal stalking its prey. As he holds his weight with locked arms over my body, he gazes at me with hooded eyes, revealing his desire for me with no words spoken.

To declare my own need, I rip off his shorts and boxer briefs in one motion, throwing them to the side.

Cole leans into my ear and whispers, "Don't move."

He climbs off me and dashes into his house while I lay on the deck, exposed and confused. He leaves me needing to be satisfied. After I hear the roll of his slider door, he mounts himself over me again, rips open the foil packet, and secures it over his shaft. He leans his lips down to my mouth, and I suck on his bottom lip as he pushes smoothly into me. I gasp in pleasure as every memory of my nightmare melts away with him, and all that is left is the two of us. Our bodies find a rhythm as we become familiar with each other. I can feel the intensity rising as Cole's moans begin to deepen with every thrust of my hips into him.

"You feel amazing… I need to take you … as far as I can go."

I arch my back toward the pleasure he is giving me.

Cole rocks my world with a passion I have never experienced before. He would climb me to the brink and then bring me back down, making me beg for more. When I feel us approach the final moment, I cup his cheeks in my hands, and we come together, staring into each other's eyes.

We hold each other in the darkness as our heavy breathing slows and our bodies come down from the incredible high we just experienced. I've never felt this intensity before, and I know I could easily become addicted. The more I discover Cole, the more I can feel myself falling deeper into him, which exhilarates and terrifies me.

With my mind wrapping itself around these feelings again, the pain I've become so familiar with, the one of being left behind, jars my memory. My body shivers, knowing that the years of distance from it can no longer be my security. Feeling the jolt through my body, Cole retrieves a blanket from the house and wraps us in it. He holds me close, as if he knows my fears are lingering. Within the warmth of his arms, my eyes grow heavy and I begin to lose consciousness. Fused with Cole, I am finally able to find sleep where none of my ghosts can haunt me.

Chapter Nine
Who do you think you are?

"Wake up, beautiful girl."

The sound of Cole's raspy morning voice and the smell of coffee swirling through my nose welcomes me to life. I hesitate to open my eyes, realizing that the magic of last night would be tainted by the reality of Todd's reemergence. As I slowly pry them open, a sea of blue meets my grogginess and warms my heart. His sexy mess of hair is a token of our night together, as my hands owned each strand of it last night. He is gazing at me with a broad smile that draws attention to his dimples, that are only noticeable when he is fully smiling. For the moment, I pretend that I am the only girl who is able to make him grin wide enough for them to appear.

"Mmmm … good morning to you. Is that coffee you're teasing my nose with?"

"Freshly brewed. I took you for a sugar and cream kind of girl … just a guess." He hands me the coffee as I shimmy myself up on the reclining chair, keeping the blanket secured over the top of me.

"Well, good guess. Am I that predictable?"

Cole reaches over my body, so both arms are trapping me in between.

He leans in and huskily says, "After last night, there's not one predictable thing about you. And I can't wait to find more surprises."

With heat radiating off my face, I begin to shift in my seat, both blushing from his compliments and aching for more of him. If I knew that my five-year-old wasn't on the verge of getting up, I probably would jump on Cole and demand round two. I scold myself for the lack of control I've had with him since day one, and attempt to roll out of the lounge chair away from him. I have to escape, so I can avoid the need for his body entangled with mine and the desire of his mouth exploring every single inch of my skin.

Patting myself down, I notice my clothes are already back on my body, and I give Cole a confused look.

"Oh yeah, after you fell asleep, I dressed you. It killed me to cover that incredible body, but I really didn't want Gavin to walk out and see us naked and wrapped around each other. I was afraid that I'd get my ass kicked by a five-year-old."

Laughing, I add, "Thanks. Definitely don't want to scar my son with that image. That's the kinda thing that would stay in his mind forever."

As I turn toward the door, Cole grabs my hand and in a serious tone says, "Camryn, last night was amazing. Everything about it—about you—was … is … perfect."

I grin at him, feeling my body do a victory dance. "Yeah, well, perfect is how I'd describe you." I squeeze his hand and add, "After last night, I'll be glowing for days."

He lifts my hand to his mouth and plants a tender kiss on my knuckle. Years and years of aching for a connection, and I finally see the promise of something real. As I turn to walk into the house, I sense his eyes scorching into me and, for once, I feel wanted.

By the time I'm showered, dressed in scrubs, and on my third cup of coffee, Cole and Gavin are cleaned up from breakfast and waxing their boards. They are getting ready for a day of surfing with Cole's buddy, Dusty. I peer onto the deck to watch Gavin laugh at Cole's goofy faces, wishing that I could just freeze time right at that moment. But one thing my past engrained within me is to never get too comfortable being happy because something will eventually crash.

After hugs from Gavin and a lingering kiss from Cole, I drive to the hospital that I haven't stepped foot in since my first prenatal appointment—the one that still frequents my nightmares. As I approach the place that represents pain and fear, my lungs tighten, and I can feel myself struggling to breathe evenly. I pull my car to the side of the road and reach into my bag for my bottle of water, and out pops a folded up piece of paper with unfamiliar writing on it. Fumbling to get it open, I scan to the top and begin to read.

> *Camryn,*
> *When it feels like the monsters are getting too close, remember to take slow, deep breaths and realize that you are in control. "When you own your breath, nobody can steal your peace." That's when the demons will leave you alone...*
> *Cole*

Instantly, my breathing normalizes, and my body tingles at the thought of Cole. How could this seemingly perfect man understand my thoughts? Why would he even want to deal with them? I push the negativity aside and drive the rest of the way to work with a renewed sense of confidence, one that Cole has started to build in me that day in front of the lockers. I recall the night before, remembering the taste of his mouth in mine, the musky scent his body always seems to have, and the feeling of his hands all over every inch of my body. Being with him so intimately made me see that what had once terrified me is actually beginning to mend me.

Shore Memorial Hospital's maternity floor is much smaller than the previous hospital I worked at in California. My experience in a larger and much busier hospital benefits me as I am assigned head of my rotation. This means that I am responsible for any in-labor patients, and if I am with them, the rest of my rotation will have to make rounds in recovery. I always prefer those rotations because it places me right in the middle of the action. Besides, after the long labor I had with Gavin, I can understand and ride the roller coaster of pain along with the expectant mothers.

With two labors, the morning flies and I am waiting in the hospital cafeteria for Lila, who is meeting me for my lunch break. As I sit at the table poking at the bland chicken Caesar salad on my tray and sipping my almost flat Diet Coke, I see a familiar bouncy blonde with new hot pink streaks through her hair come flying in toward me. She proceeds to grab my tray and empty its contents into the trash can and then place a large brown paper bag in front of me.

"You can thank me now." She winces at the spot where the tray used to be. "I just saved your ass from eating shit."

I shake my head at her and mockingly reply, "Thanks, Li. What would I ever do without you?"

"Well, you'd be eating ass and sure as hell not about to dive in to the best sushi on the East Coast." She swings the bag in front of my face.

My eyes widen and I gasp. "*Spanks*! Ohh… I may seriously have an orgasm after the first bite!"

"Hmm … speaking of that, you wanna tell me about last night? Or is that orgasm not up for discussion just yet?"

Fumbling with my chopsticks, I meet her stare and stutter. "Huh … um … well … how'd you know?" I can't seem to hide the goofy grin that is plastered to my face every time I think about the night with Cole.

"Well, besides your very noticeable afterglow, I

went to see Gavs today, and Cole had that same goddamned grin on his face too." She shrugs as she steals a piece of California roll from my plate. "You and Cole reek of sex, and by the looks of both of you … fuckin' amazing sex!"

"I think you need a job."

Waving me off, she answers, "Ahhh … the salon runs itself and, anyway, I have a more important job right now. Finding out about your night with studley."

Grinning at the memory of the night before, I gush, "Well, it was perfect … he's perfect. Let's just say, there were no grocery lists being made!"

She snorts, probably recalling the few times I've had sex in the last five years that would always equate to cabinets and a refrigerator full of food. "Well, thank God the supermarkets won't benefit from your sex life anymore! Cam, seriously, I'm happy for you. I think you guys might have something here. I mean, you never forgot about the guy since high school, even though you talked to him for like a total of five seconds." Her expression stiffens, and she leans in toward me. "But I have to tell you something before you go back to wiping asses or whatever you do here."

Ignoring her reference to my job, I say, "What's wrong? Is Gavin okay?"

"Yeah, yeah … it's nothing really … but Carter said some guy came into the shop yesterday and started asking his employees about you. Like if you were living back in your house, if you were with anyone, asking about Gavs … some creepy shit. Carter wasn't there so he didn't see what he looked like."

To hide my panic, I try to shrug off this information. "Probably just some guy from high school who saw me at Carter's during opening weekend. I'm sure it was nothing."

Not completely convinced by my casualness over this information, Lila adds, "Well, if I find out who the stalker is, I'm kicking his ass first, then having Carter and Cole finish for me."

I nod to appease her, then proceed to rush her out by getting up from the table to throw out my trash. We say our goodbyes, and I follow her to the rotating door that leads to the parking lot. When she is out of sight, I hug my arms across my body, fighting the tears away. Todd had made his rounds before he appeared on my beach yesterday, and now I can only prepare for what misery he is planning for my life.

My mind races for the remainder of my shift. Why did Todd come back, and what does he want from me? No matter how many reasons I conjure up in my mind, I keep going back to the one that has become my worst nightmare, the one that will rip me apart with no chance of being put back together, the one where he wants my son.

Right after he walked away, I would dream about ways he'd come back to us, apologizing for the mistake he made. But as Gavin reached his different milestones, I only grew angry that Todd wasn't a part of them and then fearful that he would one day regret his choice.

Feeling paranoia overtake my thoughts, I reach for my cell phone and text Cole.

Hope surf's up! Just checking on my boys. How's my mini one?

Realizing Cole and Gavin will most likely be in the ocean and not close to Cole's cell, I force myself to focus on my last few hours of work. I'm able to push thoughts of Todd aside to manage two more labors and three more rounds of recovery.

By the end of my shift, I find myself missing Gavin and craving Cole. Peeking at my phone, my heart flutters as I see the reply text from Cole.

Tasty waves today but not even close to how good you taste. We can't wait to see you at Jilly's tonight!

With a grin on my face, I rush out of the hospital, anxious to meet up at Gavin's victory dinner. As I approach my car, my excitement is quickly replaced with terror. Aqua eyes that I once adored follow me until we are standing face-to-face. Shock registers through every part of my body as I stare straight at Todd.

Todd speaks first, saying, "I always knew you'd come back to me." The rage in him last night on the beach is replaced by a look of defeat.

With anger simmering, I snap back, "I didn't come back for you … never for you."

"Then I guess you're back for Cole Stevens?" Todd's jaw tenses as he says his name.

Having no intention of answering him, I glare at him with utter disgust seeping from my face.

He shrugs, disregarding that I ignored his question. "All that matters is you're back, and our son's here."

"He's not *our* son." My voice drips with venom. "Who do you think you are? You don't fucking get to call him 'ours!' You don't even know my son's name! Where were you, Todd, when I first heard his heartbeat, when I was in hours of labor, when he took his first step, or said his first word? *Nowhere…* That's where! So he's not ours, he's mine, and you can't have him!"

My body is trembling and tears are streaming down my face as my frustration and anger seeps out. After my rant, Todd steps closer to me and reaches out as if he's trying to soothe me. I quickly jerk back from his close touch.

Clenching my teeth, I threaten, "Get the hell

away from me, and don't ever try to touch me again."

Wincing at my harsh words, he leans in to close the space I just put between us. "Cammy girl, I'm not going anywhere. You can't push me away. He's ours, and I have a right to see him."

I cringe at the name he always called me and fire back, "It's Camryn, and don't ever talk to me about your rights. You gave those up when you walked away."

"I know I walked away, Cammy, but people change. I changed. I want a second chance." He lowers his eyes to the ground and murmurs, "I miss you … you and him."

"You're five years too late. You got rid of us when you ran away. We will never want you."

Throwing his famous last words to me back at him, I push past his towering body and jump into my car as he stands watching me in the parking spot next to my car. When Todd is no longer in my sight, I pull to the side of the road to attempt to slow my breathing and grasp the note from Cole. "When you own your breath, nobody can steal your peace." I keep repeating it over and over again in my head while I take deep breaths in and out, but nothing can eradicate the anger that bubbles deep in my soul. I have to face the truth that Todd came back to break my family apart for a second time.

By the time I reach my house, fury is in control of my body and my thoughts are scattered everywhere. I dart into the house, searching for comfort underneath my covers. Thoughts of Gavin drive me to his bedroom before I can sink into the deep abyss of my bed. I scan the room, seeing everything that represents him, that makes him my son. His surf boards illustrating his favorite hobby, pictures of the ocean, his favorite place to be, his turtle dream light because Gavin's always been afraid of the dark, and a stack of J. Mullen books on the bottom of his bed because he can't go to sleep without reading at least one. Todd doesn't know these things. He wasn't there for the family fun days or the sick days, for the beach days or the rainy days, for the play days or the cuddle days. He gave up on us, so he could focus on himself. And now he thinks he can just show up in our lives and have us back? No. Fucking. Way.

Inching closer toward Gavin's hutch, I catch sight of the picture of Todd and me that my mom insisted he have. I fight back her voice in my head that tells me to keep it a part of Gavin's life, and I take it into my hands. With force, I throw it into the hallway, smashing it against the staircase. Hearing the glass crack against the tiles, I slump to the floor and wrap my arms around by bent legs. I break down, sinking my head into my knees, and allowing the anger and terror to pour out of me. As I turn my head toward the broken frame symbolizing my past, I see a white envelope peeking out from underneath the photo that is now separated from the frame.

Grabbing the letter, I tear it open as I make my way toward my bedroom. I throw myself on my bed, craving my mom's most recent words of advice.

Dearest Camryn,

I feared this "moment" since our little prince entered the world five years ago. It has been the foundation of your nightmares, and now it will become the cornerstone of your reality. You will cry, fight, and scream as your past merges with your present. You will want to push the ones you love or are beginning to love away, thinking that you have to fight this battle on your own. You may even want to run again, believing that distance will make it disappear. Camryn, don't. Find your inner strength and fight hard. Do what's best for Gavin, even if it kills you. Own your breath, then find

your peace.
    All my love,
    Mom

I center on the same words that Cole had just written a few hours before, which makes me feel closer to him. Anger begins to melt away, leaving me with uncertainty, which almost feels worse. I lay back into my pillows, feeling a weird mix of energized and defeated. Unsure of how Todd being in his life could ever be best for Gavin, I attempt to push those thoughts aside and motivate myself to do what I know is best for him right now: to meet him for dinner.

After showering, I am surprised to find my best friend sitting on my bed. Her head is down, looking at something in her hands. When I approach her, she meets my eyes, and I notice tears streaming down her cheeks. Startled to see her crying, panic begins to rise in me. Lila never even shed a tear at my mom's funeral and, come to think of it, there is really never a time I've ever seen her fully cry. She is always the strong one, and I'm always the wreck.

"Li, what's wrong? Is it Carter?"

Sniffling and shaking her head, she holds up what is in her hand. "He came back, didn't he? It was him who Jace and Judd saw at Carter's, wasn't it?" She lowers her voice and says, as more of a statement than a question, "And he wants Gavvy?"

As I recognize the picture of Todd from the broken frame, all I can do is nod at my friend.

She stands up, straightens her long, cotton dress, and wipes the tears from her face. "Not happening ... no fucking way he's getting him." She turns and walks out of my bedroom door. With the reassurance of her allegiance to Gavin and me, there is nothing left to do but prepare for battle.

Chapter Ten
Fix You

I spend the car ride to the boardwalk trying to convince Lila to keep the Todd sighting a secret from everyone. Exposing my resurrected past frightens me more than tucking it far out of sight, knowing that with it in clear view, I can lose so much, including my son and Cole. I know he is dealing with his own demons and adding one of mine seems unfair and wrong on every level. Or maybe I just don't want him to see how broken I really am and send him walking out of my life.

"Li, no one can know. Not yet." I look down to my lap and study my thumbs that are nervously rubbing against each other. "I mean, it's not fair to submerge him in my clusterfuck of a life."

"Cam, are you mental? He needs to know. He'd want to know! He's already heard all about the fuck-ups of your past. He's had his chance to jet and he hasn't." She slows the car and leans into the steering wheel.

Stunned speechless, I just shrug my shoulders and inspect the red marks my thumbs are leaving on my skin while Lila continues to rant.

"Cole can help fix this. He can make that shitbag crawl back in the hole he came from."

Frustrated with the conversation, I stomp my foot on the floor of the car. "No! This is my decision, and I need to protect Gav first. Not one person finds out about Todd until I figure out exactly why he's back." I repeat myself to Lila to ensure she understands that I'm serious. "No one finds out. Not Gavin, not Carter, not Cole. You understand?"

She nods as she looks straight out the window, trying to appease me.

"Li, I'm begging you to keep this a secret."

Desperation continues to seep from the shakiness in my voice. "I just can't forget about all those times Gav would ask my mom why his dad wasn't there. Or when he told Carter that if he could have one super power it would be to make his daddy come to see him. I just need my baby to be safe, that's all. Just please keep it quiet for now, okay?"

She lets out a heavy sigh that reveals her frustration with my request, but knows better than to press the issue with me.

"Fine. But the minute you look like you're breaking down or thinking about running again, deal's off."

I bob my head at her, grateful that the secret is safe with us ... for now. I know I don't have much time until Lila will break down and tell someone about Todd, so I have to work fast. What kills me the most is I'll have to talk to him, let him into my life in some way. *Do what's best for Gavin, even if it kills you.* That lingering message perplexes me, like I should actually consider letting Todd into Gavin's life. Ahh ... why can't the decision be something simple, like deciding on skinny jeans or maxi dress? But instead, as my mom's words continually swim through my thoughts, I struggle to find their true meaning with this more substantial problem, and am left treading in unknown water.

Entering the combined pizza shop and arcade, I feel like I'm in a time warp that takes me back to my childhood. I scan over the same vinyl-covered counter stools where I spent many Friday nights eating pizza with my dad while my mom coached lessons on the beach. Behind the last booth, the two-player Mrs. Pac-Man machine still stands, a reminder of the many days my dad would challenge me to "only one game," which would always turn into hours and hours of playing. The permanent marker sketches that reveal the newly-paired school couples decorate the row of Skee-Ball machines that line the back wall. Out of the corner of my eye, I see Lila smirking in that direction, probably remembering the many high school nights she spent betting with cute guys on who would win. She was the reigning champion, and I benefitted, never having to pay for a slice of pizza throughout our four years of high school.

As I search through the swarms of teenagers, I catch sight of Cole sitting in the large, corner, wrap-around booth. His naturally tanned skin has a hint of pink, revealing the hours he spent today on the beach. His hair is sticking up in different directions, a darker hue than normal, probably still wet from the ocean. The usual sky-blue of his eyes glistens even brighter against his sun-kissed skin. Surrounding the curve of his smile, scruff from one day without shaving lines his sculpted cheekbones, which coaxes my lips to feel the roughness of it. Lila's voice startles me out of my gawking.

"Carter's definitely a hot ass, but damn, Cole's one fine sight!"

I playfully elbow her in the ribs as she checks out Cole.

"And who's the new hottie sitting with him?"

Next to Cole is a man I assume to be his friend, Dusty. His long, sandy-brown locks fall loosely to his chin. While his eyes are not nearly as captivating as Cole's, they somehow invite you in, a kindness drawing you to them. Muscles, made evident by the sleeveless t-shirt he's wearing over his board shorts, stand out in relief from bronzed skin. Both men sitting together clearly define sexy, and I can't help but appreciate the women who keep inching closer to their booth.

"I think that's his best friend, Dusty Smith." After answering Lila, I notice she's trying to place if she knows him from growing up. "Don't think we'd remember him. He's a year older than Cole."

"Oh, that makes sense … no way I'd forget something that sexy." She grins as she eyes Dusty up and down.

"One word, Li … Carter."

She snaps her head back to me. "Oh, silly Cam, there's no harm in eyeing the candy. Just as long as I don't take a lick."

We both break out in laughter, generating some stares from people around us, including Cole and Dusty. As my eyes meet Cole's, the electricity that has surged through us since that first day on the beach returns with a zap. He is unraveling me, and I know that soon I'll be completely undone.

I hold his stare the entire way to the table and tuck myself into the arm that is stretched toward me. He draws me into him and places a tender kiss over my lips. As he pulls his lips away and tilts his forehead into mine, he whispers, "I may need to kiss you again, if that's okay?"

I smile as his question warms my heart and respond, "Better not be just one time."

Dusty clears his throat as though to alert us of his presence. Forgetting that someone is sitting right across from us, I pull away and put my hand in front of Cole's mouth. He looks at me, then to Dusty, and introduces us. With flames bouncing off my cheeks from our moment of affection, I manage to extend my hand to him and smile. Dusty proves to be much better at speaking at that very moment.

"Gotta tell ya, Gavin's a real natural on the board. The skills he has and only being five … damn, it was impressive. I'm sure he'll tell you all about it when he gets here with Carter."

Glowing from his compliment of my son, I reply, "My mom was a great teacher. She insisted that surfing was more important than learning to walk."

Cole and Dusty both nod their heads at my statement as Lila plops next to me.

She stretches her hand out to Dusty. "We haven't met yet. I'm Lila."

After Dusty introduces himself to Lila, they start talking about how the Jersey beach scene has changed in the last five years. He has just moved home from upstate New York, where he was earning his doctorate in Clinical Health Studies from Ithaca College. He is a physical therapist and came back here to work with all the top-notch athletes in the area. He and Cole's sister, Heidi, are living together, and from what he is saying, she seems to be the real reason for the move back.

As Lila and Dusty are entrenched in a conversation about how successful Carter's shop will be among all the Atlantic surfers, I cuddle close with Cole, who still has his arm draped around my waist. His fingers are rubbing in a circular motion over my hipbone, making every part of my body sizzle. I am beginning to realize that he can touch me in any sort of way and my body will automatically want more of him.

I lean in so Dusty and Lila can't hear me and ask, "Were you always okay with your sister dating your best friend?"

He shrugs his shoulder. "I actually met Dusty through my sister. They weren't really dating at that point, but I knew there was something between them. He kept me straight and stopped me from pounding faces. Stuck with me through a lot of shit. Helped me use surfing as my therapy. So I knew when his whipped ass followed my sister to school, he'd be back." Cole looks out over the boardwalk to the beach. "You might think you can stay away from the waves forever, but you find out you need it … like it has healing powers or something."

Sensing an emptiness about him, I can feel the pain in his words. I place my hand over his and lay my head on his chest. As he kisses my forehead, I ask, "Why'd you leave surfing?"

I can feel his body stiffen and hear his breathing become heavy. I have just found an entrance to his past, and I want so desperately to break in. I lift my head to see a stone-faced Cole staring into space. I cup his cheeks and force him to look at me. "Hey, Cole, it's okay. I'm here when you're ready to talk, all right?"

Snapping out of his daze, he gives a slight nod. As I stare into his eyes, silently pleading with him to open that door to his past, I can feel my desire for him deepen as I struggle to stay in control. I'm taken out of the moment when, suddenly, weighing down on me is a jumpy little kid who is shouting out loud.

"Mommy! Cole! Guess what! Guess what!" Before we can even answer Gavin, he continues, "We got the invite!"

We both look at Gavin with confusion. "Invite? What are you talking about, buddy? To what?"

"Not sure, Mommy. Uncle Carter said we were invited to some Atlantic thing or something."

Trying to sift through the meaning of what Gavin is saying, Cole adds his own thoughts.

"Gav, do you mean Carter's shop is sponsoring the Atlantic Classic?"

Gavin's face is now beaming and he leaps off the booth seat.

"Yes, yes! That's what I meant! Mommy, we get to go to that big surfing thing!"

My thoughts travel to the many summers I

attended the largest surfing competition on the eastern coast. The earlier years left fond memories of my past, as I would go to support my mom and the surfers she coached to get there. Yet, in the later years, I was there to cheer on Todd as he competed, sitting out in the sun all day long as I held onto his lucky bandana and gave his surfboard a kiss before every run. I shudder at the thought of how naïve I was to believe in him.

"Hey, bro, you want to introduce me to your friend, or you just gonna sit there staring at her?" A high-pitched voice following behind Carter and Gavin interrupts my reminiscing thoughts.

A petite woman in a short sundress stands in front of our table. Her long blonde ponytail swings from side to side as her attention bounces from me to Cole. While every feature is opposite of Cole's, there is no mistaking the color of her eyes—the same tint of sky blue that Cole's has. This must be Heidi, Cole's sister and Dusty's girlfriend. Beating him to the introductions, I stand up and greet her.

"Hi, I'm Camryn." Reaching around, I hoist Gavin into my arms. "And this is my son, Gavin."

Gavin is already furiously shaking her hand, making her laugh. "Well, I'm Heidi, Cole's older, much cooler, sister."

Gavin shouts, "Cole, you just got burned!" The whole table breaks out into laughter while Dusty and Carter slip in high fives to my son. His smart-ass comment even brings life back to the dismayed Cole who, moments ago, was trapped in his past.

Gavin's victory dinner mirrors a larger and louder family dinner, and Heidi and Dusty seem to fit right in our little group. Gav takes an instant liking to her, especially after he finds out that she will be his kindergarten teacher in the fall. My son is savvy enough to know to start brown-nosing months before the start of school. She even invites Gav to her summer camp group, so he can meet some boys his own age and, as she puts it, "stop hanging out with old dudes." Once I agree to camp, he begins chomping into his very large slice of pizza.

While Lila is trying to recruit Heidi as a customer and Dusty and Carter are discussing plans for the upcoming surfing competition, I notice the distant look in Cole's eyes has returned and am certain his past secrets are toying with his thoughts. I reach my hand to his leg and rub his thigh with the tip of my nails. He jolts when my touch meets the thin fabric of the board shorts that cover his legs. His arm that is draped across my back hooks me in closer to his chest.

"Cole, man, what brand do you want to represent from Carter's place at the Classic?" Dusty and Carter are staring at him inquisitively.

With confusion setting in, I jump into the conversation before Cole can answer. "What do you mean?" I turn my attention to Cole. "Are you surfing in the classic?"

He gives a modest shrug and replies, "Yeah. I made it in after Dusty at the Winter Qualifiers, and now we're training together."

I lean over and embrace him. "I'm so proud of you! The Atlantic Classic is big time!"

Congratulatory hugs follow from Lila, and then Gavin joins in by leaping over me to jump on Cole. We all celebrate by toasting our sodas in the air, and then, getting up from the table, Cole, Dusty, and Carter challenge Gavin to a game of Transworld Surf in the arcade. Cole places Gavin on his shoulders as they all strut toward the video game, leaving us girls in the booth.

As we bask in Cole's exciting news, the three of us begin to plan our summer around the competition.

Because all three guys are involved, we will have guaranteed tickets and all-access passes. While Lila and Heidi are prematurely planning the victory party, I watch Cole from across the pizza shop. He seems to isolate himself in his own thoughts and hope I can somehow break through. Then, Gavin's high-pitched voice suspends my musings.

"Aunt Lila, can you play Skee-Ball with me, puhlease? Mommy says you're the bestest ever!"

Never able to turn down a chance to show off her skills, Lila jumps up from the table and whisks Gavin away toward the back wall, where she held the title for countless years, bragging to Gavin about the "good ole days" all the while. Once they've moved off, Heidi scoots close to me.

"I've been waiting to get you alone. I've heard so much about you already." Heidi is smiling from ear to ear, displaying the same dimples as her brother.

Unsure why her comment causes me embarrassment, I turn my head and lock my eyes on a father and son pair playing the Mrs. Pac-Man machine together. Fond visions of me with my own father flood my mind, as well as possibilities of Gavin's future with Cole. I manage to find comfort with these thoughts.

"Hmm ... not sure if that's a good thing. I mean, according to Lila, I'm crazy."

"It's a good thing, Camryn. Crazy's the only way to be with Cole. Trust me. He'll drive you there anyway." Finding humor in her sarcasm, she tilts her chin up and raises her glass to a glaring Cole. With a tight expression, he gives a slight nod and returns his attention to his video console.

"It's not possible. I'm as crazy as they come." I switch the topic and then add in a more serious tone, "Why doesn't he talk about the Classic?"

"Well, he left the sport for a while and that competition was sort of the reason. But that's his story to tell." In a whispered hush, she continues, "Camryn, he's letting you in—no, he's wanting you in. And he's just … different. Like he's alive again with you."

Heidi's gaze travels to Cole, and I notice tears welling up in her eyes, as if she is having her own walk down memory lane. I am familiar with that expression because I would often catch it on my mom and Lila, pining for the old me, needing her to emerge from the heartache and pain that I was buried under.

I link my arm with Heidi's and comfort her. "But he's already doing that for me—he's helping me find a reason to love coming home."

Still staring at her brother, she wipes a tear that escapes down her cheek. "I just want my brother back. I know this is a lot to ask of you, considering we just met, but… " She turns her gaze to me and chokes out, "Camryn, can you please just take care of his heart and help him be the person he once was?"

Shuddering at the intensity of her words, I can only reply, "I'll try."

She grabs my hand that is on her elbow and gives it a tight squeeze. At that instant, I know I will do anything to bring that spark back to Cole. Just as he tore down my walls, I can only wish to do the same and rebuild his foundation—give him a new beginning. But how can I possibly heal him when I also need mending?

Chapter Eleven
The Ghosts Within

Our heart-to-heart chat is abandoned when Cole and Gavin approach the table. Gavin's energy is fading as I notice him in Cole's arms, his head leaning into his shoulder and eyelids growing heavy. He is mumbling the words to the book—his favorite—that we read every night at bedtime. Cole is repeating them back to him which causes my heart to stutter. Every facet of this man is sexy, but nothing is more appealing than seeing him interact with my son.

"I think my sister has done enough damage for one night," Cole says loud enough for Heidi to hear.

She looks at us, bats her eyelashes, and cups her chin with her hands, adding with a tinge of sarcasm, "Me? I would never do such a thing to my most favorite brother." She then traces an imaginary halo over her head and fold her hands in a praying motion like an angel.

"I guess that's easy when I'm the only one you have. Dusty and I have an early training session tomorrow, so it's time to get him to bed."

An evil grin spreads across her face. "Well now, I can definitely do that."

"Heidi, I told you already, I don't want to hear you, Dusty, and bed in the same sentence... Ever!" He kisses her cheek. "I'll see ya tomorrow."

Heidi leans in and embraces me. "It was so great to meet you and I can't wait to see Gavin at camp!" She lowers her voice and continues, "And Camryn ... thank you."

With a comforting smile, I say goodbye to Heidi. Lila and Carter follow with their farewells. Aware of the tension in Lila's hug, I'm the one hurrying her out the door, hoping she won't crack about Todd's reemergence.

Finally, with a broad smile and extended arm, Cole turns his attention back to me and reels my body into his again.

"So, you ready?" He repositions my sleeping boy on his opposite side so he can hold me closer to his chest. "Because I'd like to take you home."

I stretch my arm across his lower back and hook my thumb into the band of his board shorts. "Definitely. There's nowhere I'd rather go right now."

As we leave the screeching bells of the arcade, we stroll down the rickety wood planks of the boardwalk and are inundated with the signature smells of French fries and funnel cake. Cole squeezes me tighter against him and rubs my exposed arm, sensing my chill from the cool, early-summer breezes swirling from the ocean.

"Sorry Heidi dominated your time tonight. She can be a little much sometimes."

"No worries! She was great! I had a lot of fun tonight." I peek up at Gavin. "Looks like he did, too."

"Uh, yeah… He definitely did but can't say the same for me." He lowers his voice to a husky whisper. "See, I spent the night staring at you, thinking of every way I could remove your dress."

Turned on by his instant switch to intimacy, I add, "Oh yeah? Well maybe I can help you choose the best way as soon as we get home."

He kisses my forehead. "I was hoping you'd give me some assistance with it."

A sexy smirk appears that furthers my desire to ravage this man right here on the boardwalk. Thank God he's carrying Gavin. My feet start to pick up the pace, as I'm craving for some alone time with Cole, and I can feel the hustle in his step as well. Before I know it, Gavin is slouched over in his booster seat in the back of Cole's Wrangler, and we are cruising down the boulevard.

It's a mass exodus from his Jeep once we are

parked in the driveway, with Cole rushing to our outdoor showers to wash the grime of the beach from his body and me tucking my little angel into his surfboard bed for the night. Tossing the unopened mail onto the counter, the idea of a glass of wine sounds more appealing than sorting through the realities of the cost to living in a beach town. I am just grateful that my mom's control-freak tendancies led to a paid-off mortgage and a hefty inheritance left to Gavin and me.

While I sip my wine and thumb through a Pottery Barn catalogue, the soapy scent of men's body wash and the warmth of broad arms engulf me. I pivot my body around to eye the taut muscles of a shirtless Cole. Beads of water drip from the ends of hair still damp from the shower, and his eyes shimmer the clearest blue against his tanned skin. I trace my finger down his jawline and follow the slope of dimples created by the wide grin that is stretched across his face.

Cole inches his mouth toward my ear and whispers, "I'm going to kiss you slowly, if that's okay? I don't want to miss one second of you."

My body explodes with desire as I crush my mouth into his. Granting his wish, I allow him to explore my mouth at a slow pace as I graze my teeth across his bottom lip. His hands travel down the length of my body, stopping at my waist to hoist me up on the counter, closing the difference between our heights. Our eyes meet, and we hold each other's gaze as he claims every part of me in that moment.

Giving into desire, I ask, "Cole, please stay with me tonight?"

"Camryn, I'm finding out that when it comes to you, the answer will always be yes."

He lifts me off the counter, and I wrap my legs around his waist as he carries me downstairs to my bedroom. After kicking the door closed with his heel and reaching back to lock it, he places me at the foot of the bed. While his lips travel down my neck and across my collarbone, my skin tingles with ecstasy. When he reaches my shoulders, he kisses the top of each them, and then slides the straps of my dress off, causing my it to slip down my body and pool at my feet. Cole covers every inch of me as he plants soft kisses everywhere.

He travels up my body, leaving a trail of goose bumps behind. He reaches my ear and murmurs, "I already told you that I want to go slowly. I need to savor every moment with you … like it's my last."

With his arms wrapped around me, I guide him down to the bed and hold him close against me, the sync of our bodies revealing that this is so much more than attraction. We are tiptoeing into a different realm, knocking over any barrier we have ever built up against it. With Cole, my past doesn't stand a chance against what we can become together.

I lift my head from his chest and whisper, "As long as you want me here, there will never be a last time."

"I've always wanted you and always will … until the last breath I take."

With that, our bodies tangle, swaying together to a single rhythm. We move as slowly as our hunger allows, with passion paving the way. Our hands explore, and our lips touch every feature of the other's body, always coming together at our centers. Sleep eventually claims us in each other's arms.

Beads of sweat dripping, knotted sheets strangling, and shrieking jostles me awake. The stillness of the night has become my worst enemy over the years, but tonight I'm witnessing what usually occupies my sleep. Cole is in a battle with his own demons, thrashing his body as he throws punches into the air. Something so familiar to me feels foreign as I struggle to rescue him from his storm.

I roll on top of him and pin down his violent arms. "Shhhh, Cole … it's okay … come on … wake up, it's just a dream."

As he fights to release his body from my resistance, he tosses me to his side, still deep within his nightmare and begins mumbling scattered phrases. "Tara … oh Tara … why this … always love … can't let go."

My breath catches when I hear her name, knowing it's the beautiful bitch from the salon who I saw with Cole that night at the bar. Did he once love her? Does he still? I want this tussle with his tormented dream to end, so I throw myself back on top of him and repeat his name over and over until he starts to come out of the nightmare. Once he stops thrashing, I crash my mouth into his. His sharp movements immediately soften, his jaw unclenches, and his hands slide up my body once recognition sparks.

His desire is evident through our kiss as he tries to bury what he has just seen in his dreams. Attempting to slow down the passion, I sit up on him and straddle him across his lap. I feel his excitement through the thin fabric of his boxer briefs.

I run my hands through his sweat-soaked hair and say, "Wasn't a good one, I guess?"

With a heavy sigh, he replies, "You know that happy ending we're looking for … well, that definitely wasn't it." He places his palm over my cheek and continues, "I didn't mean to wake you. I guess the ghosts don't like to stay away."

"Cole, I get it." I rub a bead of sweat from beneath his eye. "Talk to me about it. I want to know about the ghosts."

Sitting up and positioning the pillows against the headboard, I can see the pain in his eyes, reflected in the small sliver of moonlight that's peeking through the windows. Heidi's words echo in my head as I watch him crumble from the darkness that looms over him. I want the Cole that existed before his nights terrorized him, the man who Gavin already knows, the one who owned me the first moment I set eyes on him.

"I had a good life growing up. We lived in this huge brownstone in Society Hill in Philly. Heidi and I never wanted for a thing. My dad owned a string of very successful Irish pubs and restaurants, and my mom was in real estate. I had just celebrated my fifteenth birthday when my mom died in an accident. She was driving late that night—picking up an old friend of mine who needed help. His mom died when he was a baby, and my mom looked after him as if he were her own. On her way to him, she was struck by a car and died instantly. Doctors said they had no chance to revive her. After that, my dad went numb. His success became his weakness as he turned to the pubs for an escape. And I just turned … angry. I got pretty good at using my fists—it was the only thing that brought me comfort. I guess it was the one thing in my life that I could control."

Tears begin to well up in my eyes as he bares his soul. I grasp his hand between mine.

"One day, my dad dropped me and Heidi off here at our grandparents' house. He was supposed to pick us up at dinnertime but never showed. He never even kissed us goodbye. It was like we were just a painful memory of his past and it was easier to just forget about us."

I kiss the top of his forehead, encouraging him to tell me more.

"I just did the same shit here that I did at home, but my grandmom wasn't as accepting of it. That's when she brought me to your mom, who introduced me to surfing. It became my therapy, and I didn't feel so … lost."

I smile at the thought of my mom becoming such a healing presence in Cole's life. She saved him from completely falling, and I find myself thanking her for that. I shudder at the possibility of Cole not being here had my mom not made an impact on him. She, in her "Milena, control-freak, way," has connected us.

"By senior year, surfing was my life. I still brawled but only when I was challenged. Your mom somehow got through, kept me straight. Rather than throwing a punch, I jumped on my board. Made the ghosts disappear for a while." Cole's head sinks and the emotional confession of his past exhausts him as he becomes silent.

Relating to the agony of his past and experiencing his pain along with him, I tilt his mouth toward me and forcefully kiss him. Shifting my body off his lap, I glide his boxer briefs down his legs and toss them to the floor. His readiness for me is evident, and I begin at his lips and trail kisses down his body.

When I reach the line that leads to his core, he pulls my head up and mutters, "Camryn, you don't have to do this. Just being here—holding you—is enough."

I place my index finger to his mouth. "Shhh … I want to be the one that takes your pain away tonight … the one that makes you forget."

With that, I continue my journey down his body and taste every inch of him. My tongue explores every line, and my teeth graze across every groove. His body shakes with each touch of my mouth. I slowly bring him to his point of bliss, my hunger raging for every part of it. After his climax, I lie on his chest while his pulse slows and his heartbeat steadies. We welcome a dreamless sleep draped with each other's body, our arms unwilling to let go.

It doesn't take long for morning to find us, as the sun creeps its way into my bedroom. The brightness isn't the reason for my wake-up but rather the empty spot next to me. I find solace wrapped together with Cole, and without him next to me I feel alone again. Knowing a twelve-hour shift awaits me, I stagger out of bed and hope to find my two boys and coffee. Down the hallway toward Gavin's room, a faint murmur of voices is heard. Peeking my head through the crack of his door, I melt at a sight that is so representative of my own childhood. Cole and Gavin have constructed a tent on his bed out of pillows and blankets, and they are cuddled together reading *Abigail Lug and the Story of the Lightning Bug*. I listen at the door as they recite the catchy rhyme from the book:

> *Foozley, doozle, bubbles and bay.*
> *Noodles and poodles, blubber and gray.*
> *The tricking will stop; the trouble will cease.*
> *You will become one of the least.*

The smile across Gavin's face is unending, and, looking at Cole, I am sure the visit with his past spirits is a distant memory. As I watch Gavin, I can see my own five-year-old self hiding away with my dad behind a tower of pillows from the sofa or sitting on his back while he was sprawled out on the floor putting together the never-ending, thousand-piece puzzle. Seeing that Gavin has found this with Cole, that fear of abandonment begins to fade away as the feeling of security slowly embraces me.

Sensing my invasion of their male bonding time, Cole's glistening eyes meet mine, and his dimples sink deeper into his cheeks. It just makes me want him even more.

"Good morning, beautiful!"

Gavin follows Cole's lead, mimicking the same phrase, "Good morning, beautiful Mommy!"

I hurry in, lean into the tent, and give Gavin a kiss. I shift to Cole and stay a bit longer on his lips than I want to in front of my son.

"Eww, Mommy! I hope you brushed your teeth. You might make Cole throw up."

Cole begins to fake a gagging sound that makes Gavin laugh. "You're right, buddy. She's got stink breath!"

They start chanting "stink breath" together until I grab a pillow and stage an assault on both of them. Within seconds they have me pinned down and are tickling me to the point of breathlessness. I throw my hands up in surrender.

"All right, all right. You win! Time for me to get ready for work, anyway. Gavs, you have surf lessons with Cole, and then he'll take you to Miss Heidi's camp for the rest of the day. I have a twelve-hour today, so Aunt Li will pick you up and feed you dinner."

Hearing the gagging noises again, I notice the sickened look on Gavin's face. "What's wrong, buddy?"

"I just hope Uncle Carter cooks. Aunt Lila tried to feed me sushi the other day! Do you know what sushi is? Her cooking sucks, Mommy."

My mouth drops while Cole purses his lips to prevent himself from breaking out in laughter.

"Gavin! The language, buddy. We already talked about this. Next time I hear it, I'm going to hold you down and make you eat Aunt Lila's cooking all day long!"

He slaps his hand over his mouth at the terrible threat I just made. "One more chance, Mommy, puhlease! That would make me just die!" He holds his neck in a chokehold and pretends to collapse to the floor.

I turn toward the door, amused by my five-year-old's dramatic show and add, "Boys, clean up your mess, and I'll see you for breakfast in a few."

I leave his bedroom with both of them cracking up and saluting me with a few "yes ma'ams." Feeling content with the dismal parts of last evening being replaced with teasing and humor, I hop into the shower and brush my teeth to make the "stink breath" disappear.

Upstairs, a cup of coffee and a steaming plate of scrambled eggs greets me. Cole and Gavin saved me a place at the table between them, and the three of us enjoy breakfast together. We talk about the upcoming surfing competition, and Gavin and I ask Cole questions about his training and sponsors. He asks Gavin to be his training manager, symbolically of course, which leaves me in awe of how he always thinks to include my son in his life. I clear the table and leave Gavin and Cole discussing strategy for the competition.

After stuffing the dirty dishes into the dishwasher, I come across the mail I threw on the counter the previous night. A formal-looking envelope catches my eye as I thumb through the various bills, magazines, and flyers. Once I recognize the return address, my body tenses and my trembling fingers struggle to open it. As I skim over the contents of the letter, my body slumps over, becoming weak, which forces my elbows to hold my weight over the countertop. When he notices my distress, Cole rushes to my side and wraps his arms around my waist.

With concern, he asks, "Hey, Cam, what's wrong? You look like you've just seen a ghost."

Bringing my voice to a low mumble to assure Gavin wouldn't hear, I reply, "More like the devil … and he wants my son."

Chapter Twelve
Right Where I Need to Be

Cole snatches the letter from my hand and begins to skim over it, his expression darkening as he reads. His eyes would occasionally backtrack through it, as if he needed to reaffirm the contents. I watch his calm concern slowly mutate into anger as he reaches the end. With his jaw clenched, Cole stares at Todd's signature at the bottom. Startled by his reaction, I wonder why he would freeze at seeing Todd's name. If maybe the memories of him come flooding back. With Cole's transformation and my inability to think straight, I rush Gavin to his room to pack his bag for the day to avoid any eavesdropping on the inevitable conversation that is brewing.

Lifting his glare from the letter, Cole asks, "How long have you known he was back?"

With a heavy sigh and a telling look on my face, I reply, "He was watching me from the beach that day we came back from the inlet. Then he…" My voice begins to quake.

"Goddammit, Camryn. What made you think you could deal with this bastard on your own?" Cole turns away from me and slams his fist into the counter.

"He was waiting at my car last night when I left work. Told me he was back for us … that he had rights to his son." I reach over and rip the letter out of Cole's hand and crumple it up. "Obviously he's going to use his power as a lawyer to prove those rights.

The letter is addressed from Connelly and Connelly Law Firm, owned and operated by Todd and his father. They are requesting a meeting with me to discuss the custody of "our son" and Todd's rights to him as the biological father. I'm expected at their office tomorrow evening to discuss a plan of action.

He turns back toward me, grabs my shoulders, and bends down to my level, his anger softening as he gazes into my eyes. "Why didn't you tell me? I don't want you to feel like you have to handle something like this on your own. I already told you that I want all of your heart, even the parts that have been broken into millions of pieces. I swear that I'll spend the rest of my life putting every last piece back together, if that's what it takes. I promise you I'll make it whole again."

Tears begin to drip down my cheeks, and Cole pulls me into a tight embrace. "I'm so sorry. I just didn't want to scare you away … I mean … my life is a total mess. And Todd being back makes it worse. You shouldn't have to deal with it. You should just walk away from this now…"

"Stop! Don't ever think for one moment that I wouldn't want you. Camryn, don't you see it yet? I want the broken high school girl who I met so many years ago. I want the strong, capable woman you are now. I want it all. No. Matter. What."

My previously dripping tears become more like a waterfall that soaks the collar of my scrubs. Palming his cheeks, I look straight into his eyes and say, "Cole, I need you."

Cole leans into my mouth, our lips desperately finding each other. For a few minutes, we are healed of our past heartache and living in our own world, one where our mistakes stay well-buried. Holding me against his chest long after our kiss, he whispers in my ear, "We'll get through this … I promise you … he won't ruin us." Deep under his breath I'm sure I hear Cole say, "not again," which leaves me to wonder what he means by it.

Comforted by his vow to stay with me through this, I squeeze his body tighter against mine. No matter the uncertainty that Todd has just thrown into my life, I am sure of one thing: Cole is willing to fight alongside me for Gavin's sake and for what we're building together. Todd may have destroyed me five years ago, but no way in hell am I going to let that happen again.

Feeling stronger, I break apart from Cole and attempt to leave for work, despite the early-morning drama. Cole begs to drive me to the hospital, probably hoping a panic attack won't manifest while I'm alone with my thoughts, but I need him to handle Gavin and avoid anything that is out of the ordinary. He eventually gives in but only when I agree to let him come to the meeting with Todd and his father. At least I still have twenty-four hours to talk him out of that. I need to keep his anger from spilling over and "fighter Cole" from re-emerging.

Before I can escape, Cole has me trapped in his arms again, unwilling to let go. He is holding me so close that I can feel his heartbeat against mine as it merges into one sound. His hesitance to let go is evident. My past actions have only shown me to break down or run away from hardship. I have to show him that I'm not the same girl from five years ago, that he is worth staying for—worth fighting for.

"Eww, do you guys always do that?" Gavin, with his backpack fastened around him, stares up at us with his nose scrunched.

Smiling, Cole answers, "What? Hug each other?"

Gavin nods with the same look of horror on his face.

"Buddy, one day you'll be chasing the girls around to try to do this!" He gives him a wink.

"No way! Never ever! So gross!" These assurances are delivered with all of the confident indignation that a five-year-old can muster.

We are laughing while Gavin makes gagging sounds, as if he is on the verge of throwing up. Cole reaches around me one more time, leans into me, and whispers, "Remember, own your breath today."

As his warmness circulates through me, I fix my eyes upon his and repeat those words back to him. I force myself out the door and peek behind to find Cole holding tight to Gavin, irrevocably stating that he is never letting go of either of us.

I try to push all custody battle thoughts from my head throughout my morning at work. I concentrate on assisting with births throughout the morning. I try to imagine having another baby one day, but this time with Cole at my bedside, holding my hand and helping me breathe through contractions. By the time my lunch break comes, I've almost forgotten about my impending meeting with Todd—almost.

Nibbling on a soggy bagel, I watch Lila storm through the cafeteria, attracting glances from every male doctor in the vicinity. After she disregards every look and flips off a few who whistled, Lila plops down across from me and throws a brown paper bag on the table.

"What's this?"

"It's lunch and your reason not to eat that shit in your hand. Seriously, Cam, how do you even manage to place that slop anywhere near your mouth?"

"It's not that bad. It's just sort of bland, that's all. What did'ya bring instead?"

"I never knew horseshit was bland, but whatever. I brought you a home-cooked meal, straight from my kitchen."

"Ugh, that's okay, Li. Horseshit sounds more appealing next to your home cooking!"

She rips off a piece of my bagel and throws it at my face as she shrieks, "Biotch! What's wrong with my cooking?" She grabs the bag from the table. "Your loss. Carter made it."

Reaching out to snag the bag back, I giggle. "I'm not the only one who questions your cooking, sweetie. Gav was traumatized when I mentioned you were feeding him tonight."

"Hmmph … whatever. So are we gonna sit and bullshit about food or talk about shitbag's custody letter?"

"What the hell? How do you find things out so quickly?"

"Oh, I don't know, genius, maybe I can read your fucking mind." She sarcastically rolls her eyes. "Obvi Carter told me, and he heard it from Cole. Not the point. Tell me about the letter."

"Come on, Li. You know Todd. Has to show he's in control. Wrote this formal letter from his father's law firm that said I have to meet with them to discuss his rights as Gav's father."

"Bullshit!" Lila's shrill, indignant voice rings off the cafeteria walls and gains us a few more stares. "He's the farthest thing from a father. The pussy had to run to daddy to take care of this, just like he always did. Gav doesn't need him, and the fuckbag knows it. He doesn't care about being a father to Gavin. He never has and never will."

I extend my arm with my palm up to signify "stop." Between Lila's lack of a filter and Cole's ability to brawl, I have to be the one in control of this issue. It's my son whose life can be severely altered by any decision. The last thing I need is to show the courts, if it goes that far, that Gavin is raised in a questionable environment. I've seen Todd's father in action, and he can turn absolutely nothing into a criminal offense.

"Just relax. I can handle this. I'll meet with them,

and we can work something out. You just have to accept the fact that Gavin is going to meet Todd at some point—he may even form a relationship with him—and it sucks. But he did help create him, so I guess he has a right to see him."

Lila bitterly interjects, "Asshole! Somebody should drown his sperm so he can never reproduce again."

As she continues her rant, adding more and more colorful words to it, my world screeches to a halt when I notice Todd in the cafeteria doorway, staring at me with what seems like regret. I abandon the table in the middle of Lila's tirade and approach him, curious as to why he is showing up at my workplace. Lila is close on my tail when she realizes who I am walking toward. To fend her off from an all-out assault, I swing my arm back to keep her behind me.

Before I can speak, Todd throws his hands up in defense. "Cammy, it wasn't my idea. I told my dad to give you a few days … to wait for you to come around. You know I wouldn't use the law against you or our son."

"Goddammit, Todd! His name is Gavin. Okay? Gavin Michael Singer. Please stop calling him *our son*. He has a name. I don't care whose idea it was, but it's done. And now you've backed me into a corner … forcing me to drop the earth-shattering news on a five-year-old that his father, who never wanted him, now does. So yeah, a few days was the least you could've given me."

From behind me Lila adds, "Some father … doesn't even know his name."

"Li, enough! Thank you for your support, but I need to talk to Todd alone."

"I'll shut up but don't think I'm leaving you alone

with this asswipe for a second."

Todd cranes his neck to see Lila, who is half-hidden by my body. "Well, hey, Lila. See you haven't changed all that much since the last time I saw you. Still so eloquent with your words."

"Yeah. I see you're the same douchebag who can shove the word eloquence up your…"

I raise my voice before she can insert her last word. "No more!" I draw my attention back to Todd, and with an annoyed tone ask, "What exactly do you want? I think anything you have to say can be discussed in the meeting tomorrow."

"I just wanted to see you … make sure you're okay … let you know this isn't how I wanted it to go down."

A humiliated smile crosses his face, and a very tiny part of me, one that is concealed by anger and disgust, feels sorry for him. I am always aware of the control his father had over him, as he would constantly batter him over grades, surfing, and clothing. Todd was never smart enough, fast enough, or perfect enough for his father, even though he was a straight-A student and a top surfer who only wore designer clothing. His father expected him to become a lawyer, and nothing less than Villanova University would do to achieve that.

"Todd, you haven't cared for five years, so don't insult me and act like you do now. I'll see you and your dad tomorrow."

By that point Lila is gripping my wrist so tightly that the feeling is long gone from it. Todd leans in and attempts to close the distance between us. He lowers his voice to try to cut Lila out of the conversation.

"Let's try to figure something out. Then we can forget this meeting nonsense."

Lila yanks me behind her like a protective mother

trying to shield her child from the monsters that lived under the bed.

Short, heavy breaths are beginning to overtake my body, and the need to end this conversation becomes a priority. "So, if I let you see Gavin, the meeting doesn't happen?"

Todd nods as he reaffirms, "Exactly. I'll even rip up the original paperwork to prove it."

"Fine. Meet us at Pirate Island Golf tomorrow at seven o'clock."

"Thanks, Cammy. I promise you, my dad won't interfere."

With a victory smile on his face, he turns to leave, but before he reaches the doorway, I call out, "Hey, Todd!"

He turns back toward me.

"Don't ever pull this shit again."

With his smile fading, and a quick nod, he struts out of the building, and I bend over, begging myself to breathe, but my lungs won't comply. I sink my hand into my pocket of my scrubs to search for the inhaler I carry. With one inhalation, I can feel my chest loosen, allowing the air in. At that moment, I picture Cole telling me to own my breath, and slowly, life circulates through me again.

I stand on my feet and smooth out my wrinkled scrubs. "I'm fine. I'm good. Just have to get back to work."

Before I can break away, Lila pulls me into her arms and hugs me in support. She walks me to my floor to ensure my panic attack will not rear its ugly head again.

"Cams, I'm waiting for you until you're done your shift. I'm not leaving you like this."

"No, I'm fine, and you need to take care of

Gavin, anyway. The guys have an important sponsor meeting for the competition, so Gav needs you."

She hesitantly agrees. "All right … then call me the minute you leave. I am staying on the phone with you while you drive home."

Pushing her toward the exit, I comply. "Sure. Now please go and take care of my son."

As she strolls toward the elevators, she calls back to me, "Oh and, Cam? Never ask me to stay quiet for that fuckbag again. Any future deals are off."

Always ending drama with "Lila" humor, I watch my best friend leave while I prepare for the rest of my shift. The last few hours of work will definitely be spent thinking of ways to explain Todd's reappearance to Gavin. Will he even understand or accept him into his life? Regardless, my baby boy is going to face what I have spent five years protecting him from—his own father.

At seven o'clock, I race from my locker and bypass the elevators to the stairwell to run down four flights toward the exit. After the day I had, I am eager to pick up Gavin to give him a never-ending hug, dreading the news he is about to face. As I rush through the lobby toward the parking lot doors, I am stopped in my tracks by the sight of a smiling Cole with a bubbly, blue-eyed boy on his shoulders.

While I'm busy watching female nurses gawk at Cole during their shift changes, his eyes never leave me. They follow each step I take toward them. "Hey! What are you two doing here?" I reach up to Gavin's leg that is tucked next to Cole's neck and give it a squeeze.

Gavin giggles at the ticklish pinch and replies, "I already told you, Mommy! I don't like Aunt Lila's dinner. Yuck!"

Cole adds, "And we both thought you could use a

nice surprise after work." The obvious worry on his face, covered by his fake grin, speaks so many words. It's apparent that he found out about Todd's visit at lunch.

My gaze leaves his and drops to the floor in shame. "How'd you find out?"

Knowing the answer before he even replies, we simultaneously say, "Lila." I shake my head, thinking how intrusive my best friend can be, but how I would never want it any other way.

Cole extends his arm to mine and guides me out the door. "Ready, beautiful girl? We have a real home-cooked meal waiting for us at my house."

"Sounds delicious! But don't you have a meeting tonight with your possible sponsors?"

"Ahhh, those sponsors will be there tomorrow and the next day and the next. Besides, there is nowhere I'd rather be right now." He leans into to me so I can only hear him. "I told you, baby, every last piece of your heart will be put back together."

With our close proximity, lust is burning through me, and I am barely able to control the flames. Our attraction is so strong, like a magnet that keeps pulling me in. I realize how much Cole has already sacrificed for Gavin and me, which causes a wave of guilt.

"Are you guys gonna kiss? Again?" Gavin snaps us out of our lust-filled moment. "Because I'm so hungry!"

Cole laughs and assures him, "We're at your service, buddy! Let's go home and eat!" He leads us out of the hospital, bouncing with every other step as he makes Gavin go airborne off his shoulders.

When we reach my car, Cole puts Gavin into his car seat, and then opens the passenger door for me, taking the keys from my hands. I'm staring at him in confusion.

"Where's your car?"

"Lila insisted that she drop us off so you didn't have to drive alone."

Amused by her persistence, I shake my head and plop into the passenger seat. Turning around to Gavin, I freeze for a minute to watch the pure bliss on his face, trying to find a way to be grateful for this moment and not worry about the ones to come. Cole reaches over the console and grasps my thigh after likely noticing my anxiety.

I push my negative thoughts aside and ask Gavin, "So, buddy, what's for dinner tonight?"

"It's a surprise! Cole and I have been cooking all day!" He wipes his arm across his forehead, pretending to be sweating from his long day in the kitchen.

"Oh yeah? Well, I can't wait! And then, at dinner, you can tell me all about camp with Miss Heidi."

He claps his hands together and adds, "And surfing too!!"

Stepping into Cole's house is a mirror image of mine, except it lacks the color and décor my mom worked so hard to put into ours. His furniture is sparse with a slipcovered couch and matching chair surrounding a very large television. Whereas our breakfast nook houses an oversized, extended table to comply with my mom's rule of family dinners, his has a round table with four chairs that looks a bit small for the large space. Technology is not lacking in Cole's house. He has a state-of-the-art stereo system and a desk topped with a Mac laptop and iPad in the area that Gavin's toys are at in our house. A small laugh escapes from me as I'm probably looking at what Gavin's play space will look like in the future

Cole and Gavin drag me over to the table and sit me in the chair that overlooks our shared deck, and I catch a glimpse of the calm sea as it rolls with the low tide. Within minutes, the table is overflowing with rolls, meatballs, lasagna, and salad, and we sit together and devour everything. As Cole brings the strawberry shortcake to the table for dessert, I am brought back to our first dinner together when that cake landed on everyone as our food fight unfolded.

Cole must have been reading my thoughts because as he begins to slice the cake he says, "Tonight, let's make sure this cake lands nowhere but in our stomachs." Gavin and I both giggle as I stick my finger into his whipped cream and smear it onto his nose. "Anyway, we don't want to spend a lot of time cleaning up because I have a surprise for both of you."

Gavin's mouth drops open, and he starts stuffing the cake into his mouth at record speed. It isn't long before his plate is clean and whipped cream is all over his face.

While I try to wipe it off with a napkin, Cole drags both of us out of our seats toward the sliding door that leads to our back deck. Shrieks and squeals come out of Gavin as he notices a hunter-green camping tent set up in the sand that makes up our back yard. Astonished, I peer up at Cole.

"How'd you know? He's always wanted to go camping, but my mom started to get really sick, and we never got the chance."

With a knowing smile he reveals, "Camping out—it's every boy's dream."

I grab him and bring his body to mine, not wanting to let go. Gavin had opened up to Cole, told him about his wants, his dreams, and perhaps things that sit heavy on his heart. Realization sets in that Cole has breathed life back into my deflated soul, and he has won over my son's heart in the process.

Gavin's excitement is overflowing as he races down the deck stairs and unzips the tent. Inside, he finds brand-new sleeping bags, flashlights, and ingredients to make s'mores. Cole sends Gav inside for warm pajamas while he gets the fire started for roasting the marshmallows. As Gavin disappears into the house, Cole scoops me up, lays me down in the tent and covers my mouth with his. When I separate from Cole, tears appear in my eyes.

"Thank you for making one of his dreams come true tonight."

He pulls me in for one last kiss and says, "Well, you coming back home has made my dreams come true."

When Gavin comes flying back out wearing his Batman pajamas, Cole and I get the marshmallows ready on the roasting sticks. The night is spent eating s'mores, singing campfire songs, and telling ghost stories—all things my mom promised for their first camping trip. Despite Gavin's excitement, he somehow finds sleep, snuggled deep in his new sleeping bag. Cole and I sit in front of the fire, kissing and holding each other. I know he wants to ask about Todd, but he probably doesn't want to ruin our perfect evening together.

As the silence of the deep night filters in and our bodies become drowsy, we find our spots on either side of Gavin to cuddle him tight. After I catch Cole's hand in the darkness, I rest it on top of Gavin's body, begging for his security all night long.

A peaceful sleep finds us—one that doesn't allow the monsters of the night to frighten us. Both Cole and I know that the real one lurking will rear its ugly head tomorrow, so we bask in the serenity of our evening together. I feel the change that is about to break into our lives, and fear what that will do to each of us. Nevertheless, Cole has shown up, and has once again guided me to right where I need to be.

Chapter Thirteen
Confessions

I am face-to-face with the day I have dreaded since Gavin was first placed in my arms, and I can't shake the feeling that our lives might spiral headfirst into the ground. I lay awake for a few hours and watch my sweet baby's chest rise and fall with each breath, as I rehearse over and over in my head how to tell him that his dad now wants him. Gavin never asked me too much about Todd in the past, but he had opened up to my mom many times, wondering why he only had an Uncle Carter and not a daddy.

I search for any good that could come from Todd's return, but I keep being led to the day that Gavin might be a burden to his planned-out life. I can never fathom how easily he walked away before, as if he was throwing away a pair of pants that no longer fit.

Rolling out of my sleeping bag, careful not to wake up Gavin and Cole, I stumble out of the tent. Met by the beauty of the endless ocean and the pureness of the salty air, I hope it will be the magical cure to help clarify my jumbled thoughts. My mom always believed the ocean had healing powers, that negativity would be taken out to sea and hidden treasures would wash ashore. But today, I only can see the vastness of it and all that can be lost in its depths.

Feeling his strong presence behind me, I apologize. "Sorry for waking you. I just couldn't sleep."

Cole appears next to me. "You didn't wake me. I was lost in my own thoughts. You wanna talk about yours?"

"Yes … no … oh, I don't know. I just wish I could see the good this could do for Gavin. No matter how I feel about Todd, if I believe my son will benefit from a relationship with his dad, I can learn to accept him in our life. But I don't see it. I know how destructive he can be. He could ruin him."

He steps around to face me. "Gavin will be able to do this. Kids are more resilient … more accepting. You need to trust that no matter what Todd does, you are doing everything Gavin needs to feel loved. Cam, focus on what you can give your son, not what Todd can take away."

I stand on my tiptoes and place a tender kiss on his lips. "How do you do it? You make everything … make sense."

With pain evident in his eyes, he replies, "I had to lose a lot … that's how."

Avoiding giving an explanation for his response, he scoops me up into his arms and carries me back to the tent. He sets my feet in the cool sand and says, "Tell him. I'll be right here when you get home, waiting for you both."

With a deep breath, I crawl into the tent next to Gavin, who is already awake and petting his brand-new sleeping bag. His happiness is comforting to see, and it gives me the confidence to tell him about Todd.

"Good morning, sweetie! Did you have a good night?"

With a huge smile that exposes his upper gums, he squeals, "Yes! It was awesome!"

"Great! Make sure you give Cole a big, fat hug for this one!" I pull Gavin up into my arms. "But I need to talk to you about something first."

He nods as he stares wide-eyed at me, with those aqua-blue eyes.

"Umm … tonight we have plans to go mini-golfing."

Gavin jumps out of my arms and lunges toward

the tent door. "Yay! Is Cole coming with us? I can't wait to tell him!"

"Hold on, buddy. Actually, Cole isn't coming. Umm … your dad wants to come golfing with you. Does that sound okay to you?"

His nose scrunches up for a moment as he pieces together this information. "So, my dad wants to meet me?" His confusion quickly passes, shrugging his shoulders after I nod my head at his question. "Cool! I'm gonna meet my dad."

"So you're okay with this … with meeting him?"

"Yeah, Mommy." He brushes me off and continues to fiddle with the zipper on his sleeping bag, while I take a few deep breaths.

Relieved at his reaction, I carry him out of the tent to where Cole is waiting. Signaling to him that Gavin is okay, he snatches him from my arms and swings him around. Once he makes him dizzy enough that his head is bobbling, he asks, "So, how was your first camp out?"

"Whoa! It was so cool!"

"Buddy, I'm so happy you liked it. How about we do it again soon?" He leans in a little closer to Gavin's ear. "Next time no girls allowed!"

Gavin hooks his arms around Cole's neck. "Yes, yes, yes! I can't wait! You know what, Cole?"

"What, buddy?"

Gavin lays his head on Cole's shoulder and declares, "I love you."

My breath catches and instantly my heart melts at the sincerity of my son's words. With my gaze jumping to Cole, I can see that he is also taken by Gavin's affection. I watch as Cole squeezes Gav tighter against him and closes his eyes, repeating the same words right back to him, "I love you, too, bud. I love you, too."

The sight of them within each other's embrace will forever be imprinted in my mind. Three words. That's all it took for my worries about Todd to disappear. No matter what might come from Todd and Gavin meeting, I know my son loves Cole on his own accord, and Cole wholeheartedly returns the love back to him.

Gavin leans back into Cole's arms and asks, "Can we go surfing now?"

With a huge smile stretching across his face, Cole replies, "You got it, little man."

****

I must have glanced at my watch fifteen times in the last minute, even knowing that he still has five minutes until it's seven o'clock. Gavin has already picked out his putter and a neon-orange ball. He is practicing his swing next to the bench where I'm sitting while I prepare for the storm to blow in. Gavin doesn't show any signs of anxiety, which is a small blessing in itself. Startled at the sound of my phone beeping to signify a text, I frantically search through my bag with the anticipation of Todd's cancellation.

Stop staring at your watch and BREATHE.

My head jolts up and I begin to look around. I scan the growing crowd of people walking the boards until I spot Cole leaning against the railing with one leg propped up on the bar. His gaze burns through me, flickering with concern, as he refuses to turn his eyes away. I check my phone after it beeps a second time.

I'll be right here waiting for you, beautiful girl. See you soon.

I blow him a kiss that leaves him smirking, his deep-seated concern erased for the moment. I hate how Todd's reappearance has somehow brought back a painful memory for Cole, but I love that he is standing a few feet away, pushing it aside for my sake. Placing my phone back in my bag, a new sense of confidence sets in, making me feel like I can conquer the world. I take in the sight of Cole one more time in his gray t-shirt and low-hanging jeans that fray at the bottom. However, noticing his attention has shifted away from me, I can only guess that Todd is right on time.

He is dressed to the nines in a striped button-down shirt that is rolled up at the sleeves and tucked into pressed designer jeans and loafer-type shoes, which probably cost more than my car payment. His sandy-brown hair is perfectly spiked up, the gel glistening in the sunlight. He is looking away from me in the opposite direction, which gives me a chance to catch a glimpse of him before he walks into the mini-golf course. I hoist Gavin in my arms to prepare for the introductions. As he turns and meets our faces, the edginess that was prominent in his features is replaced with softness as soon as he spots his spitting image clutched in my arms.

Todd slants toward me, places his arm around my waist, and brings my cheek to his lips. "Hey, Cammy, good to see you again."

I wince at his greeting and peek over his shoulder to see an annoyed Cole who is glaring at him with clenched fists. Trying to avoid a scene, I pull away from him to mark a large space between us, and introduce Gavin.

"Todd, this is Gavin."

Todd extends his hand and waits for Gavin to return his, but instead, he has a five-year-old jumping into his arms.

"Hi, Todd! Want to play some golf? I already picked my ball—it's orange."

"Perfect choice! Orange is my favorite color." With an annoying smile stretching across his face, Todd places Gavin on the ground and bends down on one knee in front of him. "You want to pick my ball for me?"

Gavin leaps over toward his choices and decides on the blue one for Todd and the pink one for me. His comfort with this stranger amazes me as he takes his hand and leads him to the first hole. I feel a sense of relief that Gavin is so accepting, but at the same time, I am also disappointed because of that easy acceptance. As I wrestle with these mixed emotions, I take one last glance toward Cole, and he traces an "X" over his heart, which is all the strength I need for the night.

To an outsider, Todd and Gavin look like the perfect father-son combination, but I know that my son is too pure and good for him. Todd may have been playing the part of father really well with Gavin, throwing out high-fives, laughing at his jokes, and asking questions about his interests, however, I also know Todd is all show. Behind the fancy clothes, expensive car, and pretty face is a monster—one that always gets what he wants even if it means walking away from his unborn child.

As Gavin warms up to him, I find myself more and more bitter over why he decided to come back in our lives. With every joke told between them and every future playdate planned, anger seethes beneath my surface, screaming to lash out.

While we follow Gavin from hole to hole, in a hushed but vehement tone, I blurt out, "Why, Todd? Why now? Do you just want to fuck with our heads?"

Todd turns toward me with eyes that I used to love, yet now just bring reminders of my nightmares, and replies, "I made a lot of mistakes, Cammy … ones that I'm ashamed of. But I know I can fix them. I can bring you both back to me."

Tears of frustration and pent-up anger well in my eyes. "But you walked away so easily. You said you'd never want him. Why? I think I at least deserve that answer."

Todd reaches his hand around the back of my neck and tries to pull my head to his shoulder. I shove his hand away and take a step back from him, assuming by the look on his face that he is annoyed. "You won't even try, will you? I'll always be the jerk that left you alone and pregnant, right? Well, what about the good times we had? Did you forget about those? The night we danced under the stars on my parents' deck because you were too sick to go to prom or letting you always win our feet fights so you could pick the latest chick-flick to watch or the night we gave ourselves to each other and you moaned my name all night long?" He takes a deep breath to regain himself. "You know, Cammy, I think you're just too goddamned hypnotized by that piece of trash who's waiting for you out there. What? Did he think you needed a bodyguard to come tonight?"

Checking to see that Gavin's attention is still focused on the final hole, I point my finger into his face. "My life, the people I choose to be with, are not your fucking business. Just worry about Gavin … I mean … if you really, truly want him back."

"Of course I do. That's why I'm here. What do you think I am? A liar?"

I glare directly at him. "I think you're nothing."

He backs away with pain obvious on his face and whispers. "I never meant to hurt you. I just couldn't stay. It would've never fit in with my father's master plan for me. He could've been a problem for you … for us … if I didn't leave."

"So you were a coward who couldn't stand up to daddy? Not good enough. Todd, it's too late for me. Focus on him." I point toward Gavin, who is now on his hands and knees trying to roll the ball into the hole.

"But you need to understand. My hands were

tied. If I'd given up law school for my pregnant, teenage girlfriend, he would've come after Gavin, just to spite you. You know he's not a good person. You remember the hell he'd put me through if I didn't live up to his standards. The best thing I could've done was to walk away."

Regret reflects in his face, but his tone carries an insincerity that can't be masked. His dad is lethal, but never once did Todd ever deprive himself of anything. What Todd wanted, Todd got. If he truly wanted to be with me, to love us, he wouldn't have left so easily.

"No, Todd, you're wrong! The best thing you could've done was to be a man and stay. We could have handled your dad—hell, we could've taken on the entire world together. Instead you made the decision that was best for *you*. And now that Gav can fit into your life, you want back in."

"I don't just want back in. I want you back … both of you.

Sounds of shrilling joy startles us from our intense conversation. Gavin is leaping in the air to celebrate the free game that he just won on the final hole of golf. I am grateful for the interruption and the escape from Todd as he refocuses his attention on Gavin. They are busy giving each other high fives while I pray to God for the night to end. I can see the connection already forming between Todd and Gavin and am sure only trouble can lie ahead.

"Way to go, buddy! What do we say we play that free game this weekend?" Todd carries Gavin toward the exit, and I cringe at the sight of them together but keep remembering my mom's cryptic advice to me: Do what's best for Gavin.

"Mommy! Can I, can I?" Gavin asks with excitement.

I plaster a fake grin across my face to hide my pain from him. "Sure, sweetie. You can definitely golf again."

"Todd, she said yes!" he shouts across the miniature golf course. When I hear Gavin's excitement directed toward Todd, it strips me to pieces, and the need to get out of there rushes through me as I begin to quickly throw out goodbyes.

"All right, buddy, it's time to go home. Early surf lesson and camp tomorrow."

Gavin wraps his arms around Todd's neck and whispers something in his ear. I cringe at the sight of it. With a quick wave, I manage to avoid a confrontational goodbye. After we part ways on the boardwalk, I hurry over to where I had seen Cole earlier. Disappointed that he isn't there like he promised, I turn my body to leave and slam right into Dusty.

"Hey, Gavinator ... want to play some Transworld Surf with me? We need practice so next time we can beat Cole!"

I nod my head to Gavin's pleading eyes, and he takes Dusty's hand and waits to be led to the arcade. As Dusty passes by me, he points toward the beach and mouths, "Go to him." My legs can't move fast enough when I see the worry evident on his face. I have hundreds of different scenarios running through my head. Ever since he found out about Todd's reappearance, I've watched parts of Cole crumble even as he tried to catch each piece before I could see his struggle.

Cole's towering body leans against the leg of the empty lifeguard stand, and his hands rest lightly in the pockets of his jeans while he stares out into the now desolate ocean. He is a figure of masculinity with the definition of his arms emphasized by a form-fitting t-shirt and jeans that hang perfectly around his backside.

He stands with his shoulders slumped, reflecting his somber mood. I come up behind him and weave my arms through the space next to his bent elbows. Squeezing tightly around his chest, I clasp my hands together and rest them over his heart.

"You want to talk about it?"

He takes hold of my hands and begins tracing circles over my knuckles. "You've had enough for one night. I can handle my own head. I'm just worried about what's going through yours right now."

I shift my body around so I am face-to-face with him. "Cole, the only thing going through my head right now is you … how to fix you like you've fixed me. Please let me try."

Lifting me by the waist, he sets me on top of the lifeguard stand. He climbs up next to me and pulls me against his body so that my head is nuzzled underneath his neck. He starts to speak, and I can feel the vibration of his deep voice penetrating through my body.

"I knew you were head-over-heels in love with Todd. I mean, I could see the way you looked at him every day. He was the only person that existed in your world. Like I said, I accepted that, even though every bone in my body ached for you. So I tried to move on, but I always knew if he left, you could be mine. That's when Tara came back into my life again."

I wince at the sound of her name as my mind reverts back to the night I saw them together, causing Cole to question me. "Camryn, what's bothering you? What did I say?"

"It's just … she's the one I saw you with at Big Daddy's, the one whose name you called out in your nightmare. Do you still think about her … about you two together?"

"She means nothing to me now. My feelings for

her are long gone. She was only someone to escape the pain and wait with until you finally came into my life." He convinces me of this with a deep kiss that is full of urgency. Hesitantly breaking away from our passion, he continues, "Tara and I were together, and I did have feelings for her, but she always questioned my commitment. How could I tell her that I wanted you, the girl who stuck up for me but never even spoke to me? So I played the game, and we stayed together. She was happy I committed, and I used surfing as my outlet, a place where my thoughts could be focused only on me. After practice was canceled one day, I walked into my grandmom's house, where Tara would often wait for me while I surfed. But this time she wasn't alone. I found her in bed fucking someone else. She would always lie to me about being out with friends, so I always suspected she had someone else—kinda funny since she always questioned me about cheating. So I reacted the only way I knew how back then. I pulled him out onto the back deck and just kept throwing punches over and over at him, destroying him. I couldn't find a way to stop, and that's when your mom stepped in and saved me from killing him."

Heartbroken at the thought that he has been holding on to this for so long, I try to comfort him. "You can't carry this with you forever. Everyone makes mistakes when they're young. I mean, you saw someone you loved betraying you. That's enough to make anyone go crazy."

"You don't understand. I didn't go crazy because Tara cheated. I went crazy because of you."

I lift my head from the crook of his neck and stare at him with a puzzled look. "Why me? What do you mean?"

Cole inhales deeply, trying to muster up the

courage to speak. "Camryn, the guy Tara was with … the one I almost killed was … Todd."

Chapter Fourteen
Stuck Inside a Memory

The second these words leave Cole's mouth, my world halts. Every ounce of feeling leaves my body, and my ability to speak disappears. I can hear each cracked piece of my damaged soul shatter again. For some reason, the only thing my mind will comprehend is my mom's favorite saying, "silence is golden," but at this moment, it's tainted and murky.

Cole embraces me, but I can't return the affection. I feel limp when his arms wrap around my body like his confession somehow instantly weakened me. I just sit on the lifeguard stand and stare at a yellow plastic shovel being taken away with the tide. I see the old, faded toy as the life I once thought I had now drifting away out of sight.

His solemn mood has changed to worry as he clutches my shoulders and calls my name. "Camryn … Camryn… Come on, baby. Say something … talk to me!"

As I jerk away from his grasp, I watch terror form in his eyes. He must know he's losing me, but I don't know how to find a way back to him.

"You knew Todd cheated on me and didn't even bother to tell me? You kept this from me? We're supposed to face things together, Cole … not hide these life-altering truths from each other." My anger bubbles over like a boiling pot that has been heating up for years.

When he tries to reach for me again, I swat his hands out of the way. He inches toward me to close the space between us and pleads, "I wanted to but I couldn't. You have to understand… I just couldn't watch you suffer any more than you already have from that bastard. I wanted to protect you from what he is … from what I am. Please believe me."

I turn away from him to avoid looking into his eyes. "I … I just need time to be alone. To figure this all out." My body gives in to the pain of pushing him away as it begins to tremble and silent sobs echo through my head. Yeah, silence is definitely not golden. I feel Cole's eyes on me as I dash off the beach, but I can't turn around, knowing that when I see him I'll want to run back into his arms.

When I reach the boardwalk out of his sight, I collapse on a bench and fight back the tears with every ounce of strength I have. I want to unleash every tear, every scream that my body can produce, but I have to push it away so Gavin won't see. Pulling myself together before facing him, I frantically scan the crowd in front of the arcade. I spot Dusty and Gavin and quickly rub over my cheeks and smooth the dress I changed into after work. Gavin darts to my arms and starts going on and on about making it to the next level in his video game. While he doesn't notice the evidence of my mood change, Dusty stares at my sullen expression. I need to go home and be numb under my covers. I take Gavin's hand and lead him toward the parking lot, sinking my gaze to the ground as I walk by Dusty, which signals to him that I have failed.

As Gavin falls fast asleep on the ride home, my actions begin to weigh heavily on my mind. The heartache of the evening sets in, and guilt quickly takes over the grief and anger I initially felt. I walked away from the one person who sees beyond how broken I am. It's tearing me apart that I left him alone to fight his own inner battle. I ran because I'm hurt and confused, and it's easier to do that than accept any anguish that will come from Cole's confession.

Lila is sitting on my front porch when I pull up

the driveway. After twenty-three unanswered texts, she finally left me a voicemail warning me that if I didn't return her call I would have a surprise waiting outside for me. I guess she's the surprise. She follows me in as I place Gavin in his bed. Leading me upstairs, she pours two glasses of wine and hands one to me.

"By the looks of you, you're gonna need a shitload of this. You best not tell me that Todd's the reason you left Cole because I swear I'll kill him first, then you, if that's the case."

"Li, please don't talk about killing Todd ... not tonight."

With her ability to see right through me, she demands, "Tell me what's going on, Cam. You look like hell."

"Where do I start? The part where I watched my son bond with his cheating father, the fact that Cole's past involves Todd and he failed to mention it, or maybe that my fucking heart is broken because I left Cole breaking apart on the beach and never once looked back?"

"Wait, Cam. Slow down. What are you talking about?"

"Cole knew. He knew Todd cheated on me and didn't bother to tell me."

"How'd he find out? Is he sure?"

"Oh yeah ... definitely sure. He walked in on his girlfriend, Tara, with Todd. When he saw it, he beat him until he was unconscious and practically dying." I took a swig from my wine glass, hoping it'll soon start to calm my racing nerves. "Remember that week Todd was in the hospital for surf injuries? Well, he didn't collide with a jetty. He collided with Cole's fist."

Lila pulls the wine glass out of my hands and leads me down to my bedroom. As she lays the covers over me, she strokes my hair to the point of my eyes growing heavy, which eventually calms me to a full sleep. However, my nightmares still find their way to me, as I envision Cole and Tara together in my bed while Todd laughs from the corner of the room.

****

153, 154, 155, 156…

This is how many seconds I sit awake in bed, staring at a baby spider crawl across my bedroom ceiling. Sickness swims through my body when I wake up to an empty bed and an eerie silence. My journey seems to have taken a sharp U-turn. I am headed back to the last place I want to be—alone. After I muster up the energy to shift onto my side, I discover my cell phone lying on the sheets next to me. Knowing Lila left a message for me to find, I pick it up and hold it above my face.

Get your sorry ass outta bed, stop the pity party, and march your scrawny legs next door to hot stuff. Tell him you fucked up and then just fuck. ☺

My lips tilt upward at her candidness that gives me the push I need to get Gavin ready. I stagger sleepily into his room to find him already set to go to lessons. After I send him upstairs for breakfast, I throw on a bikini and cover-up and pack a beach bag. The fluttering in my stomach indicates that I will have to face Cole today. Last night, my anger consumed me and caused me to betray him and myself. Admitting that causes my body to ache and the realization sets in—I may have pushed him away forever.

Just as I round the staircase, the doorbell rings and makes my body jump. I freeze and stare at the solid wood door, longing for Cole to be on the other side of it with his arms outstretched, telling me everything is just a twisted dream. Instead, Dusty and Heidi greet me when I open the door. My glum look mutates into shock mixed with anxiety. Why are they here? Has the worst happened to Cole?

Heidi's cheerful voice breaks the staring contest we are having with each other. "Good morning, you look gorgeous, as usual." She leans in and kisses me on the cheek while Dusty gives a quick wave.

I chuckle, knowing full well I look like shit, but it's the price I have to pay for pushing away the best thing that happened to my life since Gavin was born.

"Thanks. What brings you to the south side so early?"

Dusty swings his thumb toward Cole's house and opens his mouth to talk, but Heidi interrupts him before he can explain. "Well, I ... er, we were thinking that maybe I could bring Gav to the beach today since Dusty is covering lessons for Cole anyway. And Dusty sort of wanted to talk to you about something before he starts the lesson."

A confused look spreads across my face. My gaze snaps toward Dusty, who eyes me with a kind gaze. I leave his best friend on the beach with an open wound from his past, and he looks as though he wants to console me. What is wrong with him? I don't deserve it. He should be screaming at me for fucking with Cole's head.

I open the door wider and move to the side to let them in. Heidi proceeds to walk upstairs with a wide smile on her face, but I can see the worry that is masked behind it. When Gavin notices our visitors, he bolts toward them and leaps into Dusty's arms. Heidi snatches him away and disappears out the back door, leaving the two of us alone.

I toss him a bottle of water and say, "I know what you're about to say. How much does he hate me?"

He unscrews the cap and takes a swig of it as a grin forms behind the top of his bottle. "Do you really believe that? I haven't talked to or seen him yet, but if I know him, the only person he hates right now is himself. He always worried about losing you when you found out. That once you knew what he's capable of doing, or should I say what his fists are capable of doing, you'd run." He leans back against the counter and crosses his arms in front of himself. "You need to understand that's not him. He's gotten past all that shit in his life. And I have you and Gav to thank for bringing him back."

My mouth drops open with disbelief over what Dusty is saying. "That's not the reason I ran. I'm not afraid of Cole. I'm just hurt, confused … I don't know … maybe I'm just scared of us … together. He was holding back something that we needed to face together. He should've told me Todd's part in his past. If he wants this to work, we need complete trust in each other. He can't face everything alone."

Dusty nods his head in a way that reveals he understands my muddled thoughts of anger and guilt. "Let me ask you something. What if he would've come clean about his past with you when you first met? Do you think you would've treated him differently? Maybe tried to protect him because you knew that asshole, Todd, is just as much a part of his pain as yours?" He takes another sip of water while I think about his rationale. "Cam, your past happened for a reason, so did Cole's. But it's time for both of you to move forward … too much fucked-up shit in both your lives to get hung up on." Dusty walks toward the trashcan and tosses his empty water bottle in. "But you see, the one thing about Cole is you have given him a little push in the right direction. You have to show him what you need. Because he sure as hell needs you, Cam. He needs you to stay."

I come to realize that I ran again from my pain when Cole is trying to face his head on. "I don't know how to stay and face everything. I'm just not strong enough."

"Do you really believe that? C'mon! You raised a fucking amazing kid on your own, you faced the death of your mom, and then returned to the place you feared most. If that's not superwoman shit, then what is?"

I smile at his comparison of me to a super hero, something I never once saw in myself. Lila and my mom were always my lifesavers, the ones who kept me afloat. I relied on strength from both of them. It wasn't something I feel that I possess.

Dusty reaches into the pocket of his board shorts, pulls out a folded white envelope, and extends it toward me. "Do me a favor. Before you give up on him, read this."

Recognizing the familiar white envelope, I grab it from his hands, certain my mom's words are folded in it. Afraid that if I open it all my weaknesses will be exposed, I grasp it in my hand to the point of white-knuckles. Noticing my uneasiness, Dusty starts toward the door to leave and says, "Remember, it's okay to feel the anger, just don't live with it for too long." I smile as he leaves with the the very first thing that Cole said to me standing in our school's hallway, the one thing that helped me find myself again.

Exhausted from what has unfolded over the last twenty-four hours, I throw myself into the pillows on the couch. I prop my feet on the coffee table and rip open the letter, bracing myself as I begin to read aloud my mom's most recent advice.

Dearest Camryn,
I never wanted you to have to see this one. It means you're suffering alone again. It means you're in pain—the kind that is so deep within that you can feel it

through your bones. It means you abandoned someone in his time of need. It means I'm not there to help pick up the pieces. Know that not all truths should be spoken at the time of conception. Life is chaotic, yet everything in it needs to have order. While you are angry and confused, understand that this was told to you when it was supposed to fall into place in your life. Gavin was meant to be your son, and you were meant to be his mom. Remember, running is easy; it's moving on that can feel impossible.

> *Love and support,*
> *Mom*

Her words echo in the silent room. I drag my sluggish body downstairs and flop on my bed, hating myself for leaving Cole lost and alone. He's been reaching out to me, opening up a door to a difficult part of his life, and I slam it in his face to spare my own pain.

Grasping the angel charm that has never left my neck since Cole gave it to me, I stare at the wall that separates our bedrooms, as my mind wanders to where he is right now, what he's doing, and if being apart from each other is as excruciating for him as it is for me. Heidi made it clear that Cole is skipping lessons, and I can't help but think that he is avoiding me. This world of "what ifs" my mind conjures up eventually knocks me into a sound sleep.

****

Clattering dishes and the thumping of Gavin's feet on the floor above me wakes me from my daytime slumber. I peek at the clock and notice it's after five o'clock. I have slept the entire day away. Bummed that I missed out on time with my son, I crawl off the bed, splash some cold water on my face, tie my hair back in a low knot, and throw on a short summer dress with flip-flops.

In the kitchen, Heidi is laughing at one of Lila's stories as they sip margaritas and stir pots on the stove. Dusty and Carter, Coronas in hand, are discussing the baseball game on the television with Gavin dribbling his Nerf soccer ball around their legs. Gavin spots me first and yells, "Aunt Lila, she's awake! Hi, Mommy!"

Everyone's heads turn toward me, and my cheeks flush at the attention. Lila sprints over and reaches out to me, looking as if she's ready to catch me if I shatter into a million pieces.

"Hey, sunshine. Glad your lazy ass could join us for family dinner."

Confused I say, "Li, it's Friday, not a family dinner night."

She takes my hand and leads me to the counter where Heidi has poured a fresh margarita into a glass. "Well, since we missed one last night, Gavs thought we could do one tonight. He asked for Mexican-themed … your favorite!"

I smile at Gavin and blow him a kiss, appreciative of how much he values these dinners. "It's perfect. And everyone, thanks for today … taking care of Gav, making dinner, and everything else." I look directly at Dusty to assure him I'm referring to our earlier talk. He nods and gives a slight tilt of his beer toward me.

All of us surround my kitchen table and chow down on enchiladas, tacos, and nacho dip. Gavin entertains with jokes that he obviously learned from Carter, Heidi brags about the advanced skills my son is exhibiting at camp, and Lila complains about a bride and her bridal party who left crappy tips for all the stylists.

I pretend to be involved in each conversation, but my mind is on the one person who is missing from dinner. Even with a full house, I've never felt more alone. Cole should be here. He deserves the company of family and friends. In the middle of another Lila story, I stand up from the table and escape downstairs to the front porch. Leaning against the railing, I watch as surfers strut off the beach, balancing their boards on top of their heads and wet suits hanging off their bodies. When I hear the door close behind me, I know I'm no longer alone in my thoughts.

"You know, he's just giving you the space you need." Heidi moves in next to me and rests her back against the railing to face me.

"I'm sorry, Heidi. I shouldn't have been so distant with him. It wasn't his fault. I promised you that I'd be there for him."

She places her hand on my shoulder. "And I have no doubt in my mind that you'll do just that." She walks back inside and as the door opens, I can hear laughter emanating through the entire house, leaving me to wish that Cole and I are part of it.

It drives me straight to his front door, incessantly repeating over and over in my head how I'm going to explain my reasons and apologize for leaving him. Focused on my knuckles meeting the wood pane of his door, I am startled by a familiar voice behind me.

"He's not home. I heard he broke someone's heart last night and was thinking of a way to put it back together for her."

I twirl around and see Cole in his wetsuit with red, swollen eyes that match his raw knuckles. "You see, he promised that he'd never disappoint her, but he failed. Now he's just completely lost without this beautiful girl in his life."

Guilt swarms me as I take in Cole's state, knowing I'm to blame. His scabbed-over fists indicate that my reaction drove him to old places, ones where he came face-to-face with the darkness of his past.

"I'm so sorry. I ran when you needed me the most. I shut down when you bared your soul. How can you blame yourself? How can you still want to be here, with me?"

"Camryn, I already told you, I won't give up on you. No matter what, you own me forever."

I wrap my arms around his neck and coax him down to me. "This has been the worst day of my life because you weren't with me."

"Oh, beautiful girl, I was with you. Every day I'm right here." He kisses over my heart and then glides his mouth to meet mine. When our lips connect, a shiver travels through my body as if we haven't felt each other for years. Our tongues become more forceful with each touch. I hop up on him and wrap my legs around his waist while he holds me steady underneath my backside.

Being with him is instantly healing, and I know that without him I'm left with a wound that will never stop bleeding. He broke through my barriers to find the person I used to be, the one I want to be, and I am somehow able to give him a reason to bury his own past mistakes.

Squeezing him tighter around his neck, I lean close to him and whisper, "Cole, I want you right now. And tomorrow. And the next day. And the next…"

His dimpled smile spreads wide across his face, and he carries me through his door, kicking it closed with his foot. After we bump into the wall and make our way to his room, we collapse into his bed. With our bodies entwined and our hearts reconnected, we find our way back to each other.

Chapter Fifteen
Goldfish

Cole spends the entire weekend with Gavin and me, not leaving our sides except to train with Dusty a few hours each morning. Every time he kisses me, another part of my heartache breaks off and disappears. Our weekend together erases any remnants of the drama we faced over our connection with Todd. It's as if that marred part of our lives ceases to exist for the time being, and we are left with just each other.

As I sit on a bench, looking up for Cole and Gavin in the multi-colored Ferris wheel that blinks alternating red, green, and blue lights, I am grateful that I managed to avoid Todd all weekend, which allowed for Cole and Gavin to bond outside of surfing. He had called Friday morning, but I convinced him that Gavin wouldn't be up for anything since he was scheduled for his required vaccinations needed to enter kindergarten. By the time he called back on Sunday, we were already in the middle of a picnic on the beach and had plans to come up on the boardwalk tonight for the amusements. With all the pain he created in my life, I was satisfied when I heard the frustration in his voice, seeing it as a small victory in revenge.

A mass of people exit the ride at once, but I am able to easily spot Cole and Gavin. My handsome son is sitting atop Cole's shoulders as he bounces him through the line of people forming for the bumper cars. I can't help but notice how much attention Cole attracts from women all around him. Even a young mom standing in line with her husband and daughter loses the balloon she's holding when she strains her body to get a better look at him.

Growing up in a beach town, you become

accustomed to the sights of buff, shirtless guys and pretty boys who spend most of their free time lifting in the gym, but Cole isn't typical. First of all, he towers above the average surfer, amazing me with how acute his skills are on the board, which allows him to become top-notch in his sport. Also, Cole doesn't don the usual surfer fashion of tribal tattoos and bleach-tipped hair. He is more natural with his toned-down blond hair that is currently growing out from a previous buzz but is long enough for me to run my fingers through and grab. He is a dream guy for most women, but he's mine in real life, and that thought makes me smile as they approach.

"Mommy, we were up so high. I could see Aunt Lila and Uncle Carter's house from the top!"

"That's so cool, buddy. Wow! And you weren't even scared up there!"

Cole lifts his thumb up to Gavin, who is still sitting on his shoulders, and he meets his own thumb to Cole's, rubbing them together to create their own thumbs-up handshake. "My man scared? No way. He owned that ride!"

Gavin did an exaggerated nod of this head and repeats Cole. "That's right. Owned it!"

We all laugh as we make our way out of the amusement pier to Cole's car. I lock hands with him, feeling like my world has finally found some balance. As I glance from Cole to Gavin and to the beach that lines the boardwalk, a sense of peace swarms me as I realize I finally found the one person who completes me. While we drive down the boulevard into the calm end of the island where we live, I silently say goodbye to our amazing weekend.

****

Monday morning comes in the blink of an eye, and I am getting ready for another start to a three-day rotation at the hospital. Dressed in my stork scrubs, I sit at my vanity and plait my hair to the side in a low braid. I stare at the reflection in the mirror of Cole sleeping, wishing I was still snuggled in his arms. We spent the entire night just talking and holding each other. And for once we enjoyed a dreamless sleep with our bodies refusing to let each other go.

"Did I ever tell you how sexy you are in those scrubs?" The hoarseness of his voice startles me from reliving the previous night.

"Ha, Ha, Mr. Stevens. Sexy and scrubs can't possibly go together. Not even a sexpert like you could find a way for that!"

A vibrant laugh bellows from Cole to expose his prominent dimples. "Did you really just call me a sexpert? What, exactly, is a sexpert?"

I stand up from my stool and traipse over to the bed where Cole is leaning on his elbow, sheets wrapped around his waist, his bare chest exposed. As I sit on the edge next to him, I begin to rub my hands over his chiseled abs, moving up to tickle his chest with my nails. "This is all part of being a sexpert."

"So sexperts have a stomach and a chest? Wow, that really explains it!"

I playfully swat at him. "Shut up! You know what I mean. You define sexpert—hot, solid, and a pro in bed."

"Oh yeah. Well, this sexpert looks at you in those scrubs and pictures you with nothing on underneath. It gets me pretty hot."

A grin spreads across my face. "Well, Mr. Stevens, I stand corrected. You found a way to make scrubs sexy. Not only are you a sexpert … you're a sexpert champion."

"You know how this champion feels about you

calling him Mr. Stevens. I'm sure he's pretty solid right now and can show how professional he can be."

I lean into his ear and add, "Maybe that champion should know there's nothing underneath these scrubs."

Cole's eyes widen, and he flashes a sexy smirk. He pulls me down and rolls me over him so my back is against the mattress as he positions his body on top of mine. He holds his weight up with his flexed arms and says, "Did I ever tell you your surprises are such a turn-on?"

I run my hand through his hair and reply, "I'm pretty sure everything turns you on."

"Not everything ... just everything about you." He leans into my mouth and claims it. I can feel his readiness brush against my leg as I begin to slide his boxer briefs down. His hands are frantic as they jump from my breasts to my stomach to my core. Just as his thumbs are dragging my pants down, the doorbell rings.

Cole mumbles into my mouth, "Just ignore it. They'll go away."

After the third ring, I hear Gavin yell from his room, "Mommy! Somebody's at the door!"

Between the intrusive sound of the doorbell and the awakened five-year-old, our sensual mood quickly dissolves, and I scoot out from under Cole with a disappointed groan.

Retracting my body back to his, he says, "We'll continue this later."

I nod but still make a pout with my lips.

He pulls me against him again he adds, "And that means the scrubs too!"

As my pout changes to a giggle, I grab the pillow and smack him in the face with it. With the doorbell on its fifth ring, I put myself back together and trudge to the front door. Any remaining desire that was hanging on is instantly stripped away when Todd greets me on the other side.

"Well, good morning! Happy to see you haven't mastered the art of avoidance in your own home yet."

I shut the door slightly to shield our conversation and his sarcasm from Cole's ears. Since I am already bubbling with annoyance, there is no telling how Cole would react.

"Oh, I guess I'll have to try harder next time."

Todd huffs, frustrated with my remark. Before he can retaliate and achieve the almighty last word, Cole appears next to me, still shirtless but covering his boxers with low hanging gym shorts. He positions his arm behind my back and grasps onto my hip while staring at Todd like he has just marked his territory. Fury overtakes Todd's features, and through clenched teeth, he speaks to Cole through me. "Cammy, we have parental issues to discuss. Maybe you can ask your friend to leave."

Cole sneers at Todd's comment. "Parental issues? Are you fucking serious? Last time I checked it takes actually being a parent to have those types of issues."

The acidic nature between them is so prominent that it suffocates the space between us, which causes me to take a step back. When Cole senses my uneasiness, he squeezes me tighter while circling his thumb along my hipbone.

"I guess you would know from all that experience you have with parenting." The iciness of Todd's comment startles me, especially with its effect on Cole. His body becomes rigid, every muscle tense, and his fists are clamped, ready to strike. The rage that consumes his features is unyielding, even sending a chill down my side. Hoping to extinguish the fire that is spreading between them, I wrap my arms around Cole's waist and whisper into his ear, "Own your breath." As he sucks in air, his body relaxes and light returns to the darkness that has blanketed him. Grateful that I saved him from whatever past demon reared its head, I cut to the chase with Todd to avoid any more mishaps.

"What, exactly, do you want? Obviously, it must be important enough to show up at my home this early, uninvited." My abruptness is apparent.

"Anything that involves my son is important." He glares at Cole when he speaks, digging in the dagger a bit deeper. "I want to take him to the beach today. I know he's into surfing."

Just as I'm about to give an excuse as to why my son can't go, Gavin bolts down the hallway and hurtles directly into Todd's arms.

"Todd! Come here! You have to see my room. Me-Mom made it so cool!" He jumps into a surfer stance and pretends he's riding a wave.

Todd smiles and replies, "Sure, bud. But first I wanted to see if you'd like to come surfing with me this morning."

"Yes!" Gavin's face turns toward me, his eyes wide with excitement. "Mommy, can I puhlease go with him?"

Goddammit, why did he put me in this position in front of my son? With a tight smile, I give my son permission to go with Todd but only if Dusty is willing to be there with them. As Gavin rejoices, high-fiving with Todd and brushing past us toward his bedroom, my heart tears out of my chest. It has become apparent that he wants this person in his life, this person who once rejected him. Cole's arms, still swarmed around me, become my security blanket, and I feel his breath in my ear humming, "Focus on what you do … not him."

After I settle the plans with Dusty over the phone and Gavin gives a tour of his room, he leaves with Todd, surfboards in tow for their morning together. I know the sight of them walking away hand-in-hand will stay branded on my mind, most likely to become a fixture in my nightmares. Before it's time to leave for work, Cole leads me to the swing on his front porch and cuddles me as we glide and sip our morning coffees together.

"As much as it kills me to admit it, you did the right thing. Gavin will be great. It's you who will feel the agony of it."

As I snuggle my head into his chest, a stray tear escapes from my eye, knowing he is right.

"I just wish he was here swinging with us and telling his goofy but inappropriate for a five-year-old jokes." Both of us smiling at that thought, I lift my face from him and look into his eyes, which have softened since Todd left. "I'm still reaching for that happy ending. Can't seem to let that dream go."

"I'll get you there. I promise."

We spend a few more minutes swaying together in silence, and I'm hesitant to let go of the satisfaction the weekend had brought us. We have taken a huge step toward becoming the family I always wanted for Gavin, one where love is the driving force that conquers everything. With my head upon his shoulder and our bodies both physically and emotionally connected, I wonder if this journey we are taking will ever find its happily ever after.

****

Between the maternity floor bustling with births and the erotic text messages from Cole describing how he plans on finishing what was interrupted this morning, the morning flies. I welcome the craziness since it keeps my mind away from Todd and Gavin and focused on the laboring moms who are in need of my full attention. With summer in full swing, Lila's salon is packed, so I am stuck having my lunch alone. When I enter the cafeteria, I can't help but notice a very familiar blue-eyed boy sitting at my usual spot.

"Hey, Gavs! What are you doing here? Are you okay?" I can't hide the panic that escapes from my mouth.

"Silly, Mommy! Me and Todd are surprising you!" He has a gleam in his eyes that speaks pure excitement and happiness, the same gleam I saw over the weekend when he was with Cole. "He's over there buying me chocolate milk." He points to where Todd, who gives a modest wave resembling a peace offering, is standing in line.

I return with a quick wave and turn my attention back to my son. "How was your morning? Was everything okay?"

"Oh, Mommy, it was so much fun! Todd's an awesome surfer, just like Cole! We went out deep, and I got to paddle his board for him, and I stood up for three whole seconds!" He holds up three of his fingers in front of my face.

I grab his fingers and place a kiss on them. "You're absolutely incredible! You'll have to show me next time we go to the beach!"

Todd sits down on the other side of Gavin with chocolate milk and two waters in hand, and passes one to me. He has a tied-up plastic bag with him that he places on the table.

"One whole wheat roasted veggie wrap, no onions, with a side of fat-free honey Dijon." He sets it in front of me and asks. "Still your favorite, right?"

With a slow nod of confusion, I manage a "thank you" and begin eating. Gavin and Todd share chicken fingers and fries while they lead the conversation with talk about surfing and the upcoming Atlantic Classic.

Todd breaks into my stunned silence and says, "You know, Cammy girl, I'm competing again this year. I may need you as my good luck charm again … like old times."

"If you want old times maybe Tara can help you out." I concentrate on my food, avoiding the death stare I can feel Todd giving me.

"Hey, Gav, buddy, why don't you go pick out some dessert at the counter? I have to talk to Mommy about something for a minute."

"Anything I want? So cool!"

When he is out of earshot, Todd leans in closer so that I am looking into those deep eyes that at one time captured me at first sight.

"It was a huge mistake that meant nothing. You were my everything then. You still are, and now he is as well." He points in Gavin's direction. "I have no excuse except that I was young and stupid and she would talk to me about how horribly Cole treated her. I was trying to be her friend."

"Last time I checked you don't usually stick your dick into friends. I wasn't everything to you, Todd. Who are you kidding?"

"I screwed up, but I came back. Doesn't that tell you something … anything?"

"Yeah, it tells me that we conveniently fit into your life now." I start to collect my trash, hoping he'll get the point that I am done discussing the past.

"Cole should have never said anything to you. Did he also tell you he nearly killed me? Actually committed a crime?"

"Come on, Todd. You were sleeping with his girlfriend in his grandmom's bed! You deserved an ass beating."

"Is that all he told you?" Todd's expression turns

pale. "That I slept with his girlfriend?"

Sensing that there is more to the story, I reply, "Should I know something else? I thought it was just one time."

He takes a gulp of water as color returns to his face. "No, I just figured someone like him would make up some bogus lies to turn you and Gavin against me."

"Todd, you walked out on us. I think you did a pretty good job of turning me away. You're just lucky Gavin is young and doesn't know why you left."

"Well, speaking of Cole, listen. I don't want him around my son. I think his past shows that he's dangerous."

I leap up from the table and slam my palms onto its surface, which cause a few people around us to jump. "Don't you dare make demands! You have no right! Cole will never hurt us." I gather my things. "I should've known you came here with an agenda. You'll never change."

I turn my back to him to find Gavin. "Make sure Dusty gets my son to camp."

As I scamper away, I hear Todd threaten, "Maybe we'll see what a judge has to say about that low-life."

My rage flings me back to him. "You fucking promised me no courts would be involved. I gave you Gavin. What else do you want?"

"Simple. You, him, us. I want to be a family."

"It's too late, Todd. I don't want that anymore. I don't love you anymore."

"So you want that worthless piece of crap? You're so much better than him, Cammy. I don't want you and Gavin around a criminal."

I crouch down toward his face and lean into him as close as I can. "Then maybe we shouldn't be near you, since you were the one who killed me five years ago." I

171

throw my trash onto his plate and rush to Gavin, giving him a hug and a kiss, then scurry out of the cafeteria to my floor.

Once I reach the nurses' station, I sink into a chair behind the high desk and inhale slowly, trying to get my rapid heartbeat back to normal. I am livid that Todd came to my work and actually thought he could threaten me. I grab my cell phone from my pocket to text Lila about my standoff when a recognizable voice is heard from over the desk.

"Hey, Goldfish. How long have you been back in town?" Knowing only one person in the world ever called me that, my head snaps up to bring me face-to-face with my father.

Chapter Sixteen
Let's Forget the World

It's amazing how quickly perfection can be erased from human memory, but all my mind can process is the misery of the day. Between Todd's sneak attack and the sight of my father standing over the desk, the high from my flawless weekend morphs into a day from hell. It seems that my past won't leave me alone. It keeps creeping back, trying to knock me on my ass. I am beginning to think that I might never find a way to move on and forget the hardships. Peering at the man who at one time had been my idol, all my aggravation from the day comes to the forefront.

"Well, Jack, why would you know I came back? I mean, it's only been … I don't know, a decade … since you checked in with me." I twirl my chair around and open up the metal drawer to file some paperwork, hoping it will cue him to leave me alone.

Instead, I hear his feet brushing the carpet around the desk and planting themselves next to me. I knew he wouldn't let me off that easy. It's not Jack Singer's style. My father, who already towers over me at nearly six-foot, feels even more out of reach while I sit in the desk chair below him. Height definitely is not a trait I inherited from him, as I stopped growing when I reached five-foot-four. He still maintains a slim figure, apparent even in his baggy scrubs, which he always attributed to his dedication to swimming. While my mom lived and breathed surfing, my dad swam two miles a day. Many of my fondest memories as a child were when he would return home from the hospital, scoop me up, and carry me to the beach for his nightly swim. He always ended the evening by challenging me to a race that he always let me win.

"Sweetie, there's so much we have to discuss, so much for you to understand. But it's going to take time. I just wanted to stop up here because I kept hearing about this beautiful new nurse on the maternity floor, and I knew it had to be my baby girl."

Annoyed with his sentiments of affection, I correct him. "Well, you can see I'm not your baby anymore. I grew up over the last ten years. Somehow I managed to do it without a father." The bitterness is spilling from my mouth.

Jack doesn't seem flustered by my resentful tone toward him. His dark eyes carry sorrow and regret, and his lips are curved upward with a soft smile. He won't take his gaze off me and never once winces at my backlash.

"How's that grandson of mine? I hear he takes after his grandma at surfing." A full smile appears on his face to expose his large, straight teeth while his hand combs through black hair that is peppered with patches of gray, which give him a very chic look.

"You have no right to know anything about him! You haven't earned the title of father, let alone grandpa." My annoyance is beginning to raise the volume of my voice. "You're just a guy who walked out on his family, so you could screw some bitch behind Mom's back. So, Jack, did she reach drinking age yet, or is she still using her fake ID to get into the bars around here?"

Still calm with no reaction to my outburst, he shakes his head and squeezes the bridge of his nose. "It wasn't like that. Things were complicated. Amanda was there during a difficult time. She was my support system, and we fell for each other. Didn't mean to, it just happened. But, if you care to know, she's not in the picture anymore." He crouches down to my level. "Goldfish, I never wanted to leave you, but I respected your mom's wishes. It killed me every day, not seeing you, watching you grow up. But it had to be done for your mom's sake."

My eyes narrow, and venom spews from my mouth. "She was your support system? What about my support? Mom had just fought through cancer, I was still a kid, and you just left us! I've haven't had a dad for ten years of my life. In that time I had a son, moved across the country, and watched mom die. And I did it without a father!" The tears I was fighting back began to flood my cheeks. "So, don't you dare talk to me about needing support because you can bet your ass my son will always have it from me, and he will never feel an ounce of the hurt you inflicted."

The force of my attack causes him to back away and gives me the space to swing out of my chair and stomp away. His words reverberate in my head and infuriate me so much that I need to punch something or scream. Feeling the latter would be less painful, I trudge to the break room, press my forehead against my locker, and belt out my frustrations. With a bit of stress lifted, I search for my cell phone and typed a quick message to Lila.

There's been a Jack sighting … may need a bottle of Jack to handle this one. TTYL.

I tuck my phone away and attempt to finish the work day, eager to keep any more ghosts from sneaking back into my life.

The increasing awfulness of my day has me anxious to get home to Gavin and Cole. I crave the ongoing but ridiculous conversation about Batman and Spiderman. If anyone can bring me out of the funk my father and Todd put me in, it will be my two guys. I spend car ride home attempting to put the day behind me, with the hope of leaving it in the past.

As I suck in the breath of fresh air that the sight of my home causes, I park in the driveway next to a number of cars, knowing my friends are also here. When I open my door and hear Gavin's laughter mixed with Lila's screeching, the punch line to Carter's joke, Heidi's delicate laugh, and the clanking of beer bottles—which are most likely Cole's and Dusty's—the tension from my day evaporates, and calm flows through me. Skipping every other step to join the party, I am first reeled in by the set of arms I have come to love. Cole places his lips on mine, and after a soft, gentle kiss, he holds me close to him, and comforts me with his embrace. Gavin greets me from his spot next to Carter on the couch, and Lila sticks a shot glass in my face.

"What's this?"

"No other than fucking Jack himself." Lila pushes the glass to my mouth, and leaves me unable to do anything but open up and embrace the burning trail down my throat.

I cough out, "Thanks, Li. Knew I could depend on you for the strong stuff."

She proudly salutes me with the bottle of Jack Daniels that she is grasping with her other hand, while Cole is watching me with a questioning glance. I smile and shrug my shoulders, hoping to quell any concerns he may be forming.

Once everyone settles down and returns to what they were doing before I walked in, Heidi approaches me, just as Cole is beginning to ask about my day. With a folded piece of paper in her hand, she slides it over to Cole and me. Confused, I ask, "What's this?"

"It's for you and Cole. From all of us."

My eyebrows scrunch together, and I peer up to Cole, who looks just as puzzled as me. After unfolding the note I hold it up for him to read along with me.

Coupon for One Night Free from Everyone but Each Other

When: Tonight

"Heidi, did you guys really make us a coupon to go out on a date?" I am laughing as I ask the question while Heidi proudly nods.

Dusty throws his hands up in defense. "It was all Heidi. I swear. And if you're good tonight, maybe she'll let you pick out of her classroom treasure chest."

She swats at his mocking comment.

"I ... er, we ... thought you guys needed some alone time. So I called Lila, and she and Carter are taking Gavin overnight, and Dusty and I are going to handle surf lessons and camp tomorrow. Oh, yeah and, Camryn, you have tomorrow off. I asked one my nurse friends there to cover your shift, and she happily agreed."

Shock registers on my face at the extent our friends have gone to concerning our date night. "You guys are amazing! This is exactly what I needed!" I feel Cole squeeze the top of my arm, knowing he needs this as well.

****

The view from our restaurant is breathtaking as we watch various boats sail through the marina against the pink-streaked sky. Across the table from me sits a delicious-looking Cole, dressed up in gray pants with a fitted button-down shirt rolled up to his elbows. I'm used to seeing him in surfer shorts or jeans, so when he "picked me up" like this, I was close to ripping off his clothes and keeping him in the house all night.

The conversation shifts to the events of my day while we are sharing our key lime cheesecake dessert. "So my dad stopped by my floor today."

Once I hear the clatter against the plate, I know I had made him drop his fork. "Why didn't you tell me?

Was everything okay? Were you okay? Dammit, Camryn. You should've called me."

Appreciative that this man is so in tune with the triggers of my past and concerned how I am regarding them, I take hold of his hand and force him to look into my eyes. "Cole. Stop. I was fine. I handled it. Don't beat yourself up over it. I can't call you every time my past feels the need to show up." Mindful to avoid divulging Todd's little surprise lunch and threat, I keep the conversation focused on my father. "He heard I was back in town. Asked about Gav. Then spit out some bullshit that my mom asked him to stay away from us. I wish he would just let her rest in peace."

"Now that you've seen him, any thoughts on wanting to have a relationship with him?"

"No. He left us. He cheated on my mom and walked out on his daughter. How could I just forget that and let him back in?"

He circles his thumb over my knuckles. "Well, you know, my mom used to tell me that forgiveness was a super power and if you were special enough to possess it, pain would just disappear." The memory of his mom causes the sides of his lips to curl up.

Smiling back at him, I add, "You're wise beyond your years, Mr. Stevens." I wink, knowing that title is a turn-on for him.

Cole smirks and continues, "Camryn, what I'm trying to say is that it's okay to want a second chance with your dad. Even with the shitbag move my dad did when he walked out on Heidi and me, I know that if he came looking for me, I'd want to give him a chance."

In awe of how easily Cole can piece together my muddled thoughts, I stare over his shoulder in silence, trying to grasp what he has just revealed to me about his past.

"No, I can't forget. I just can't go against my mom. He left her stranded in her time of need. How would I even begin to get past that?"

Cole nods his head and squeezes my hand, showing his acceptance of my loyalty to my mom. However, I understand the desire for his dad's place in his life, especially after I watched Gavin yearn for a father figure in his own life. For many years after Jack left, I grabbed hold of anything that could bring him back to me, anything that could show him that I was worthy of his love and care. But those thoughts have long passed, and I am left to wonder what is worse—why he left or what made him come back?

****

The next stop of the evening is a swanky beach bar that is actually on the bay rather than the ocean. After we remove our shoes, we walk hand-in-hand across the cool sand to a couple of lounge chairs that are surrounded by tiki torches and a personal fire pit. Once we order our drinks, rather than lying in my own lounge chair, I snuggle with Cole in his. I want to feel him against me and inhale his scent. His presence alone can heal me, and help me let go of the stress I faced during the day.

"I used to think about what it would be like to hold you, touch you … well everywhere." His gaze travels up and down my body. "You were the only good thing I saw in my dreams. Sometimes I wonder if it's still a dream. And if it is, I better never fucking wake up from it."

I tighten my hold around him and nuzzle my head into his neck. "Well then, I guess we have the same problem because you're the first dream I've had in five years, and there's no way I'm waking up any time soon."

I meet my lips to his and become lost in the

moment. We have a way of forgetting everything around us and existing in our own world. I stop kissing him only when I feel his lips tense and his body freeze. As I follow the direction of his gaze, I am led to the sight of Tara standing at the water's edge.

Tara is a vision of sophistication and elegance with her tall, slender body and perfectly-styled blonde bob with bangs that sweep to the side. She always seems to be wearing an A-line dress or skirt that hangs at a modest length, paired with a short-sleeved cardigan and strand of pearls around her neck. I won't be surprised if she is a descendant of the Kennedy family.

She is standing just a few feet away from our lounge chair and seems to be waiting for something or maybe someone. Her eyes are glued to Cole, but she has a very noticeable scowl on her face that is most likely directed to me. Her presence has caught his attention and manages to make the intimacy between us vanish. Drawing my gaze back to Cole, he speaks to me but never takes his eyes from her.

"I'm sorry, but I have to handle this. Will you be okay for a few minutes?"

Annoyed that he's allowing her to intervene on our night, I shift my body around so my back is to him. "Yeah, sure, it's fine."

The coldness of my tone must snap him out of his trance, and he grabs hold of my waist and nibbles my ear before whispering into it, "Remember, there's only you. Now and forever." He places a kiss on my ear and lifts himself off the lounge chair, moving toward her. I peek back over my shoulder to watch and notice her scowl turn into a full-fledged smile when Cole approaches, which only deepens my hatred for her, realizing that she has some sort of control over my man.

As they disappear into the dark, no longer

illuminated by the torches that line the chairs, I find myself drinking my apple martini a bit faster. The warmth it causes is a welcome feeling in my stomach that erases some of the aggravation I have been feeling since he left our date with her. Just as I polish off the last sip, a voice startles me from drowning in my cocktail.

"I have to say I warned you, Cammy girl. I told you he's no good. He just can't be faithful. He'll always run back to her." Todd stands behind me, watching me sulk into my empty martini glass. His words pierce me more than I want to admit.

"Really, Todd? You're accusing someone of being unfaithful? Not sure you should throw those stones."

"The difference between him and me is I've learned from my mistakes, and I'm trying to make up for them. He just runs to her every time she calls. Even after she slept with me, he still wanted her. I mean he actually begged her to come back to him."

Whether it's the alcohol clouding my mind or the hurtful words spewing from Todd's mouth, dizziness comes over me and I have to get away from him. My mind needs to process what Todd has said when it is clear and not in a drunken fog. I stumble out of the lounge chair and make a dash toward the gazebo that leads out of the beach bar. Before I can make a clean exit, an arm hooks my waist and whips me back. Todd has come after me, and now I am trapped in his embrace. With anger consuming me, I start to swing my arms at Todd, punching him repeatedly in the chest.

"You come back in my life, and everything goes to shit again. Why can't you leave me alone? Why can't you just stay away?" At this point, I am in full hysterics, screaming in his face. Luckily, the cover band is so loud that I'm not making a noticeable scene.

Todd grabs my shoulders to stop my assault on him and steadies my shaking body. Brushing the hair from my face he says, "Because I'm in love with my son and his mother."

I jerk away from him, but my alcohol-induced reaction is too slow, and I find his mouth covering mine, his lips begging for me to respond. His touch, once so intimate, is now foreign and unwelcome. It is clear that only one person has control of my heart, and he is off with his ex-girlfriend somewhere.

I sober up from his horrid kiss and push him off me with enough force that sends him stumbling backward. Irritation and confusion plague me as I watch him gain his composure. With my mind unhinged and my body constricted from his mere presence, I start to back myself to the stairs that lead out of the bar. Todd is stalking toward me, blurting out apologies, but at this point they're just empty. Before I can escape, a tall body blocks my way out.

Glaring from me to Todd, fury blazes from Cole's eyes. With his jaw tense, eyes narrow, and fists clenched, he is ready to release the Cole of old, the one Todd has already met. Terror is evident in Todd's face as he realizes what Cole has just witnessed. However, he pumps up his chest and rolls his sleeves as he prepares to come to blows with him.

Eager to restrain this side of Cole, I maneuver around his body to the exit, praying that he'll come after me rather than give in to his rage. I race four blocks to the beach, hoping to lead him out of his danger zone. Nestled against the lifeguard stand, I pull my knees to my chest and stare out into the dark depth of the ocean as I try to understand how our seamless date unraveled so quickly.

"I'm sorry, beautiful girl." Cole's voice soothes

me as he squeezes in next to me. "I keep disappointing you, and you keep running from me."

I feel blood stream down his knuckles as it drips onto my leg when he secures his arms around me to calm my trembling body. "Tell me how to fix this."

I stare straight out to the ocean, and fearing his answer, I ask, "Did you hurt him again?" I cringe at the thought of me being the reason for bringing back Cole's past demons.

He slowly shakes his head from side to side. "I couldn't do that to Gavin."

With a sigh of relief, I swirl my fingers over his bloody hand. "Did he hurt you?" I silently scold myself for not asking that question first.

"Nah … just the wall outside the bar."

I sigh in relief and look into his eyes. "Cole? Will you just lay here with me and help me forget?"

Cole guides me down into the sand and pulls my body into his. We stare at the starry sky while listening to the waves crash against the shore. Together, we find a way to forget the world for just one night.

Chapter Seventeen
My Only One

The chaos from the previous night doesn't allow us to sleep a wink. With the sun peeking up over the horizon amidst the pink- and orange-painted sky, Cole remains attached to me, reveling in the peace of the early-morning sunrise. He hasn't mentioned what happened at the beach bar, as he kept his promise to help me forget everything, but I know we'll have to face that aftermath today.

"Thank you for coming after me last night and for not letting your anger take you to those places again."

He presses his lips together, which reveals the battle he is fighting with his conscience. One side of Cole would have felt pleasure pounding Todd's face while his other side loves and respects my son enough not to hurt him, which only adds to the many reasons I love him.

"It took every ounce of my willpower to not kill that bastard. I saw the look on your face, the tears rolling down your cheeks, and I wanted to end him. But I thought of Gav and couldn't take it if he looked at me differently. If he saw me as a villain … I just couldn't fail him."

I admire his affection for my son and pull his face into mine to place a kiss on his forehead. "That one is for thinking about Gavin." I move to his cheek. "That one is for protecting me." I pause my mouth in front of his. "And this one is for being the man you are." I catch his bottom lip in my teeth and run my tongue across it before plunging completely into his mouth. I push Cole back and straddle him, pinning his body to the sand. A rush of need fills me as my hands travel down his unbuttoned shirt, over his defined stomach muscles, reaching underneath his pants to take hold of his manhood. With his excitement evident, I begin to stroke him while I try to undress him at the same time. He catches my wrists and holds them still.

"Camryn, I want this, but not here. I want to be the only one who can see you squirm and hear you moan."

Grabbing a striped beach blanket hanging over the side of the lifeguard stand, he reaches for my hand to lead me away. As the houses that line the beach begin to disappear from sight, I have an idea about where we are going. When we reach the inlet, Cole boosts me up on the jetty and then leads me to an opening that is hidden behind the flat-top rocks that are exposed to the rough waters. He unfolds the blanket and spreads it over the damp sand between the rocks that hide us. The privacy of this spot makes me wonder how many teenagers sneak here for heavy make-out sessions.

As a small laugh escapes me, I tease, "So how many women have you brought here and had your way with?"

He guides me down and places me gently against the blanketed sand. "None at this point. But I'm hoping I can add one to my list by the end of the day."

His muscles bulge from his chest and arms as he holds his weight over me. I sweep his arms away, slamming his body into mine. He inches my dress up over my neck to expose my braless breasts and black lace panties. My desire for him is uncontainable. I want to prove he is mine only.

"Cole, I need you inside of me. I want you to show me I'm the only one." I moan as his bare chest grinds against my breasts. The erection beneath his boxers rubs against my core, making my body crave him.

He teases my mouth with his tongue as he travels down to my breasts, and grazes his teeth over my nipples. On top of my stomach, he circles around the edge of my belly button, causing my skin to tingle with every touch. As his head descends between my legs, I grab hold of his hair, knowing that where he is going I will need something to hang on to.

Cole torments me with slow, short licks in and out of my center. Not being able to control my urgency, I pull his head in closer to me as he unleashes his assault, my screams echoing off the rocks that encloses us.

I guide his head away from the center of my legs back to my face and begin inching down his boxer briefs with my foot. I need more of Cole, need to feel the way I swell around him when he is inside of me, need to feel that our connection isn't severed from everything that happened last night. Grabbing hold of his ass, I arch my back to meet him but pause when I sense his hesitation.

"Cole, what's wrong?"

"When I have you like this, nothing's ever wrong. But I don't have a condom with me."

With a grin, I assure him. "No need for one. I think I learned my lesson about birth control years ago. I've been great friends with the pill for a long time now."

A sexy smirk lights up his hungry eyes, and he slowly enters me for the first time with nothing in between us. The sensation of his skin so intimately apart of me drives me to the point of no return, and I lose myself completely in him. Feeling my heat radiate around him, Cole grinds with force as he strives to reach his own climax. This second time of bliss ends with the echo of his screams against our hidden safe haven.

Cole drifts off to sleep in my arms while we remain hidden under the jetty—our jetty. Since my body won't allow itself to find its own slumber, I lie next to him and admire his strong jawline, plush lower lip, and curled eyelashes. When I run my thumbs across the dark circles that line his eyes, it becomes evident that he's still haunted. With my mind reeling, I become restless as different scenarios race through my thoughts. A sick feeling arises as Todd's words pop into my brain, "Is that all he told you?" I know there's more to their connected pasts—something that has the power to take Cole from me.

Quickly dressing in my clothes from the previous night, I lean down and shake Cole's shoulders. "Wake up, hot stuff. It's time to get home before Li sends out a search party."

In a groggy state, he brushes his hand at me and mumbles, "Hmm … ahh … okay… I'll be right there." He turns back to his side and falls back to sleep.

Accepting the futile attempt of my wake-up call, I grab his boxer briefs and pants, pulling them up his legs and then fold over the blanket from the sand to cover his upper body. With a kiss on his cheek and a note on his smartphone telling him I will see him soon, I leave the privacy of our cave and speed down the beach through groups of vacationers and reach my house in record time. I pull out my cell phone and scroll down my contact list to find Heidi's name. I click on it to send her a text.

Can you meet me at the music pier in twenty minutes?

Before I have time to stuff my phone back in my purse, Heidi replies, agreeing to meet.

I quickly wash the sand from my hair and face and throw on my workout clothes before heading to the the pier to meet Heidi. When I arrive, it's bustling with people, some coming in and out from the elite business offices there that boast an ocean view, while others are strollling up and down the long wooden pier, hoping to catch a glimpse of a morning dolphin swim. As I maneuver past the small groups of people who are crowded around the observation viewers, I find an open bench that faces out toward the ocean and plop down. With a heavy sigh, I stare out to the rippling waves, wishing my worries will somehow be washed away with them.

"Hey, Camryn. Is everything okay?" an out-of-breath Heidi asks.

Startled, my head snaps around as I take in her red cheeks and concerned eyes. I inch over on the bench and motion for her to sit down next to me.

"I'm not really sure." I look down to my lap where my thumbs are nervously rubbing together. "I don't know… I'm just worried about your brother. I know there's history between him and Todd. But the minute I try to talk to him about it, he just shuts me out."

Heidi reaches over and places her hand over my twitchy thumbs as she flashes me a comforting smile. "Trust me, he's not shutting you out. He's just trying to protect you."

Growing frustrated with everyone's need to coddle me, I jump up from the bench and step toward the railing. I lean my elbows against it and focus on the rushing water funneling around the leg of the pier.

I growl out, "Well, I never asked to be protected."

Heidi moves next to me and leans her back against the railing to face me. "Camryn, you know as well as I do that's what he does … that's who he is. It's how he cares."

My frustration melts into understanding. "I'm sorry. You're right. I just can't stand to see him hurting, knowing he's dealing with something on his own."

Placing her hand on my shoulder, she calmly states, "Time. Just give him time. Everything he's been through… It's his story to tell. Not mine."

I nod with understanding and after some small

talk, I wave to Heidi as she leaves. I take one more glance across the endless sea, hoping it will suppress the overwelming feeling of helplessness that continues to gnaw at me. As I turn around to leave, I am met by the sight of Todd standing behind me with only the wooden bench seperating us.

He is dressed in black suit pants, a crisp, white shirt, and charcoal tie that looks straight out of an Armani ad. A few women are buzzing around him, but his stare is on me.

Unable to stand the sight of him, I bite out, "It's impossible for you to leave me the hell alone, isn't it?"

"Cammy, just give me a minute. I want to apologize. I misread you last night, and I was wrong."

"I doubt you think you're wrong." I start to walk away but he steps in front of me to prevent me from leaving.

He leans in close to me assuring my eyes are on his. "He's no good for you. Trust me when I say he'll hurt you and Gavin."

A sarcastic laugh escapes me. "Trust you? Are you serious? After all you've done, you actually think I'd trust you?"

His gaze drops to the ground and he squeezes his eyes together. "Cammy, whatever he's told you about me … it wasn't my fault. I swear. I never meant it to happen. I would never…" He steps toward me and mumbles some random words and phrases that don't make sense. "He did this. Not me."

Confused by his puzzling confession, I ask, "Did what? What wasn't your fault?"

He shakes his head and backs away. "Cammy girl, let the past go. And let him go." He quickly turns away and begins to hurry off the pier.

"Todd, tell me. What did you do?" I yell out to

him in desperation as he rushes away.

Rather than run home with no answers, I decide to take a long walk to sift through what happened with Todd. Never meant for what to happen? The idea of asking Cole about this enters my mind, but I quickly shut it out. He had the chance to come clean with everything the night he told me about Todd, but he chose to only tell me a part of the story. So, obviously he's not ready to divulge the whole story yet.

As I enter town, my legs seem to walk me directly into Milena's Salon and Spa for some necessary Lila advice. When I greet Gabby, who is sitting in the reception area, she points up, which means Lila is in her office. I trudge up the steep wooden staircase and turn the corner to barge into her office. I interrupted her skimming the pages of her *US Weekly*.

"Li, how do you do anything in here? It's total chaos." I step over a pile of gossip magazines, which are sliding into empty pizza boxes and Chinese cartons.

"It's organized chaos, and business is fab! So who cares if my office is a tad messy?" She does a once-over of me once I'm in full sight. "Cam, what happened? It's not Gav, is it? Did something happen with lover pie on your date?"

"Why do you think something's wrong? Maybe I just wanted to visit my best friend."

"Cam, you're dressed for a run. You never go running unless you're dealing with shit. C'mon and just spill it."

I sink into a loveseat that is covered in dye-stained towels and crumpled foils and pour my heart out.

"There's something more between Cole and Todd. It just doesn't stop at Cole beating the shit out of him. I just know it. I can feel it."

"You sure you're not being paranoid? I mean,

since the assclown came back, you always seem to be on edge."

I sigh, knowing she's right. "Yeah, Todd has that effect, but I just saw him at the music pier and he shut down when we were talking. He was blurting out strange accusations."

"Cam, what made you think it was a good idea to talk to him ... and actually believe a word he says? He's a fucking liar. Didn't Cole prove that to you?"

"Yeah, he's always been a liar. That's what makes him a good lawyer. But the one thing with Todd is he can't hide his emotions. He wears them on his sleeve."

"Hmm ... well, did you think to maybe ask Cole about this?"

"Of course, but I can't. I don't know ... maybe I'm scared to hear his answer, or I don't want this image of him being perfect to go away."

Lila pushes some combs and brushes off the other side of the loveseat and sits next to me. "That's your problem, Cam. Cole will never be able to live up to your standards. All this shit with Todd is in the past, and then he comes back in and stirs it all up again. It was like he wanted it to come to the surface to contaminate your relationship with Cole. Just stop looking for something wrong, stop wanting perfection. You know what I always say... Perfection—Perfucktion ... it doesn't exist."

Cocking my eyebrow at her, I say, "You always say that?"

"Now I do." She puts her arm around my shoulders and guides me out her office door. "Stop running. First of all, it can make your calves hideously big, and second, you need to learn how to deal with shit, not tuck it under the rug and flee."

I nod as I hug my best friend. "Thanks, Li. I

needed this."

"Sure, babe. Anytime. Now go get that day-old sex smell off you, and get ready for family dinner. We'll all be there in an hour."

Rushing to get home, I hop the trolley car to the south end of the island. In the distance, I can see Cole swinging on his porch swing. His hair is tamed, and he is in different clothes, making me assume he has been home for a while and has showered and dressed. I pulled out my cell phone and notice there are no missed calls or texts from him. A tad disappointed that he didn't check in with me, I begin to pick up the pace, hoping to talk to him about everything in my head. As I approach, I notice Cole isn't alone, but rather is sitting shoulder-to-shoulder with a blonde bob, who I know full well is Tara.

My brain tells me to trust him and walk right up the porch stairs to my home and give a wave and a friendly hello. But my heart is breaking, telling me to kick him in the balls and mess up her perfect haircut. I end up in the middle, as I decide to sneak to the side of the porch and tuck myself where I can't be seen but can hear some parts of their conversation.

Cole is talking sternly but comforting at the same time. "You have to stop just showing up. I made my choice. She's it." He whispers something I can't hear, but he has said enough to melt my heart.

Tara begins to plead. "Please, not her. It's always her. What's so great about her, anyway?"

Before she can continue her battering of me, Cole interrupts. "She's perfect, and you'll never come close."

Tara laughs. "Perfect? Let's be serious. She's trash. Cole, you're just reaching for what could've been with me." She starts to sniffle, and I can't tell if it was fake or not. "You know you're trying to fill the void of losing…"

Cole snaps, "Don't! We're not dredging up the past anymore!" He reins in his emotions and lowers his voice to an almost inaudible volume. All I can make out is the word "gone."

I hold my breath as he escorts her off the porch and then slams his door. As I listen to his feet pound up the stairs, I am sure of one thing—I trust this man with every bone in my body. This isn't the type of relationship that girls my age try to find on a drunken night in the bar, but the kind that can be seen with a clear head and an open heart. I am perfect through Cole's eyes, and I find myself starting to really love Lila's idea of perfucktion.

I run up the front porch steps and fling open Cole's door. Shouting his name as I run up his stairs, he appears in the doorway at the top with a panicked look on his face. I leap into his arms and wrap my legs around him.

"What happened? Are you okay?"

I grab his face with my hands and hold his gaze with mine. "Nothing happened. I'm perfect! I'm just absolutely and completely amazed by you, Cole Stevens!"

I lean into his lips and give him every bit of passion I can gather from my soul. After we separate I say, "I just wanted you to know. See you at dinner. And bring dessert!" I hop out of his arms and wink at him as I descend down the stairs over to my house, leaving Cole likely staring at me like I've completely lost it.

****

I wake up early for work to get there before my scheduled time. I have a pile of papers waiting to be filed since I put it off to do yesterday but had the surprise day off. The maternity floor has been busy with the larger population here for the summer months, so I wanted to be prepared for nursing the laboring moms rather than having to focus on tedious paperwork.

Cole and Gavin are still sound asleep after the crazy family dinner the night before. Since Dusty and Heidi are new members to our dinners, I thought it would be a good time for my mom's third rule, the occasional food fight. Needless to say, my two sleeping guys reigned as victors. As champions, their chosen prize was a late-night movie, with Gavin even letting Cole choose *Spiderman*.

I love the impression Cole leaves on Gavin, especially knowing that in a few hours Todd will be here to pick him up for surf lessons. Now that Todd is competing in the Classic, he is determined to have Gavin train with him. Although I know it's just a way to keep him away from Cole, I also see how excited Gavin is to surf with his father. It's just another example of me having to swallow my pride and let go of the reins when it comes to my son.

After a kiss to both Gavin and Cole and my coffee to go in my "World's Greatest Mom" travel mug, I am off to work while the sun is still rising. Thinking back to the previous morning when Cole and I watched and made love under the rising sun, I rub the charm that hangs from my neck and know that I've already found my angel.

The maternity floor is still quiet as the overnight nurses end their shifts and the daytime ones take over feeding the babies and checking the birthing moms. I plant myself in the same chair my father stood next to a few days before and wonder if he'll come to see me again. Maybe he took the hint and decided to go back to leaving me alone.

While I file birth certificates and records in the letter "C" drawer, I am curious when I come across a random envelope. Pulling the entire file out, I am startled to see the envelope has my name written on it in my mom's handwriting. With shaky hands, I manage to open the letter, terrified that the answer to what I've been searching will be found in it.

Dearest Camryn,

First, I need to commend you on actually taking the time to file birth records. It's such a tedious job, and most of the nurses refuse to do it, which always leaves endless piles for others to handle. I need you to read this one many times over just to fully embrace all I am asking you to do. I placed this letter in a particular file for a reason. It represents loss—one that is beyond what you have felt in life. Understand that your mere presence is important for moving past this loss, and therefore, you need to be part of the grieving, the healing, and the honoring. I ask that you don't run or push, as you are the only person that will be able to "mend the broken soul."

Love and strength,
Mom

I inspect the file underneath her letter and gasp as I read it over and over just to verify that I'm not having a terrible nightmare. I start back at the top of the file for what feels like the tenth time, somehow hoping the information will change.

File name: Chambers
Mother's Name: Tara Chambers
Father's Name: Cole Stevens
Baby's Name: Rose Marie Stevens
Baby's Sex: Female
Baby's Birthdate: 6/11/2005
Date of Baby's Death: 7/01/2005
Cause of Death: Blunt trauma as a result of

mother suffering severe fall, sending her into premature labor. Baby was born and placed immediately in NICU with trauma to head, chest, and lungs.
    Manner of Death: Accidental

Chapter Eighteen
What It Feels Like

My body stands frozen, my eyes staring at the scattered file papers strewn across the carpet below me. The ache that creeps through my body is unbearable, as I struggle to find a chair. Thinking of Cole, my heart breaks into a million pieces, knowing what he must have lost—a loss I would never live through. I then shift to the short five years of life that Gavin has lived and find myself counting my blessings for each day I have spent with him and the promise for many more in the future—a future that was ripped away from Cole's baby girl.

The head nurse, Melva, rushes over to me and crouches down in front of me. "Camryn, dear, you're so pale. Are you sick?"

When I don't respond, she picks up the papers that are spread across my lap. She scans over the file, noticing the letter from my mom that fell with it. "Oh dear, you found your mom's letter. This is your Cole, isn't it?"

I can only give a slow nod, still feeling the aftershocks of what I have just discovered.

"Oh, sweetie, I think you need to go home. Call it a sick day. I'll cover your shift myself. Who can I call to come pick you up?"

I reach for my phone and extend it to her. "Lila … call Lila."

I sit on the chair at the nurse's station, with my mom's letter gripped in my hand. When I spot Lila, I fall apart, releasing the shock and grief through heavy tears. Holding my face into her shoulder, she strokes my hair. Once I have nothing left in me and my eyes are too swollen to see straight, Lila guides me away from the maternity floor.

"Cam, let's go home. I'll carry you on my back if you want."

I picture how ridiculous that would look and a small giggle manages to escape. "Thanks, Li. But I think I can handle walking."

Lila doesn't push me to talk during the car ride home, and I am grateful for the silence. It gives me time to pull myself together and figure out a way to talk with Cole. My mom's letter said I'm an important part in his healing process, but I'm confused since it's obvious Cole is keeping this from me.

Handing me a glass of water once we are home, Lila asks, "So a baby who died? Goddammit, that's one shitty pill to swallow."

"Yeah, and then there's me, who's been tossing all my problems into his lap, just expecting him to make it better."

"Cam, stop right there. I don't see him bitching about it. Besides, he seems just fine when you're climbing into that lap."

I roll my eyes at her and change the subject with more guilt evident in my tone, "What about Tara?"

"She's a bitch. What about her?" She holds my shoulders and shakes them. "Don't be concerned about her. Focus on Cole. Got it?"

Lila advances toward the door. "Cams, go to him. Don't run. Don't break. Remember, perfucktion…"

With a heavy sigh I toss her a quick wave and watch her leave. I need to process everything before seeing Cole, so I decide a walk on the beach will clear my mind. Besides, it will give me a chance to peek in on Gavin, who is surfing with Todd.

The warm, summer breeze feels refreshing on my face, and the ocean water I kick up keeps my exposed legs cool from the blazing sun. I watch the surfers ride the rolling waves to the shore, wondering if it was how Cole dealt with the loss of his child. When I reach the beach where Gavin is, I peer out into the ocean and spot my five-year-old paddling out with Todd mounted on the board behind him. Backing my way up to the top of the sand, I stumble over a stranded bucket but am caught by strong arms.

"Camryn, what are you doing here? Why aren't you at work?" Cole is grasping me tight as his eyes flash with concern.

After I regain my balance, I pull his lips to mine and kiss him. "I'm fine. I just wasn't feeling well."

His worry melts into heat as he eyes me up and down. "You know, I'm feeling pretty selfish right now. I'd much rather have you come home and have you all to myself right now."

I whisper into his ear and say, "If only we were in our secret little cave like yesterday." With a slight moan from Cole, I grab his hand and lead him down to the sand to sit with me facing the water. "Do you come watch Gavin every time he's with Todd?"

His cheeks flush pink and he shrugs his shoulders. "I just want to see he's safe ... that's all."

I hook my arm with his and bend my body into him. "Thank you. He's never had anyone care about him this much ... well besides the usual suspects—Lila, Carter and my mom."

He tilts my chin and stares at me with twinkling eyes. "It's more than caring. I love him." He then looks out into the ocean toward Gavin, exposing the pain deep within his eyes. Only this time, I know its cause.

As he smiles with pride at Gavin riding a small wave in, my eyes lock onto his tattoo, which I now know to represent great meaning. I graze my fingernails over the black outline of the rose, then onto the broken heart that surrounds it. I place a kiss on the rose to pay homage to someone who will always be part of the man I love.

At this point, Cole's head is turned toward me as he follows my every move. Both confusion and terror are evident across his face, most likely realizing that I now know the meaning behind his ink.

"Who told you?" he asks in a hushed voice, barely able to formulate his words.

"Talk to me, Cole. Tell me about her. Let me help you. No secrets between us. Okay?"

His breathing becomes jagged, and he shuts his eyes tightly, trying to hold back the tears. The pain must be as fresh as if his wound is sliced open every day, and he doesn't know how to stop the bleeding. I stretch my arm across his back and massage his shoulder and arm, trying to give him some form of comfort.

With a deep breath, he begins to divulge his loss. "The day I found Tara and Todd together, I was ready to walk away from her. Let him go back to you and just be alone. But later that night Tara came over with a pregnancy test—it was positive. At first, I slammed the door in her face and told her to handle it with him, but she swore it was mine. That they only fucked once—that day. I didn't know what to believe, but what I did know was if that baby was mine, I wanted to be the father, and there was no way in hell he was getting close. So I stayed with her. And Todd went back to you. I stood by Tara the entire pregnancy, but my heart was still with you, and she figured it out. So she just continued to fuck him, thinking I had no clue about it. The day Rose was born, I was training for the Classic that was coming up. I stopped by Tara's on my way home, and he was there. They were having a pretty heated conversation on the deck. So I ran up and grabbed him, dragged him to the stairs. Tara was screaming at me to let him go. At some point, he reached for her, or maybe she grabbed onto him, so I let go and he pulled her down the stairs with him."

I wipe a tear from his cheek and he sniffles, shaking his head at the ground. "Rose was born at twenty-eight weeks. God, I fell in love with her at first sight. I stayed with her every single day, tickling her toes, rubbing her tiny head as she just lived on machines. The day of the Classic, Tara begged me to go. Told me I needed to get out, clear my head. I rushed back the minute I was done, and my baby was … gone."

He renders me speechless as he exposes some of the pain that seeps from his soul. I glare at Todd, feeling his knife dig deeper through my back. Todd's unfaithfulness played a part in Cole's loss, and I wonder how he can even stand the sight of Todd. That thought sprinkles me with guilt. My connection to Todd forces Cole to relive his pain every day.

As if he has read my thoughts, he glares out to Todd, who is splashing around with Gavin but very aware of our presence on the beach. "He's the reason my baby girl's not here, he's the reason you left home, he's the reason why we're just so … fucked up."

"I'm so sorry you went through that. I don't even know what to say," I say with anguish.

He weaves his fingers with mine and assures me. "Say nothing. Just stay with me."

I squeeze his hand. "Always."

****

I am determined to make the weekend a good memory for Cole, especially since sleeping has been traumatizing for him the last few nights. Ever since he opened up about the death of Rose, nightmares have dominated his sleep. I wake up to him yelling out her name, crying hysterically, and punching and kicking.

I've been hurting along with him, hurting for him, and I wonder if we'll be able to survive this pain together.

"Hey, Gav, can you please hurry up? We have to be there before the surprise, buddy. I mean, we are the hosts of the party," I am yelling from the front door down to Gavin's room.

"Coming! Almost done with Cole's present!"

I grin at the mention of the present. When I told Gavin we were going to throw Cole a surprise good luck party for the competition that is coming up in a few weeks, he bounced from the walls. He insisted he had the perfect gift for him but refused to tell me. He kept telling me it is a "guy thing" and I'll "never understand" since I am "a girl." So I let him have his secret and told Carter to make sure he didn't lie, steal, cheat, or burn the house down to get it.

A few minutes later, Gavin comes scurrying out of his room with a huge smile, holding a small gift bag. I reach down for his hand and lead him out the door to the corner of our street. We catch the trolley car to town, where we're going for the party. Lila has become friends with the owner of the restaurant and bar next to her salon, and he gave us a great deal on a private party there. We have the outside terrace to ourselves and the owner even threw in a live cover band with the discounted price. Cole had a few real estate issues to tend to, so he's meeting us there in a half hour, thinking it's just the three of us for dinner.

"Mommy, do you think he's gonna be surprised? I hope so!"

"Definitely, kiddo! Anyway, when he sees your decorations he is going to go nuts!" Gavin had begged to decorate the terrace with a Spiderman theme. Knowing Cole will get a kick out of it, I agreed and searched every party store in a fifty-mile radius, finally finding

Spiderman confetti, streamers, balloons, and the best decoration—spray spider webs.

"Todd's gonna think it's cool too! He likes Spiderman but not has much as the Hulk."

I stop still in my tracks, panicking at what he just revealed. "Gav? What do mean about Todd?"

Startled by my serious tone, a frightened look appears on Gavin's face and his lower lip begins to quiver.

"Was I not supposed to invite him? You said anybody I wanted." He attaches himself around my leg and tears begin to well up in his eyes.

Telling myself that he has no way of knowing, and he is the innocent one in this complicated situation, I force myself to relax and pat him on the back.

"I'm not mad, buddy. You're absolutely right. I did tell you to invite whomever you want. So if you want Todd there, then he'll be there." I have to bite the inside of my cheek to keep my disappointment of his invitation masked in my tone.

He lifts his head from my knee as a smile returns to his sad face, and he wipes his tears away. He begins skipping toward the trolley car that has just pulled up to the curb for pick-up. While he bounces on his seat, I squeeze in next to him and silently pray that Todd won't somehow ruin Cole's night.

Lila and Carter are already sipping on drinks from the open bar when we arrive. Gavin dashes toward them, jumps into Carter's awaiting arms, and whispers into Lila's ear. Once my son returns his attention to Carter, who orders him a root beer still in the bottle, Lila rushes over to me and places a shot glass in my hand.

I glance at her suspiciously while she demands, "It's not poison. Drink up."

I throw my head back and shudder at the burning

in my throat. "Why Jim, Li?" I ask, referring to the shot of Jim Beam.

"Well, Gav just told me he invited shitbag, so I figured I start you off early with numbing the pain that he seems to always bring with him."

"Oh. Well, in that case. Order a few more. I may need them to survive this night."

She runs in search of the waiter while I fix some decorations and check for any missed calls or texts from Cole.

Heidi and Dusty walk in next, followed by a few friends from Dusty and Cole's surf team. Jace and Judd, Carter's employees, come in after them with stylists from Lila's salon right behind. After quick introductions, everybody makes themselves comfortable at the bar and high tables that surround the stage. It doesn't take long for everybody to settle in and enjoy the warm air and music from the DJ that plays in between the band's sets.

While I sit at a high top with Lila, across from the bar stools Carter and Gavin are on, I send a quick text to Cole to tell him to hurry. Just as I am sending it, my body tenses and all the air is sucked out of my lungs because of the new presence in the room. Gavin jumps off his seat and runs into Todd's arms while those who know him stare in silence. Heidi appears behind me and tugs on my elbow.

"What were you thinking inviting him? Cole hates him!"

Attempting to explain, I tell her, "I know, but my son knows nothing about that. He invited him, and I didn't have the heart to tell him no. Besides he just broke the news to me about twenty minutes ago, so I was kind of stuck."

"Ohh. Well, let's hope he doesn't start with Cole. He's been a little on edge this week, and one comment could push him over."

I nod and quickly turn back to Lila, who is waiting with a shot in her hand. I guzzle it down to calm my nerves.

Todd approaches me just as I slide the empty shot glass onto the counter of the bar. "I see he managed to make you believe it was my fault. He's the only person there is to blame for that day. Anger management is clearly something he's always needed … still does."

I gape at him in awe of how casually he is talking around the issue. "What the hell is wrong with you? You're talking about the loss of a child's life like it was some meatheads in a bar fighting. Todd, he lost his daughter, and no matter what you made yourself believe, you are a part of it. You shouldn't have even been there!"

Todd huffs with frustration. "Cammy, I already told you it was a mistake. I was in too deep with her. After that one time happened, she became attached to me, and I was stupid enough to try to help her." He wraps his arms around my waist. "I'm making up for being an idiot. I've changed, and you'll see."

Before I can jerk back from his closeness, all the guests yell, "Surprise!" My head turns toward Cole, but his eyes are already locked on Todd's hands touching me. Rage registers on his face while his body stands frozen in the entranceway. As guests go up to greet him, he softens but still never shifts his gaze from my waist, his expression terrifying, even after I push Todd's arms away.

The injury evident on Cole's face only reminds me of how toxic I am for him. My connection to his heartbreak will only continue to lead him down this path of rage and destruction. I know it's only a matter of time until my association with Todd will break him. As much as I don't want to consider the possibility, maybe Cole needs me and the mess of my life out of his, so he can finally heal.

I hoist Gavin in my arms and approach Cole, hoping my son will help his anger subside. He gives me a closed-mouth kiss but quickly changes his disposition when Gavin jumps into his arms.

"You like it, Cole? It's all for you! Mommy even let me pick the decorations!" Gavin holds out his hands in display.

"You did all of this?"

Gavin nods with pride.

"Well, I have a little secret for you." He leans close to his ear. "It's the coolest party I've ever had!"

Gavin's smile stretches across his face and his eyes glisten with excitement. "You want to see everything? Mommy even let me buy spider web spray!"

Cole laughs in genuine pleasure, and that small sound makes me hopeful that this freeze out between us will disappear. I've never experienced this side of Cole, and realize instantly that I hate it. I never want to be the reason for his pain or anger. However, the idea that with Todd in my life I will always be the cause of his distress stays in the forefront of my mind.

Before Gavin can tear him away, he leans into me and kisses my forehead. "Beautiful girl, thank you." His gratitude shows me that, yet again, he is hiding his resentment of Todd for my sake.

The night doesn't go as I planned, with Cole keeping his distance due to Todd's presence near me all evening. It's as if he purposely stood near me any time Cole would come close. And even worse, he would have Gavin in his arms so that I couldn't call him out on it. The bastard. However, just feeling Cole's eyes glued to me all evening gives me the strength I need to deal with Todd.

"Does douchemaster over there really think he's wanted here? I mean, can't he be escorted out?" Lila plops down next to me and a sleeping Gavin. She is motioning with her crazy drunk hands that always fling all over the place when she has a few too many.

"Oh how I wish we could make that happen. Any ideas, aside from killing him?" I ask, amusedly.

"Don't tempt me with that idea. I won't tell if you won't." With a sinister laugh, she continues to ramble more titles that uses the word "douche," and I am grateful that Gavin is sound asleep to miss his Aunt Lila's foul mouth.

Belting out laughter at Lila's tirade, I am overcome by the sounds of yelling and screaming. Our heads snap up to see Cole and Todd throwing punches at each other. Heidi is screaming for Cole to stop, and Dusty is trying to jump in the middle, but the rage on Cole's face communicates that no one can stop this—except me. I peek down in the chair next to me to check that Gavin is still asleep amidst the turmoil. I hop out of my seat and rush to Cole's side and shout, "Own your breath, baby! Please. Own your breath!"

Cole stiffens when he hears me, but Todd follows through with his swing and knocks him to the ground. Before an infuriated Cole can lunge toward him, I jump into his lap and wrap my arms around him while Dusty grabs Todd by his back collar and begins dragging him from the courtyard. The bouncers quickly file in to toss Cole and Todd out. Most of the guests are quickly filing out since the fight has dampened the evening.

I back up toward Gavin and peek down at him, grateful that he has managed to stay asleep through the chaos. As Cole is being led out by the bouncer and blood gushes down from a wound beneath his eye, I can't help but think that I brought this disaster into his life. Cole has gone downhill since Todd has come back and I realize he can't possibly recover when he's faced with the person responsible for his child's death everyday.

I ask Carter to stay with Gavin so that I can run out to Cole. I begin to regret the loss I've brought back to his life, aware that my own past will only continue to shatter him. It is now my time to pick up his broken pieces and put them back in place, even if it means that I don't fit back in.

When I reach him, I begin to shed tears and my gaze drops to the ground, unable to face the the man I have broken. He tilts my chin up and brushes away my falling tears. "Camryn, please don't cry over me. It was just a lucky punch … that's all. He can't hurt me—not when you're with me."

I reach up, wiping the blood from his gash and my body begins to tremble underneath my unbearable weeping, "Cole, don't you see it? He'll always be in my life because of Gavin, and you'll just keep falling apart, piece by piece. I'm not good for you, this isn't good for you. I just can't fix you—with me you'll always be broken."

Pushing my hand away from his cut, I notice the tears welling in his eyes and the defeat etched on his face. "Camryn, please don't run away now. You see, I've fallen completely and utterly in love with you. Maybe it was that day in the cafeteria, or when I saw you on the beach, or just this very moment. It doesn't matter when it happened … all that matters is it did happen, and it will always be true." His voice lowers to a whisper. "You've brought me back to life, Camryn. You're not doing this … you can't."

The agonizing pain in my chest throbs, as I know my heart will be forever shattered without Cole in my life. "I'm not running away this time … I'm just letting you go."

He reaches for me, but I back away, fully aware that his touch will only draw me back to him. I have to walk away. It's the only way for him to truly heal.

He opens his mouth to speak, but nothing comes out as he watches me slip farther away from him, from us, from love. His eyes speak defeat, and his body shows evidence of my blow to his heart as he slowly turns and drifts away from me.

I sit motionless, my fingers stained with his blood, and stare down the sidewalk as he somberly walks away, only to glance back at me with an expression that carries a depth of hurt. As Cole fades from my sight, out of my life, I whisper to myself, "I love you too." And at that moment, I feel like I've taken my final breath.

Chapter Nineteen
Broken

I am lucky because Gavin never cries much. I would often see other moms, red-faced and embarrassed, in the grocery store as their toddlers were throwing themselves on the floor having a fit over their empty box of animal crackers. Not Gavin. He would eat his slowly, always saving his last two to play with like they were his action figures. So when my crying five-year-old, who is staring out the window, awakens me, I don't feel as lucky anymore.

"Gav, sweetie, come back to bed. You need some sleep." I am fighting to hold back my own sorrow over losing Cole, trying to stay strong for my son.

"No! Why is he leaving? I see big boxes in his car. Is he not gonna live here anymore?" Gavin takes heavy breaths as he tries to talk through his cries.

I check out the window and pull Gav back to bed with me after seeing Cole pack up his Jeep, leaving me weak and trembling. I hope my battered son won't catch on to the fact that I am falling apart. Our lives are now separate from Cole's, and that thought is agonizing.

After I walked away from Cole last night, I went numb and needed Gavin to revive me. I only allow him to sleep with me when he is sick or woken up by a bad dream, but last night was the exception. He eventually woke up shortly after all the commotion of the fight just in time to see us go home without Cole. Gavin is my only reason for breathing, all that I have left in my life, even though my heart will be permanently damaged.

I lift the covers to his neck and stroke through his messy hair. "I told you last night, buddy, sometimes adults just need to take time apart from each other, that's all. He'll come back to his house. I promise." I close my eyes knowing that I have likely just lied to my son, and to myself.

"Why, Mommy? Did he hate our party? Did he think my present was stupid?" he asks with a pout on his face.

"Buddy, this has nothing—I mean nothing—to do with you. We have to give him some time to be alone and get ready for the big competition. We don't want to bother him anymore right now. Does that make sense?"

Gavin slowly nods and smashes his face into the crook of my elbow. "I'm just really gonna miss him, Mommy."

I pat the back of his head and under my breath whisper, "Me too, buddy."

****

My eyes flash open in terror, my pillow drenched from the tears that are streaming down my face. The sheets are tangled around my body like I am a prisoner in my own bed. Beads of sweat soak me and I taste their salt. My body feels like it has gone to war and lost. The nightmares have come back, the ones Cole erased when he held me through the night.

My mind flashes to Gavin's disappointment earlier in the morning when he watched Cole move out of his house, guilty because I know I am the reason for Gavin's misery. However, letting Cole go is the only way to let him heal without the threat of Todd lurking in the background, the only way to save him. This will give me the strength to tuck that guilt away and move on without the man I love. I'd be naïve to think that watching him leave wouldn't pierce my heart, though. I know he had to go, and I know it only adds to the end of us.

Peeking out from under the refuge of my comforter, I notice pink highlights fanning across the pillow next to me. After I realize that Lila took Gavin's spot in my bed, I grab a pillow and cover my face, anticipating a lecture. I vaguely remember Lila screaming at me while I stood listless as I watched Cole walk away. With her own tears flowing down her face, it was evident she was as broken as I felt. Lila probably knew that when I let go, she would lose a part of me.

"Cam, what are you doing? Are you really letting him walk away or are you just playing mind-fuck games with him?" Her tone carries an edge to it that I'm not used to hearing directed at me.

"I just can't, Lila. I can't do this right now." My voice is muffled from the pillow drowning out the sound of my voice.

Lila yanks the pillow from my face and throws it across the room. It knocks over the lotions that are displayed on my vanity. "I don't care. You're gonna talk to me. Let's face it. I know and you know that you fucked up."

My body jolts up at her accusation. "Are you serious? You think I fucked up? I did this for him. Look what I was doing to him. He would've killed Todd last night if I didn't jump in! I had to protect him … let him find someone not connected to his horrible past." My voice softens
to a plea. "Don't you understand, Li? I had to save him."

She throws her arms up in frustration. "Cut the bullshit. You had a choice. You just didn't leave him one."

I fling myself back down to bed. "It doesn't matter anymore. I'd eventually push him away. I'd somehow break him."

She leaps out of my bed. "I'm tired of the same old shit with you. Stop letting other people control your life! One day you're going to wake up and have no one!"

I drop my gaze from hers and hang my head

while processing the harsh truth in her words.

"Cam, it's time to stop running from everything and everyone. Take what you want in life ... take what you and Gavin deserve."

Before I can attempt to defend myself, she disappears from my bedroom and is up the stairs. She leaves me speechless and unable to remember a time that her fury was directed toward me. I always knew she wanted me to face the problems of my past, but I never knew that my reactions to them hurt her as well. Wallowing in my own self-pity, I throw the covers back over my head and wonder who else I can possibly hurt.

****

As each week goes by without Cole, the fire he'd ignited in me starts to dim—his empty house a representation of my barren soul. I often peek out the window to search for his Jeep parked in his driveway or his surfboard propped up next to the door, but it never happens, and I wonder if I'll ever look into his electrifying eyes again. Every facet of Cole in my life seems to just disappear, as if he never existed. With Dusty taking over Gavin's surf lessons, I am left to wonder if everything we had was even real.

Todd shows up, as usual, to bring Gavin to the beach. He is strangely upbeat, even with the faded bruises that are still prominent from the brawl with Cole. I cringe at the first sight of him, aware that he'll always be the reason why I'm alone and miserable. He managed to slither into our lives and swallow up the happiness we were beginning to find again. As I pour my coffee into my travel mug, running late for work, Todd barges through the front door with the smug look that's been plastered to his face since Cole left.

Annoyed at his self-righteous presence, I snap, "Not sure when you felt it was okay to walk right into my house. Seems like it's a habit of yours to crash into everything of mine."

Not affected by my obvious irritation with him, his cocky smile grows wider. "Cammy girl, it's a new day. I have my surfboard, my son, and soon you'll come to your senses and realize we're perfect together. With that low-life out of the way, you'll finally be able to see that we're meant to be a family again."

Sickly amused by his overall plan, I let out a sarcastic laugh. "The only—I mean only—reason I still look at you, speak to you, and associate with you is for Gavin's sake. So do me a favor and knock the next time you come to my house." I swiftly turn around and stomp up the stairs to get Gavin ready to go.

Still uneasy about putting Gavin into Todd's hands, I stand on the porch and watch them, dressed in their wetsuits, trudge down the street toward the entrance of the instruction beach. Taking deep breaths to control my anxiety, I catch sight of the white porch swing swaying on Cole's porch. The one that held so many hopes for our future, a future that should have included Cole. I sit on it and begin to kick my legs back and forth as I close my eyes and tilt my head back. I can almost feel his body pressed up against me and his hand clasping mine as we swing together and enjoy the comfortable silence we were always able to create.

When I open my eyes, I am met with Tara's smug face and my daydream is shattered as she stands right in front of me, leaning on her right leg with her hand on her hip. "You know, you're trespassing on private property. That's against the law around here." Her iciness shoots straight through me.

I leap up from the swing and push past to avoid a conversation. She catches my arm, causing me to swing around toward her. She leans into my face and threatens,

"Stay away. You're no longer needed or wanted."

I jerk my arm from her with a small push that creates distance between us. "Guess that puts me in the same category as you ... not wanted."

I speed away while I hold onto the ache her words bring. Before I close the door behind me, Tara mocks, "I'll be out of your hair as soon as I pick up the things he wants me to get for him."

Hiding my reaction, I slam the door on her and sink to the floor, releasing all the hurt she is able to exhume. I'm slammed with the realization that I pushed him right back into her arms. Tara has shown up and pulverized the shards of my already broken heart. The only thought that is able to pull me off the floor is that I can no longer break him.

Work has become my distraction over the last few weeks, allowing me to trudge through the motions each day. But after Tara's unwelcome visit, I know I won't be able to just get by today. Everything seems darker and the agony I've been struggling to cover up for the last few weeks has resurfaced. As I stand at the circulation desk, staring aimlessly at our assignments, Melva appears next to me.

"Sweetie, you handle vitals today." She guides me away from the desk toward the recovery rooms.

With a sigh of relief, I reply, "Thanks, I guess I'm just zoning out today." Melva nods in understanding but little does she know I am slowly dying inside.

Reading and recording was the best effort I could give throughout the day. My mind continues to wander to Cole and then replay Tara's appearance on the front porch, which causes my heart to sink even more. By leaving him I was trying to keep him away from his past, not drive him right back to it.

Finishing my rounds and waiting for the

overnight staff to take over, I lean over the desk at the nurses' station to document records. Feeling a person hovering close to me, my head jolts up to the sight of my father watching me with a gentle smile on his face. My expression hardens, and my body tenses. Why doesn't he take the hint to stay away? As I continue to stare him down, he extends a box to me that is tied together with ribbon and an envelope that hangs off the top.

I reluctantly accept it and ask, "What's this, Jack? My birthday's not for another couple months."

"It's not a birthday gift, Goldfish. It's something that will make you understand."

"Understand what exactly? How not to be a father?" I ask with stinging bitterness.

Ignoring my hostility, he continues, "No. You'll see that leaving you and your mom was never my wish. That I had no choice."

"Yeah, Jack. Whatever helps you sleep at night. But it looks to me like you made a choice. It just didn't include us." I become angry with myself as I feel tears well up in my eyes.

"Just do your mom the favor of opening it. She's part of it." He leans in and places a kiss on my cheek, surprising me with his affection.

My coldness toward him won't deter him. Just like Cole, he is determined to be a part of my life no matter how hard I push against it. He is trying to crack the wall I built around me when he left, and I can only wonder if the contents in the box will be enough for him to break through it.

I couldn't have felt more alone on my way home from work. The day revealed more than I'm capable of handling. Todd is now a regular part of Gavin's life, Cole seems to be letting Tara back in, and my father wants a second chance. Each scenario leaves me completely shattered. Frustrated, I bang my hand against the steering wheel and scream out loud, "Mom, why did you want me to come back here? To just watch me fall apart?" I angrily slam my fist down on my steering wheel in a fit of frustration. I am more lost now than when I left five years ago.

With my father's box clutched close to my body as I walk into my house, I am met by the sympathetic eyes of my son. Gavin's two arms are outstretched, begging for my embrace. I enclose my arms around him, holding on to the only person keeping me from running away. With his face scrunched against my shoulder, he mutters, "Mommy, I don't want you to be sad anymore."

At that moment, the guilt punches me square in my face. For years, I have been able to tuck away any pain for Gavin's sake. I made sure he always came first and he never saw how broken I am. I failed this time, hurting him with the same things I have spent every day protecting him from.

"Aww, buddy, with you right here I can never be sad. How about we have a picnic on the beach … just you and me?"

He grins and runs to his room to grab his sweatshirt while I thank Carter for bringing Gavin home from his day with Todd.

After we pack dinner and a blanket, the two of us head to the beach for some family time. Gavin seems more upbeat as we walk across the sand, but I can see the worry on his face. I have to show him that all I need is him—all we need is each other. But first, I have to somehow convince myself of that.

Amidst our conversations about surfing, camp, and Gavin's newest jokes, he, out of nowhere, asks, "Mommy, do you miss Cole?"

Startled by his question, I stutter to think of the

best way to answer him. "Umm … yeah, of course I miss him. Cole is very special to me."

"Didn't you love him, Mommy?"

Sighing, I surrender to him and say, "Yes, sweetie. I still do."

I hold my breath, awaiting the next question, but it never comes. He just stares at me with his beautiful, sapphire eyes, as if he's trying to piece together loving someone and not being together with that person. Curious on how this is affecting him, I ask, "Do you miss Cole, honey?"

"I don't miss him. I see him every day." He laughs as if I have asked the most absurd question.

"Gav, what do you mean you see him every day? I thought Dusty was coaching you now?"

He takes a deep breath like I should already know what he is about to say. "No, Mommy, I see him when I surf with Todd. He watches me. I don't think Todd likes him very much, but I told him that I love Cole, so Todd lets him stay."

My chest tightens as I realize that Cole still wants Gavin in his life. Letting him go didn't stop him from holding onto us. As Lila said, I didn't give him a choice, but he is taking it anyway. It becomes clear to me that Cole needs Gavin, just as much as I do. He is our connection to the future and our way to right the wrongs of our past. For me, Gavin is my reason to start over. For Cole, he is his reason to move forward.

"Do you talk to him?" I ask hesitantly.

"Duh … yeah. He says stuff about you. I think he misses you just like you miss him."

I smile and pull Gavin into my chest. Gazing out into the ocean with my son close to me, I finally find a reason to stop running.

After a two-man game of Wiffle ball on the

beach, I carry an exhausted boy home and put him to bed. As I walk into my bedroom, I focus on the box that my father had given to me earlier. Now that I gained the confidence from my son to face life head on, I pick it up and plop on my bed. Fiddling with the ribbon, I nervously open the envelope that is secured on top. At first glance, I am startled to find the handwriting isn't my father's, but rather, it's my mom's.

Dearest Camryn,

This is the toughest letter to write, and my biggest regret is not doing this face-to-face. That's the least you deserve, but unfortunately this is the only way. After my first fight with cancer, I cherished life and saw so many possibilities. I decided that having another baby would be the perfect start to my "new life." However, the doctors disagreed with this because I ran the risk of losing the baby or my own life. Your father agreed with the doctors, and who could blame him—he agonized as he watched me suffer through my sickness. The thought of losing me to the cancer was one thing, but to lose me to something we could control was unbearable for him. So he made sure that wouldn't happen—he had surgery without me knowing. After months and months of begging him to reconsider, he still refused, but never told me he was unable to get me pregnant. However, I was determined, and a few months later I told your father I was pregnant. That was the day your father found out that I slept with another man. Yes, Camryn ... I cheated on your father ... not the other way around. Since your father wouldn't give me a second child, I went out and made sure it happened. It was selfish, and I regretted that decision every day of my life. He tried to stay with me for your sake, and we played the part in front of you, but eventually it just became too much for him. I had ruined him, and he needed to move on with someone who could heal him. I lost the baby during the pregnancy, and my cancer went out of remission. Your father wanted to remain in your life, but I begged him to stay away ... that I needed you to take my pain away. Besides, at that point, you were so angry with your father, thinking he left his family. He reluctantly agreed but really never stopped trying. In this box you will find letters, pictures, and Christmas and birthday cards for both you and Gavin. They are things your father sent over the years that I have intercepted. I will never be sure why I allowed this lie to continue through the years, and for that, I am truly sorry. Camryn, I am not seeking your forgiveness through this letter because I don't deserve it. I am asking that you let your father in. He deserves to know the child and grandchild I took away from him.

  Love and understanding,
  Mom

Chapter Twenty
Bleeding Out

I am paralyzed by the words she wrote, the ones she held with her to her death. I should be angry with her, feel betrayed by her, but the only thing I feel is numb. She stripped me of years with my father, the man who I aspired to be like at one point in my life. However, she had been everything I needed, she'd given up her own life to make mine worth it. I stare at the box that holds past hurts and the letter that sliced them wide open again, wondering if I can somehow find a way to staunch the bleeding of a wound that is continually torn open.

Memories from my past flash through my mind. I am unable to believe that I missed the friction between my parents. It was so clear as I think back to times I spent with my father at the arcade alone, our nightly swims together without my mom, his always being on call at the hospital, and extra hours she dedicated to coaching. Suddenly, my emotions begin to take over my paralysis, and I crumple the letter and throw it at the wall. She allowed my father to represent everything I hated about my home—my reason for leaving. She watched as I cried over his leaving and then later when Todd did the same to our child. And then she led me back to this place of torment, knowing that I would break all over again.

Needing answers, I text Lila to come over, hoping she'll help reveal what I need to do. When she arrives, I hold the crumpled paper to her, and she cautiously opens it and watches my expression as she smooths out the corners with her fingers. Her eyes narrow, and her hands tremble as my mom bares her soul. Gripping the letter, she shakes her head and mumbles, "Shit, Cam. I'm so sorry."

"Li, I have to go talk to him. Can you stay here with Gav?"

She gives a slight nod, still in disbelief, and I head out the door to the place I know I can find him—the hospital. When I scour the fluorescent-lit halls of Shore Memorial, I go back to my childhood when I would beg my mom to drop me off, so I could surprise my dad with a slice of his favorite pizza. I would peek into each of the rooms and daydream about becoming a doctor, yearning to cure every person's ailments. When I would find him, he'd pick me up and swing me, then parade me around to all the nurses and doctors, while he exaggerated my abilities to swim, dance, play soccer, or any other talent he could think of. I never forgot his proud smile those days, and as I face him now, he still wears the same one.

"Hey, Goldfish. Is everything okay? You're not on night shift, and you have that handsome son to take care of at home."

"I read the letter." I begin to choke up. "Why, Jack? Why did you let her do that? Why didn't you fight for me?"

He wraps his arm around my shoulder and guides me to a waiting room chair. "My only answer is that she suffered enough—the cancer, the loss of the baby, the mistake she regretted—I wanted to give her something to help her heal."

I wipe my tears with the back of my hand. "You gave up your daughter? I could never think about letting Gavin go."

He inhales a deep breath. "Sweetie, it wasn't like that. I had no plans of giving you up. When her cancer came back the second time, she was given six months to live. I thought you could give her strength, let her live out the last months of her life with dignity and pride. I expected that when she died, you'd come back to me, and I'd know that I gave your mother the best last months of her life because they were with you." He holds his head in his hands, as if the decision he made is still painful.

"It was a miracle she lived and by then I was already painted the bad guy. I didn't fight for you, Cams. I failed you, and I have to live with that every single day of my life."

I place my palms on his cheeks and raise his face to meet mine. "But you still tried ... with all the letters and cards. You didn't fail me. She did."

"This wasn't meant to turn you against your mom. Please know she was an amazing wife and mother. All of this just got out of control, and we both made mistakes that in the end hurt you. My biggest regret is that you had to grow up so fast, that we stripped you of your childhood. So, I promised your mom I'd fix this by giving you the letter and the box. I just couldn't live another day hurting you."

Confused, I ask, "When did you talk to her?"

"Last summer, right after she found out she was sick again, your mom came out for her yearly visit, and she came to the hospital. The minute I saw her I knew she was dying, that there wouldn't be a miracle this time. She handed me everything I sent you and Gavin and all she could say was that she was sorry. For some reason, I wasn't angry, just grateful I had a chance to see her one more time. That's when I realized how much I still loved her. She always had that effect on me. She was hypnotizing." He smiles wanly, eyes distant.

"You still loved her after everything she did?"

"Goldfish, I never stopped loving her. I was just so hurt that she needed another man and then got pregnant. So for the few weeks she was here, we spent our time together, getting the house ready for you and

Gavin. After she left, she sent pictures, and I would go hang them in your house. It was the perfect goodbye. And I've missed her every day since."

In awe of his ability to forgive after so much was taken away from him, I move to hug him. I wrap my arms around him for the first time since I was a young girl, and it somehow is still so familiar. He has the same musky smell from his Old Spice aftershave, and the same long arms that feel like they can wrap around my body more than once. I can feel the roughness of his scruff against my forehead, reminding me how I always thought he had sandpaper on his face. Able to find the same comfort with him, I stay embraced with him until he is paged for surgery. I sense his hesitance to let go.

"I think it's time you meet your grandson. Family dinner tomorrow night at my house. Can you make it?"

An infectious smile spreads across his face. "I wouldn't miss it for the world. Should I be prepared for an occasional food fight?"

My mouth drops in surprise. "You know mom's three rules?"

Laughing he replies, "Know them? Pfft … I created them. Just happy you still follow them."

I hug him one more time before leaving the hospital. Bombarded by the cool night breeze and sound of the crashing waves in the background, I am able to understand my mom's belief in the healing power of this place. For once during this journey home, I am able to staunch the blood and feel a small fissure of healing begin.

****

Family dinner is bittersweet for me. I am so excited my father will meet Gavin, but I wish Cole could be here to meet him too. I can't seem to stop holding on to him or the idea of us. With weeks now between us I'm despondent, and still hurting.

Stirring the fettuccine sauce, Gavin startles me out of my daze. "Will Pop-Pop have a name for me?"

"What do you mean, buddy?" I ask in puzzlement.

"He says you're Goldfish. Can I be something cool like Shark or something?"

Laughing at the five-year-old mind, I, of course, appease him. "Shark sounds perfect. I'm sure Pop-Pop will love it!"

Gavin folds the card he is making for my dad and races down the stairs when he hears the doorbell. Carter and Lila walk in first with a case of beer and a bottle of scotch. Lila holds up the bottle and winks, reminding me of the night we drank my father's stash of scotch and smashed all the bottles in the park. It was Lila's form of therapy when I had thought my dad cheated and left us.

Soon after, my father walks in with a very clingy boy riding on top of his shoulders. With a large grin that stretches across his face, he gallops over to me, causing Gavin to yell with glee. My dad places a kiss on my cheek as he hands me a box. "Brought some of your favorite cream-filled donuts. You remember … from Dot's?"

I stick my hand in the box and lick some cream from my finger. "Perfect! Just how I remembered them!" I dab some powder from the donuts on Gavin's nose, getting me a deep belly laugh.

Grinning at the interaction between us, my dad asks, "You need any help in the kitchen?"

"No way, Jack. You grab yourself a drink and play with that crazy kid on your shoulders."

My father settles in, catching up with Lila and talking business with Carter. However, most of his focus is on Gavin, and my spoiled boy sucks up every bit of the attention. He warms up to my father quickly, and when he finds out my dad's secret obsession with Batman, he is completely won over.

I couldn't have asked for a better night for Gavin, and I find myself thanking my mom for her honesty, despite how difficult it is to hear. She's given my father a second chance with his family and the only emotion I feel is grateful. Nevertheless, even with the second chance I've been granted, I still have the heaviness in my heart. Without Cole, I am sure I will never feel complete, and I'll never be fully healed. But I love him too much to risk breaking him just so I can be whole again.

Lila and Carter leave as my father is reading Gavin his bedtime story. I watch from his bedroom door as his eyes grow heavy and his breaths even. After my dad tucks the covers around him, he kisses his forehead and whispers, "Goodnight, Little Shark," which transports me back to my own bedtimes with him.

"I can't thank you enough for this evening. It was the best night of my life." He is emotional as he pulls the door shut.

"I'm pretty sure the little guy would second that motion. He adores you already."

"Yeah, well I'm pretty sure it's the other way around." He lingers a few minutes, smiling at Gavin's bedroom door. "Will you walk me out, sweetie? I want to talk to you about something."

I nod, tuck my hair behind my ear, and walk with my dad onto the front porch. He takes my hand and leads me to Cole's porch swing.

"I have to tell you that I was sitting in this very swing when I found the love of my life. Not sure if you knew this, but your great-grandparents lived right here, and, also, your mom grew up in this very house. I was visiting my grandparents, who lived next door, when I first saw her. Your mom walked up those wooden stairs and threw her surfboard against the side of the house. She was so angry, but it was absolutely adorable. I fell in love with her that second. I needed her fire in my life, and I was never going to stop until I got her." He stares at the porch stairs, as if my mom is climbing them at this very moment.

"So I made daily visits here just to see her. But she wouldn't give me the time of day. Finally after six months, I sat on your mom's doorstep and waited for her all day to return home. She walked up the steps, opened her door, and walked around me, never saying one word. Most guys would've given up weeks before that, but not me. I knew she'd be worth the fight. One day I came to visit and noticed her sitting on this swing. I practically sprinted up to the porch to make sure I'd catch her if she tried to get away. But she didn't move, just continued to sway back and forth. So I sat next to her and swung with her. After a few hours, she finally spoke her first words to me. 'Well, you gonna kiss me or not?' I wasn't even sure if I heard her correctly. I said, 'You've never spoken one word to me but now you want to kiss me?' She looked at me and smiled with that innocence that always captured me. 'No, you want to kiss me. I just want to swing with you forever.' She had all of me that day … still does." With tears in his eyes, he gazes up to the sky like he is paying homage to the woman he loved and let go.

I lay my head on his shoulder and kick out my legs to swing along with him. "That's definitely Mom—stubborn but endearing."

He nods in agreement. "Goldfish, what I'm trying to say is if you're lucky enough to find that type of love—the one that knocks you on your ass so hard that you can't fully recover from the fall—you need to fight for it. Fight hard. Fight as if it's the final battle of your life. Because it never comes around again and if you don't get it, one day it will be gone forever."

I lift my head from his shoulder and stare into his serious eyes, searching for how he knows. I come up short and am left too shocked to speak.

"Sweetie, don't look so surprised. Dads always know the guys who want to take their daughters away. And I think you may be able to find your guy behind the house, sitting on the beach." He winks and playfully nudges his elbow into my ribs. "You up for a good fight tonight?"

I wrap my arms around his neck and squeeze my cheek against his. "You mind hanging around here? I think I have to go to battle."

"Of course. Go get him, Goldfish!"

I race down the porch steps around to the back of the house. The cool sand tickles my toes as I make my way through the dunes to the beach. With the full moon casting a glow across the rippling ocean, I am able to spot his silhouette sitting in the sand, propped up against the leg of the lifeguard stand. Dark shadows outline the muscles bulging from arms which are wrapped around knees that are pulled up to his chest. His attention is focused on the ocean, which leaves me to wonder if he is waiting, or perhaps searching, for something.

My skin tingles and heart races as I stand behind him, still able to feel the effect he has on me. With my nerves working overtime, I take a deep breath and break into his thoughts. "I'll never understand the fascination with the ocean. It's so deep and dark. Bigger than us. But we're drawn to it, always searching it for answers."

Cole's shoulders jolt as the sound of my voice startles him, but his head remains turned toward the water. I crouch down next to him in the sand and cross my legs in front of me. His gaze still remains focused on the ocean. I yearn to reach out to him, run my hands through his hair, and feel his body against mine.

His chest begins to rise and fall quickly and in a hushed tone he speaks.

"I hear your voice and feel your body next to me, but I'm afraid if I look at you, you'll disappear ... this dream will end. And I'll just be left with nothing again."

A wail escapes from me, reacting to how deep I cut him when I let him go. I thought leaving was the selfless thing to do, that walking away would only save him, that with me he'd never find wholeness again. I made myself believe that our tainted pasts could only destroy each other and leave us disfigured images of who we could be. But I've never been so wrong. It only split our already weak hearts and emptied the hunger in our souls.

I reach for his face, force him to look directly in my eyes, and plead, "Cole, I'm right here. Touch me. Kiss me. I promise you I'm done running away."

His eyes expose his pain as he takes in my words, probably seeing them only as empty promises. I stole a piece of him when I let go, and I know I would have to fight like hell to give it back to him.

"I thought walking away would save you, let you move on from your pain. With me, you'd always be stuck in the past, breaking apart over and over again. I could never live with myself knowing that I was the reason for your heartache. But I wasn't prepared for this pain, the one that pierced me the moment I let you go. The one that's more agonizing every day I'm away from you. The same pain that's in your eyes tonight."

In the midst of pouring out my heart, Cole has clutched my hand and laced his fingers with mine. His grip tightens with each word I speak, and I can feel his pulse radiate through his veins. He guides me to his lap and holds me in his arms, still grasping my hand in his. "You finally see it, don't you?"

"See what?"

"That you own my breath. Without you, I don't exist."

With force, my lips meet his and push him backward to the sand. Our tongues brush together with urgency as I crave the feel of him again. No matter the risk, I can't stay away. I'm addicted to him.

Needing him to believe in me, in us, I continue, "You make me want to stop running from what if and start running toward what is. I don't want to be lost anymore. Cole, I now know you're it. You're my happy ending."

He rubs the back of his hand over my cheekbone. "I love you, beautiful girl. Always have, always will.

For the first time, I speak the words aloud that I've known all along, "I love you too. Never stopped, never will."

He rolls his body over mine and places me in the sand below him. As he holds his weight over me, I stare into his fathomless eyes, the ones that drew me in from the very first day, and I know those three words will never be enough between us. What we have is beyond our realm, a penetrating force that keeps driving us together. Separately, we are fractured reminders of our pasts, but together we are somehow revived and able to breathe again.

At that moment, our bodies find each other again, and our hunger is screaming to be fed. His hands lift my dress up and explore every part of my body with desperation, one we both felt from being apart. His tongue follows, as he tastes my skin and nibbles on the areas that will bring me to the edge. Beneath the weight of his solid body, I am victim to his seduction while need drives through me. As I slide my hands under his waistband, I take hold of his center and force a low growl out of his throat. Holding his shaft and feeling the moisture of his readiness in my hand drives me over the edge. All I can do is surrender to him.

With our clothes balled up in a pile next to our heads, our bodies come together. The sand from the beach grazes our skin as it rubs against us. His lips never leave me. They move from my mouth to my neck to my breasts. He fills every inch of me, stretching my insides in a way that brings a satisfying pain. I want him to stay inside of me, in this part of me that is forever only his.

I thrust my hips up to him and lift my back off the sand to take him in deeper. Our bodies quake and our breaths shorten as we climb to the top of our desire. With the motion of our entwined bodies intensifying, I grasp Cole's face, bringing his hypnotizing eyes to mine. When we reach the peak, I yell those three words as we topple over the edge together, knowing that they will never come close to the way I feel at this very moment.

Cole adjusts his jeans around his waist as he guides me up from the sand, brushing it from my hair and back. He slips my dress back over my head to try to save my modesty since we have just made love on a public beach. Grabbing a towel that was left in the lifeguard stand, he wraps it around my shoulders and cuddles me close to his chest, my head leaning into the crook of his neck. He rocks me in his arms while we become engrossed with the rhythm of the sea.

A voice startles us as a figure stumbles toward us in the dark. "Well, well. Ishn't this cute. Happy couple back together. Let me ashk you, Cammy girl? How'd a low-life like him get you to become shuch a whore?" Todd slurs his words while taking gulps from a liquor bottle in his hand.

Cole's eyes narrow and he leaps up, ready to pounce. "One more fucking word and you'll be tasting a lot more than that pansy-ass alcohol you're drinking."

"Whoa, tough guy. C'mon, Cole. Hit me. You know you want to. How about you get it right thish time. Kill me … not your baby."

Before I have a chance to step in, Todd is on his back with blood spurting from his nose. Cole is standing over him, his jaw tense and fists ready for an all-out assault. I know it will be hard to reach him because he has already entered that alternate world—the one that has haunted him for so many years.

Unclenching one of his fists with my hand, I place our palms together, "Cole, don't let him take you back to that place. Stay right here with me. Own your breath. Own your breath and he can't touch you."

His shoulders relax, and his glare softens. He throws his arms around me while I anchor him to hold the weight of his body up. I kick Todd's shoe and growl, "Go home and sober the hell up. We'll talk about this tomorrow."

"Oh yeah … that's right … I have to come pick up the little pest so he can go shurf, if that's what you call it."

The second these words leave his mouth, I lunge on top of him, repeatedly slapping him in the face. Strong arms lift me away, but I continue to kick him until he is out of reach.

"Don't you fucking dare talk about Gavin like that! We didn't ask you to come back! Stay away from us … just stay the fuck away!" The anger is spewing from me, and if not for Cole holding me, I would have attempted to kill Todd.

"No way … not letting him have something that

belongs to me, even if I have to put up with the poor, little charity case who didn't have a daddy for five years. No. Fucking. Way." He stands up and spits out some blood that is dripping down from his nose. "Almost ruined the bashtard, too." He points directly to Cole. "Just my mere presence broke him down. The kid adores me, and it bothers him. So that makes Gavin my ticket to ruining that ashhole's life. You were the problem, Cammy. Couldn't get between your legs again … too busy whoring around with him. So, even though it killed me, I turned to Tara for help and drove her right to him, but still he wouldn't cave. What is it, Cammy? You suck hish dick that good that he's pussy-whipped?"

Cole pushes me behind him then charges at Todd. He grabs him by the collar and starts to unleash his fists on him. Todd manages to hook him in the eye, throwing him to the ground. Cole grabs his ankles, trips him, and then hops back on top of Todd, sending a few blows into his rib cage before returning more to his face. Blood squirts everywhere, and I am helpless at breaking it up.

Pinned underneath Cole, Todd thrusts his head toward his face and manages to crash directly into his cheekbone. Cupping his face in pain, Cole rolls into the sand next to him off of Todd's body. Free from the weight of Cole restraining him, Todd attempts to stand up but stumbles over his own feet, falling face first into the sand. Unsuccessful at walking, he begins to crawl to Cole.

My own cries grow louder when I glance over to Cole, whose cheek is swollen and a stream of blood drips down his face. Witnessing the agony he is enduring, I charge at Todd and throw my body on top of him and dig his face into the sand. He grips a section of my hair, yanking it with enough force to drag me off his back with a wail of pain.

Cole finds whatever bit of strength he has left and lunges at Todd, slamming his back flat against the sand. As he grabs around Todd's throat, he leans close to his face and threatens, "Touch her again, and I will fucking end your life with my own two hands." Cole releases his grip and pushes Todd's head back into the sand to deliver a few more punches to his jaw.

Within a second, Todd's hand reaches for the empty liquor bottle laying next to him and smashes it down into Cole's head. The sound of shattered glass echoes through my screams. I sit motionless as he stabs the slivered glass through Cole's side, his body jolting with pain and his blood pouring down into the sand. And then his body goes silent, all movement ceases, as if Cole is lifted from this world.

And all I can do is watch the man I love bleed out.

Chapter Twenty-One
The Storm

"Camryn! Come on, sweetie. Camryn! I need your help. I can't save his life without you, Goldfish."

My screams have led my father to the beach, but his voice barely registers behind my heavy breaths. His hands aren't felt as he shakes my shoulders. All I can see is Cole's marred body, his lifeless form dripping red. And right next to him, the man who wrecked my past, now close to abolishing my future, is lying unconscious from a drunken rage. The metallic stench of blood fills my nose and finally brings me back.

In barely a whisper, I beg, "Dad ... Daddy, don't let him die ... please ... don't let him die." It's the first time I've called him that since before he moved out, and it's never felt more right than at this very moment.

"I promise you, Goldfish. I'll bring him back to you." He hands me the towel that Cole had wrapped around my shoulders. "Now help me save your forever."

I drop to my knees next to Cole's battered body and bind his wound as tightly as the towel allowed. He'll have a chance if I can slow down his blood loss. Pressing in on the towel, I can feel the wetness soak my hands, and my body begins to tremble. Images of the sharp glass jutting into his side, his body convulsing in pain, and the endless streams of blood replay over and over in my head. I can't bear the pain, can't make the images disappear, can't do anything but fall apart at the seams.

Holding the wound with one hand and stroking his cheek with the other, I lay my body over his, letting my tears flow down my cheek onto his bare chest. "Cole, don't leave me ... please fight to come back ... fight for us."

The flashes from the ambulance light up the dark

beach, along with a few curious spectators. As I watch the two stretchers roll across the sand, I yank my angel charm from around my neck and secure it around Cole's wrist, placing the angel in his hand. I lean over and kiss him on his lips that are now swollen and bruised. "Your turn for a guardian angel. Fight hard, Cole. I love you … never stopped, never will."

I'm pushed to the side as the emergency personnel places Cole on the stretcher and begins timing his pulse, checking his breathing, and treating his injuries. My father comes up behind me and pulls me into an embrace. "It's my turn, sweetie, to be your hero. Go clean up, and take care of my grandson. Lila and Carter should be there by now. I'll ride with Cole in the ambulance and meet you at the hospital."

I weep into his shoulder, hesitant to let go.

Finally able to pry me off, he places a soft kiss on my forehead. "This right here … it's the battle I was talking about earlier, kiddo. You'll win. I promise you that." He jogs to catch up to the first ambulance, the one Cole is being lifted into. Hopping in the back, he blows me a kiss and slams the door closed. I watch both ambulances speed away—one carrying the future I want and the other carrying the past I hope to forget.

Chills race down my spine, leaving me immobile as I stare at the bloodstained sand beneath me. As a nurse, I see these types of injuries, watch loved ones agonize, and hear all the prayers and promises in exchange for a life saved. But tonight I'm not just a spectator anymore. I have a front-row seat. If the devil himself shows up on this beach, I'll sell him every ounce of my soul to bring Cole back.

I begin to wail into my hands, my body quivering with every shred of fear and grief I can emit. How did I let Todd get this close? My knees grow weak, and I plummet into the sand, unable to find the strength to move forward, to deal with whatever comes next. The world spins around me, and everything blurs as I close my eyes to the pain and misery I caused. The despair I am facing is no match to the guilt that has crept its way in. Collapsing into the sand, I surrender and let the pain overtake me.

Steady arms wrap around my body and lift me from the ground. I can hear Carter's soothing words but can't open my eyes to face him. The sound of the waves becomes distant as he carries me closer to my house and climbs each stair of the deck. Carter places me on the lounge chair while images of Cole's body crawling up mine floods my mind. Every part of my life here, the life he revived, is attached to him. And I am left with only one choice—to fight for his breath.

"Cams, open your eyes. We need you … all of us. You're stronger than this." Lila's voice finally reaches me and my eyes pop open.

"Li, he can't d—"

She interrupts, "Don't you dare say it! Throw it the hell out of your mind, and never go looking for it. You got me?"

Exhaling deep breaths, I stand up from the lounge chair and stumble over my words. "I … I need to wash this blood off. And … ah … talk to Gavin." Concern blankets my voice. "Where is he? He's still asleep, right?"

Lila's eyes widen at the mention of his name, and her gaze drops to a crack in the wooden deck.

"What is it? What happened to him?" My voice raises as panic strikes me.

"Cams, he's safe. I was with him in his room when Carter brought you here, and now he's down there reading books to him. It's just that…"

"What, Li! What happened to my baby?" I am screeching in terror as if I know what's coming next.

"I'm so sorry, Cam. Your dad heard you screaming and ran out to help before we could get here. Gav must have woken up at some point and followed Jack outside." Lila's voice trembles. "He saw everything. I'm so sorry."

Horror chokes me as I picture the terror that must have consumed him as he watched Cole break at the hands of Todd. He faced it alone with no one there to hide his eyes or hold him tight. It took only one night to unravel the last five years of what I've tried to protect him from. And now I will have to find a way to somehow keep the monsters from coming back again.

"I need to hold him, to let him know everything's going to be okay. Help me, Li. Help me make that happen," I beg, feeling defeated against this night.

Lila guides me down the stairs to my bedroom, where she helps me clean the blood from my skin and change into clean clothes. When we walk into Gavin's room, Carter is rocking him with his body as Gavin lays limp in his arms. His normally clear eyes, now clouded with fear, watch as I approach him.

"Hey, buddy. I heard you had a pretty scary night."

He nods with tears welling in his eyes.

"We're all here now … safe and sound. But if you're still scared, you need to tell us, so we can help you."

He sniffles and brushes the back of his hand across his runny nose. "Why did Todd hurt Cole, Mommy? Is it because I told him I loved Cole?"

The fact that he is blaming himself feels like a dagger through my chest. I lift him from Carter. I need to hold him close, to try to hide him away from the world.

"Oh, sweetie, of course not. Todd made a mistake tonight. He was very mad at Mommy and took it too far. He wasn't thinking that his anger would hurt somebody, but it did." I'm sick that I'm was making excuses for Todd after the way he spoke about Gavin.

"But I'm not allowed to hit anyone, right?"

"No, sweetie. You would never do that. If you are mad you need to come talk to Mommy, Aunt Lila, Uncle Carter…"

He finishes my statement saying, "or Cole, right?"

I nod in agreement.

"Is Cole all better? Did Pop-Pop fix his boo-boos?" His concern for Cole causes more tears to stream down his cheeks.

"Don't worry … Pop-Pop is a superhero and will fix him like that." I snap my fingers in front of his face.

Gavin embraces me as he snuggles his face against my shoulder. "Mommy, I should tell you when I'm mad, right?"

I stroke his hair that is sticking up on top of his head. "You got it, buddy."

He tightens his hold around me. "I'm really mad at Todd."

Just like that, the entire night is summed up with these five simple words from my five-year-old.

****

The emergency waiting room is a place of regret. Crying people crowd the waiting room seats, staring into space like they are attempting to piece together reason for the tragedy they are facing. Others pace the hallways to try to pry information from any nurse or doctor they can find. I just stand in the entryway, bracing myself to put one foot in front of the other to whatever comes next.

"Camryn! Camryn!" Dusty rushes toward me, his

hair flapping in his face. He's wearing sweat pants and a ratty t-shirt. He had probably been pulled out of bed. He extends his arms to me and pulls me in for a hug. "Are you all right? Did that bastard touch you?"

That his first concern is me rather than his best friend who is dying somewhere in a hospital room catches me off guard. "Umm … not really. I mean … I'm okay. Cole stopped him."

One side of Dusty's lip tilts up. "My man couldn't stay away, could he?" His expression tightens, evidence of his worry over his best friend.

"I'm so sorry. I'm so sorry. I'm so…" I break down right as he pulls me into his chest again. He doesn't try to comfort me with words that mean nothing to me, instead he just holds me and lets me shed my guilt into his shirt.

Leading me over to a chair, he sits us both down and hands me a tissue from the table next to him. "No matter what you did or how much you tried to stay away from him … this would've happened. It's a part of him, Cam … he needs to protect the ones he loves."

"But if I would've just let him move on, he wouldn't be lying in that bed, fighting for his life. I could've protected him. I could've saved him."

Dusty laughs out loud. "Move on? Are you fucking blind? The dude hasn't moved on since the first day he saw you." His tone becomes serious, and he leans in closer to talk. "Don't you see it, yet? You already have saved him."

My small smile tells him that I'm grateful for what he said. I place my hand on his shoulder as I climb from the chair. "I have to find my dad. See what's going on."

"I'm supposed to be getting coffee. But Heidi's back there hunting down every doctor she sees."

"I'll go help her. I happen to know Cole's surgeon." I walk away but after a few steps twirl back around to him. "Hey, Dusty. Thanks for understanding and just being here."

After he flashes me the peace sign, I hurry down the hall to look for Cole, the man who has saved me in more ways than he'll ever know, hoping to do the same for him.

Turning the corner to ICU, I am met by the image of Heidi and my father in a tight embrace. She is unable to stand on her own, and her face is hidden in his chest, but it's evident she is crying by the vibration of her shoulders. Afraid to move closer, I stop in my tracks to brace myself for the inevitable: Cole is dead. Unable to cope with the thought of losing him, my breath is knocked out of me, and I sink to the floor with my face into my hands. My cries will never lead to relief. I am certain that without him I will always be stuck in the darkness of loss.

My father's long arms drag me up from the tile floor and lead me away. With my head in his shoulder and my eyes squeezed shut, I refuse to look, not ready to accept my fate. Turning out of the hallway, he stops and holds my shoulders from behind me. My eyes remain closed.

"Goldfish, we'll face this together. I won't let you be alone ever again. So when I count to three, you're going to open your eyes. Okay?"

I nod.

"One, two, three…"

I open my eyes to Cole's firm body listless in the hospital bed surrounded by beeping machines. The blankets are pulled to his waist and tucked securely around his legs, revealing his defined lines. His exposed arms are straightened at his sides, and dried blood is smeared around the cuts that travel up to his elbows. The blue-striped hospital gown lies loosely over the bandage that wraps around his ribs. I shift toward him and trace my finger down the stitches along his hairline, rubbing over the peaceful smirk on his face. I wonder if in some way death has finally brought Cole the contentment he was always seeking. Silent tears stream down my face as I try to find a way to say goodbye and face life without my only one.

"He has a long road ahead, but I think he'll make it just fine." My father's words rush through me and cause me to gasp.

Clutching on to him to hold myself steady, I whisper, "He's. Not. Dead?" I swallow back more tears. "But I saw Heidi crying on you. I thought he was gone."

"He made it through surgery, but he's still critical. He lost a lot of blood and we had to induce a coma while the swelling in his brain comes down.."

I sag into his arms as a serious expression crosses his face. "He's not out of the woods yet. But he's a fighter. Go on. Touch him. Talk to him."

I leave the safety of my father's embrace and creep toward Cole. Grabbing his hand, I open his palm to the angel charm I had placed there before he left in the ambulance, amazed that it's still in his grasp. I place a kiss over his raw knuckles and in his ear whisper, "I'll be right here when you wake up. Not leaving your side until those beautiful blue eyes are looking at me. I love you." My body collapses over his, and I let every emotion pour out. I am finally able to see the light shining beyond the darkness.

****

The days are endless while I wait for his return. I refuse to leave his side. I want to be the face he sees when he wakes up. The hospital even temporarily reassigned me to Cole's floor so that I can still work but remain close to him. Dusty always brings Gavin with him after surf lessons each day and then he comes back after camp with Lila, Carter, or Heidi. Ever since he witnessed the attack, he's been haunted by his own night terrors, ones that wake him up screaming each night. However, the longer he spends with me in the hospital, watching Cole get stronger each day, his nightmares lessen, and he feels less scared. The trauma Gavin has witnessed in his short life is heartbreaking, but his perseverance is beyond inspiring.

After a week, still clutching on to hope, my father stops in and stretches his arm across my back. "Why don't you go home and get some rest? I'll stay here with him."

"No. I … I can't. I want to be here when he opens his eyes. I'm not leaving him again."

He squeezes my shoulder and nods while staring at Cole. "Camryn, I know you want him back more than life itself. But you know you have to be prepared for the person he'll be when he wakes up. He may not be the same Cole."

I look into his eyes and smile. "I know, Dad. It doesn't matter because for as long as he breathes, he'll own my heart."

"That's exactly what I want to hear, Goldfish. The soul of a fighter." After kissing me on top of my head, he leaves the room, leaving me to wait.

After checking his vitals, I sit down in the chair next to Cole and open up the romance novel I've been reading aloud to him all week. It's a perfect representation of us—a swoon-worthy male who fights for and protects the woman he loves. And it is on its way to a happy ending, just like we are still reaching for our own real-life one. As I arrive at the chapter's end, Lila and Gavin come rushing into the room.

"Mommy, Mommy! I surfed a big wave and didn't fall down! It was awesome!"

I lift Gavin up and throw out my hand for a high five.

"I'm gonna tell Cole all about it!" He jumps out of my arms, climbs up on the bed next to Cole, and starts babbling about his day.

Lila chimes in to my reunion with Gavin. "Are you still holding up? Cam, maybe you should go home for a bit. Get your life back together."

"My life is right here—on that bed ... both of them. And I'm not leaving until we all walk out of here together."

Lila sighs. "You love being a stubborn bitch, don't you?"

"And you love it."

"Damn right. It's what I love most about you."

****

After dinner, Gavin puts the movie *Spiderman* on for the third time this week. I think he believes that Cole's favorite superhero will somehow bring him back to us. He cuddles next to him and leans his head on his shoulder. Right after he falls asleep, I curl up on the chair and start to doze off, my body begging for sleep. Before I give in completely to my exhaustion, my blurred vision catches glimpse of a figure standing in front of me.

Registering the sight of Todd in Cole's hospital room, I leap up from the chair. He should be rotting in a jail cell for assault, but because his big-shot lawyer father has an in with the local law enforcement, they brushed off the incident and kept it hush-hush as a favor to his father.

With one arm in a sling, Todd puts his other hand up to motion me to stop. "Shhh ... I'm not here to start any shit." He points toward the door. "Can we go out there to talk?"

Todd was released from the hospital the same night as the fight with just a few bumps and bruises. His face still shows evidence of the blow from Cole's fist. Dark circles surround his eyes, and the bridge of his nose is still swollen from where it broke. Stitches line his upper lip with shades of purple surrounding them. Both fury and fear consume me at the sight of him.

"I think you fucking said enough last week. There's nothing that can ever change this." I point my hand toward Cole.

"I know that. How is he, anyway?" He tips his head at the bed.

"You don't deserve to know how he is."

He glares at the floor in shame. "Please just come out in the hallway and talk? For closure?"

"If it gets you the hell away from me, fine. But I'll never give you the satisfaction of closure."

He follows me out the door into the fluorescent lights of the hallway. Only a few people are milling around as the visiting hours are coming to a close.

"Cammy, the other night … it got out of control. I was out of control. I said a lot I didn't mean. And I'm sorry."

My anger is boiling over. "You're sorry!" I shriek, my rage too wild to control. "Sorry for what? Trying to kill Cole or using your son in your fucked-up revenge plan?"

"For years, Cole made me the bad guy. He blamed me for his daughter's death. Tara wouldn't be with me because of him. She always had a connection to him, and she loved him—she still does. And I hated him. I wanted to make him pay for ruining me, for not letting me move on with my life, for always being in my way.

That day I saw you on the beach with him, I could tell he loved you and Gavin cared for him. I couldn't bear to see him so happy, so I went after it, his happiness." He shakes his head and pinches the bridge of his nose like this confession is difficult. "I walked away from you five years ago because I was in love with Tara. And I still love her. I knew that she'd never want me if I stayed with you during your pregnancy, especially with losing her own. But I couldn't get her to forget about Cole, and I wanted him to suffer for it."

I grit my teeth. "You're a class act, Todd. A real fucking bastard."

"But I never intended on this. I never planned on almost killing him. You see, that night I'd just been rejected again by Tara and was drowning my sorrows in a bottle. She'll never let Cole go, no matter what I do for her. Then, I happened to stumble upon you two all loving on the beach and I just … snapped."

I stand in silence as he pours out years of lies and deceit. Unable to stand him another moment, I turn away. "Just stop, Todd. It's over. Everything about you is a lie. I won't let you ruin us anymore."

As I walk away a faint whisper leaves Todd's mouth. "Goodbye, Cammy girl."

When I step back into the room toward the sounds of Gavin's quiet snoring and the sporadic beeping of the hospital monitors, the sight of my angel charm on the floor startles me. As my gaze meets a sea of blue staring back at me, I bring my hand to my mouth and gasp, unable to move from where I'm standing. I continue to just stare at Cole, praying this is real.

"Well, baby girl, are you going to get over here and let me hold you, or you just going to stand there with your mouth wide open?" Cole's raspy voice warms my body in an instant.

I sprint to him and throw my arms around him and Gavin, who is sound sleep next to him. Cole grunts in pain as the weight of my body presses down on his injured ribs. Sobs begin to wrack my body, but for the first time in a long while, they are tears of joy.

I hold his face between my hands and begin to kiss him all over as my tears wet his cheeks. "You came back to me. You came back to us."

He grins, despite the pain it must cause him. "No way in hell I was staying away. Not when I just got you back."

I lean in to his mouth and gently taste his lips. "I love you Cole Stevens … never stopped, never will."

Raising his weak hand to my face, he strokes my cheek. "I love you Camryn Singer … always have, always will."

For a moment, we just stare into each other's eyes, finding what we had lost and knowing the storm has finally passed.

Chapter Twenty-Two
The Ghosts That We Knew

The glistening morning sun has barely grazed the horizon when my eyes pop open. My body is sore, and my head aches from the lack of sleep in a tiny bed, but looking over to Cole sleeping peacefully next to me, all those aches and pains are instantly eased. When he woke up from unconsciousness the previous night, I knew this was our second chance. I finally have a reason to move forward and to stop looking over my shoulder to the past. And last night only sealed that fate as the three of us spent the night together as a family.

Laying in the stillness of the hospital room, I look over at Gavin sleeping on the cot that the overnight nurse rolled in for him. It was the first night since the attack that he didn't wake up screaming. The heavy weight he's felt has finally lifted, and that lighthearted boy I admire with every bone in my body can return. He hasn't asked about Todd since that night, and I am ready to help him forget about the man who never deserved him.

As my gaze lingers from my son who captures me to the man next to me who completes me, I find my own relief from the ghosts who haunt me. Brushing my fingers along his sharp jawline down to his broad neck, I find his beating pulse and kiss over it, grateful for the blood that still pumps through his veins. I progress down his taut chest, stopping in the middle to savor the rise and fall as he breathes on his own. Resting my ear over his heart, I cherish the pounding, knowing that our hearts will always beat as one.

With his strong hand stroking through my tangled hair, he whispers, "If your hands keeping touching me all over, I may have to wheel this bed into the empty room next door and have my way with you."

I prop my head up to face him. "No way! You know I always follow doctor's orders. Anyway, a nurse never takes advantage of her patient, no matter how sexy he is."

"Who said you're the one taking advantage? Besides, I'm pretty sure the doctor's orders call for total and complete care of the patient." He guides my head toward him and covers my mouth with his, sending tingles down to my toes.

"Mr. Stevens, you need to rest. No rolling beds anywhere. Sorry, that's nurse's orders." This time I lean in and claim his mouth, slowly rediscovering his plump lower lip and agile tongue.

In a husky voice, he mutters, "Sorry, I'm not making any promises. Especially when you call me that."

Smiling, I press off of his body to climb down from the bed. As he grunts in pain, he grabs my hand and ropes me back toward him. "Camryn, you're my angel … the reason I'm breathing right now. I love you, beautiful."

I lean in and softly kiss his lips. "I love you." My eyes begin to water as a pang of guilt hits me. "But you wouldn't even be here if it weren't for me. I almost destroyed you. I almost lost you." My gaze falls away from his.

He lifts my chin up and circles his thumb over my lips. "Look at me. That day you walked on the beach, you gave me a reason to live again, to want again, and every day after that you showed me how to love again. Camryn, I need you to see that for as long I live, I want to get lost with you and then we can find each other every time we open our eyes."

I descend into his steady arms, and he holds me tight. He is everything I want in life, and although I don't deserve him, I know I can't live without him. Coming home set me on the path that led me to face my past and find my future.

With his lips resting in my hair, his voice sounds muffled. "I need to give you something. I wanted to do it last week when we were on the beach, but some shithead tried to kill me." Half of his lip tilts upward. "It's tucked in my shoe over there."

I stare at him in confusion as I slowly wander over to his belongings. Retrieving an envelope, I return to Cole and snuggle in bed with him. As I flip the envelope over, I notice the handwriting in an instant.

"When did my Mom give this to you?" My voice raises with question.

"One day last summer she came to watch me surf. At the end of my practice, she handed me this envelope and told me that I had to open it with my one and only love but only if it was you, of course. I could've given it to you that first day on the beach, but you would've thought I was crazy. So, if you're ready, maybe it's time to see what's inside. What do you say?"

I draw in a deep breath and nod with hesitance. "Okay, but I need you to do this with me."

"Going forward, everything is together, okay?"

Reassured by the man I love, I slide my finger within the envelope and rip open the top. My trembling hand pulls out the letter, and Cole helps unfold what could be my mom's final words. In a shaky voice, I begin to read it aloud.

Dearest Camryn and Cole,

I write this letter in the hope that my final words leave a lasting impression, one that will stay with you for a lifetime, one that you can pass down to Gavin and perhaps to any other children that may one day grace your lives. You both have traveled very different paths in life, however, in many ways they're the same. You have experienced heartache, suffered the enormity of death, endured the deception of those who were supposed to love you, and discovered how ten little fingers and ten little toes can change your entire scope of life. These paths somehow found a way to merge. They found a way to become one whole journey that you have taken together.

Camryn, honey, wake up every morning knowing you have a purpose, that you're worth it. You are an amazing mother to Gavin, one that I never even came close to being, but one that I have admired every single day since he entered our lives. Always know that you deserve everything life with Cole can offer you. Let him be the man who holds your heart in lock and key, who bears the burdens of your soul, who revels in the beauty of your mind. Let him complete your being and make you whole again.

Cole, every day cherish each breath you take. You are a strong, capable man who has overcome everything that has stood in your way. Know that you've become a better man because of it, and Camryn is beyond lucky to have you in her life. Let her be the woman who owns every bit of your heart, who carries the pain of loss you feel every day without your daughter, and who understands the small imperfections that actually make you perfect—that is, perfect for her. Let her complete your being and make you whole again.

Remember that every day is a gift that you are given, and you have the task of treasuring every moment. It's now time for you to let go of the past, drive the demons far underground, release all the ghosts that you once knew, and knock down any walls, both emotional and physical, that exist between you. Don't ever forget that a love like yours is its own perfection and that sometimes on your journey it's not until you're lost that you can be found.

> *Love always and forever,*
> *Mom*

I clench the letter in my hands, and Cole pulls me into him as he holds my body, weak from her sincerity. Through his chest, I can hear his own quick breaths, evidence that her words have the same effect on him. Somehow we have reached the end of her journey as she is letting go and urging us to step into our own. A clean slate, a new beginning is within reach, but first we have to say goodbye to what follows behind us.

The sound of a clearing throat breaks the spell my mom's letter has cast. My dad stands in the doorway, his arms crossed over his chest and a wide grin spanning from ear to ear.

"You two look comfortable over there. You want me to come back in a little bit? Give you some more time alone?"

I straighten my body against Cole. "Of course not, Dad. Why don't you come over here so you two can formally meet?"

He strolls over and extends his hand toward Cole. "Well, it's definitely a pleasure to meet you."

"I think I should be saying that to you, the man who saved my life. Thank you, Dr. Singer," Cole gushes.

"Call me Jack, Cole. And I didn't save your life. You did that on your own. You're one hell of a fighter." He positions his stethoscope over his ears. "Let me do one more check and see if I can get you out of here."

Cole props himself up in his bed, and I stand up, reaching for his hand. While they talk sports, I find myself thanking my mom for bringing these two incredible men into my life again.

"Looking good. All of your stitches are healing. The swelling in your rib area has gone down. So I'm clearing you to go home today. But you need to take it easy for a while. You might want to find a nurse who lives nearby and make sure she takes care of you." My dad turns to me and winks. My cheeks flush.

Cole smirks at my dad's idea. "I think I may know the perfect person for that job. I just hope she doesn't mind all the extra attention I may need." At this point my face goes crimson, and I choke from his insinuations.

I rush toward the door and shout back orders, "I'll go fill out the check-out paperwork, and you guys wake up Gavin. Get him ready to go home." I leave the room with both of them laughing at my embarrassment.

****

Cole's homecoming is met by a week full of family dinners, frequent visits from my father, who is growing closer to him each day, and many walks on the beach with Gavin, who insists on showing Cole all his new moves on the surfboard. He is living in our side of the house. His sits empty, except for the porch swing where we end every evening after we put Gavin to bed. The swing has become a symbol of love and family for us, just as it once had for my own parents.

With the Atlantic Classic approaching, Gavin is spending the night with Heidi and Dusty so they can make an early run to the beach in the morning. Knowing Cole's disappointment over missing it due to his injuries, I set dinner up on the porch, with hope that the sunrise and salty air can cure some of what he is feeling. After we finish, I curl up next to him on the swing and rest my head on his shoulder. "So, I was thinking. What if we knock the wall down between our houses ... make it one house … make it our house?"

With no answer following my question, my head springs up to meet his glowing eyes, which seem to be smiling at me. The expression on his face convinces me that he is just as ready as I am for this next step. I leap over his body, straddling him as gently as I can. "I love you so much. I can't wait to wake up with you every day and fall asleep with you every night."

He grabs my face and pulls me close to his lips. "You have no idea how long I've waited for you, Camryn. Just knowing we'd end up right here, right now… I'd wait ten more lifetimes for you." Our lips merge together and the urgency to feel each other again quickly rises. That addiction is unbearable, and holding back tonight will be close to impossible.

Cole's hands travel down my body and land underneath my thighs. Hooking his arm around my waist, we stand up from the swing and walk together toward his door while his lips move over mine. My hands, underneath his t-shirt, are exploring his back muscles. My nails press against his smooth skin. As his fingers travel into my jean shorts, sneaking under the lace of my panties, my breath hitches. In between pants, I warn, "Cole, it's only been a week…" I moan as his hand cups my center. "We definitely shouldn't be doing this." I choke on my breaths. "It's too soon. You still need"—my voice is barely audible when I feel his fingers teasing in and out of me—"time to heal."

I feel his lips turn upward against my mouth as I picture that sexy smirk that always appears at these times—the one that always makes my skin tingle. "This is exactly what the doctor ordered. And I'm definitely going to need more doses of it all night long." Cole backs us into his house, his fingers still working through the wetness of my excitement. Pushing his bedroom door closed with the heel of his foot, he lays me on the bed and our bodies, lips, and tongues become the medication that evening—a very strong medicine that lasts until morning.

****

Three weeks after that fateful night, the bruises clear, stitches are removed, and ribs are stronger. Scars have appeared where the wounds were the deepest: the ones on his knuckles from his continuous blows to Todd's face, the one on his hairline from the bottle that was smashed over his head, and the one on his side from the stabbing, the one that nearly killed him, the one that will forever be imprinted in his memory.

Cole and Carter are loading his Jeep with items from the surf shop that are going to be sold at the Atlantic Classic later that morning. I dress in Lila's room in a "Team Dusty" bikini that Heidi specially made for all of us to wear at the competition. We've been temporarily living with Lila and Carter while the contractors work on our house, tearing the wall down and remodeling the inside.

Lila is painting the last coat of polish on her nails when she finally mentions the elephant in the room. "So is shitwad really going to make an appearance today? I mean, does he have big enough balls to compete even when he took Cole out of it in such a pussy way?"

I shrug my shoulders at her. "One thing about Todd, he doesn't give a shit about anyone but himself. Well, he did use an innocent five-year-old, who was his birth son, for revenge. I knew I was right. That asshole really is the devil."

Lila throws her middle fingers up to the air. "Then fuck the devil himself."

I laugh and push her hands down. "I just hope Cole can handle it. I know if he sees him, he's going to want to beat the piss out of him. Especially after I told him about his little visit to the hospital that day."

"Then let him, Cam. He deserves a fair fight this time. Besides, Cole could kill that shithead any day."

Finishing the braid in my hair, I mumble, "That's what I'm afraid of."

The beach is bustling with half-dressed women who flaunt support of their favorite surfers. Children run around the blankets and beach chairs, as they throw sand and water at each other, while their parents try to calm them down. We walk on, all wearing "Team Dusty" apparel and carry merchandise from the shop. Since Carter is one of the head sponsors of the competition, we are able to set up in a prime viewing area, close to the span of ocean where the surfers will do their runs. From the beach towel I am sitting on, I catch sight of Gavin kneeling next to Dusty, helping him wax his board. It warms my heart that Dusty included Gavin even when I had pushed Cole away. Heidi and Dusty never turned away from my son during our temporary separations, and I am grateful for their presence in his life during that time.

Firm arms wrap around me, and I tilt my head up to see Cole's wide grin. His eyes sparkle against the clear sky, and even though he hasn't been surfing since his injuries, his skin remains deeply kissed by the sun. Whether he's looking at me, brushing his fingers against my skin, or touching me in places that can make scream, this man still seems just as beautiful as he did the day I crashed into him. He always put my senses in overdrive, and I lose all control just by being next to him.

"Even though I wish I were out there riding for you and Gav, I'm just pretty fucking grateful that you're in my arms right now, cheering on my best friend."

I smile and lay my head into his elbow. "Next

year, I'll be sitting in this same spot watching Gavin wax your board, and you'll be the one out there. But I'll definitely take this right now."

He kisses the side of my head. "Did I tell you how amazing you are?"

"Every day, Mr. Stevens."

His one eyebrow arches. "I don't think you know what that does to me when you call me that. I tend to lose all control."

I lean over and whisper in his ear, "Wrong, Mr. Stevens. I know exactly what it does to you. And I'm pretty sure we have about thirty minutes until we have to be in these spots. And I happen to know some private dunes a few blocks down…"

That sexy smirk of his appears, and we dash away with Lila and Carter yelling our names until their voices become a distant grumble. The beach does something to us. It takes all of our cares away, making us powerless to each other's urges. When we reach the private dunes, we satisfy every bit of our cravings, enjoying the healing powers that the ocean possesses.

Thirty minutes later, Lila stares in shock while Carter claps as we return to the group. Before any comments can be made, Dusty's name is announced, and we all make our way to our beach towels to sit and watch his runs. Heidi plops down next to me as Dusty begins to paddle out. He manages to catch three waves that set him as the current leader. Just as he is exiting the water, the announcer calls for Todd.

Cole reaches for my hand and squeezes as we anticipate seeing the man who almost destroyed us. As silence prevails over our group, all of us hold our breaths, waiting to see him enter the water. The announcer comes on again and says his name a second time. I keep moving my head in all directions to catch sight of him, but I can't seem to find him anywhere. After the third time he is summoned, a sophisticated blonde, one that Todd claims to love, who is dressed in a strapless one-piece bathing suit wrapped in a white crocheted sarong comes running out of the announcer's area and heads straight for us.

Ignoring my presence, Tara focuses her attention on Cole. Tears stream down her face, evidencing her own heartache. With a sigh, she whispers to Cole, "He's not coming back. His house is empty. You ruined him." She glares directly at me.

Before Cole can jump to my defense, I bite back, "Tara, you're delusional. I never wrecked Todd. He never wanted me. He loves you. And you used him when Cole wouldn't give you the time of day. So it seems you're the one who ruined him."

Cole drapes his arm over my shoulder. Remaining calm, he looks at Tara and simply bids farewell. "Goodbye, Tara. Have a nice life." He returns his attention to me and pulls me into his chest. With a sickened look on her face, Tara falters on her heels. Unable to fire back, she pivots around and stomps away.

At that instant, an announcement is made that Todd has forfeited his spot in the competition. Since no one is left to compete, Dusty, who is the current leader, becomes the champion. With air entering our lungs again, I peek up to Cole, who is staring into my eyes, and with no words spoken, we claim our victory at the end of the long and hard battle fought.

****

After Dusty's celebration dinner, Cole hoists my excited son into his arms and urges me away from my conversation with Heidi. He excuses all of us from the after party and tells everyone he has plans for the three of us. Confusion sets over me, but I let Cole whisk me out of the restaurant to whatever surprise he has planned.

Cole leads us down the beach, letting Gavin splash on the shoreline a few feet in front of us. We hold hands and bask in the beauty of our home: the faded pink- and orange-striped sky that just put the bright sun to rest, the gentle ripples of the rolling sea, the vast dunes that line the top of the beach hiding the homes that stand behind them. I'm convinced that I will never be more at peace than I am at this very moment.

As the powdery sand begins getting rocky beneath my feet, I know Cole is leading me to the inlet, our place of solace, a place where we once marked our love. Climbing up to the top of the jetty where my mom's initials are etched in stone, I come across a wooden box. I look to Cole with uncertainty, but he nods to me with confidence to show me he is the one responsible for placing it there. I open the box to find a note from Cole.

Beautiful Girl,
It's time to release the ghosts we once knew. It's time for our beginning. I love you—always have, always will.
Yours forever

Underneath his note is the letter from Todd and his father's law firm that states his rights to Gavin, the picture of Todd and me on the lifeguard stand, the bloodstained glass that had pierced his side, and Cole's hospital bracelet that he wore just a few weeks before. I am holding our past in my hands, finally ready to let go. With Gavin clutched in his arms, Cole guides me to the edge of the jetty. I stare at the restless water that once was a place to hide, now it is a place that has the power to set me free.

As I look up to Cole and Gavin with ready eyes, Cole begins to count down. "Three, two, one…" With force, I toss the wooden box into the unsettled water of the inlet. We say our silent goodbyes as we watch it disappear into the depths of the ocean, the ocean that somehow cured our pain.

Breaking our silence, my voice shakes as I choke out, "My mom is part of my past that's in that box and letting it go is like saying goodbye to her all over again."

Cole leans close to my ear. "I'm here for you. All the way. Every. Single. Day."

I continue to stare out into the vastness, thinking about the woman who created me in so many ways, who also disappointed me, who always supported me, and who led me home. "I'm okay. I promise. I just need a minute." Cole and Gavin back away and leave me to say my final farewell to the ghosts that we once knew.

As I turn away from the inlet's waters, I face Cole and Gavin, who is holding a small velvet box in his hand, and my breath catches. Bringing my hand to my wide-open mouth, my eyes well and I am unable to hold back the tears. With my legs growing weak, I sink down to the ground and meet Cole, who is in front of me on one knee.

Cole tucks his hand behind my head, combing through my hair. "Calm down, beautiful. You haven't even let me ask you the question yet."

Breathing through my heavy cries, I nod to him, trying to steady my emotions. Cole raises my left hand and states, "That day in front of the lockers, when we first spoke, this amazing journey began. It's been long, it's been hard, but it's been the most incredible ride of my life. Please do me the honor and take the rest of this ride with me."

He asks Gavin for the box. Opening it up, he

takes out a gleaming ring, one that I recognize as my mom's engagement ring, and places it to my finger. "Camryn Singer, I will love you now and forever. Will you marry me?" As he waits for my answer before slipping the ring over my finger, I begin to nod my head, still unable to form coherent words through my tears. As he secures it on my hand, he grabs hold of me and leaps up with me in his arms to twirl us around in circles.

Placing me on my feet, he leans down on one knee again and pulls my son in front of him. "Gavin, our family won't be perfect until I ask you something first."

Gavin's smile spreads from ear to ear.

"You are one amazing boy who has made me prouder each day. I love you so much, buddy. I would like to know if you would do me the honor of being my son?"

Gavin's head bounces up and down as he responds, "I get to call you Dad now? I love you so much, Daddy!"

My heart melts as I watch my son accept Cole completely in his life and, somehow, I fall more in love with Cole at that moment. After raising Gavin up in his strong arms, he pulls me into his face and presses his lips into mine, declaring, "You and Gav now control my entire heart. You both own me forever … our forever."

Epilogue

Gavin's laughter echoes against the slapping waters of the inlet while he and Cole skip rocks off the jetty. Watching them, the last few months flash through my mind, parts of it still unbearable but the result unbelievable. I place my hand in front of my face as I gaze at the beauty of my engagement ring, one that my mom cherished each day of her life with my father, one that I thought disappeared when he was gone. The large, round diamond is cushioned into an antique setting that is adorned with smaller diamonds all around the gold band. The sophistication and uniqueness of it screams Milena's aged sense of style.

"I knew it would be perfect on you. Now you will always have another piece of her left with you. One that brings you joy." Cole comes up behind me to rest his chin on my shoulder and admires my decorated finger.

"How'd you get this? I always thought she sold it when my dad left."

Cole kisses the crook of my neck, sending a tickle through my body. "Your dad gave it to me. After I asked permission for his daughter's hand in marriage."

My mouth drops in disbelief. "You did that? When?"

"That last day in the hospital. When you left the room all flushed in embarrassment, we woke up Gav, and I asked both of them. Your dad told me about the ring, and I knew it'd be perfect."

I turn around. Cole's hands drop to my lower back, and my arms wrap around his neck. "You're amazing. I can't wait to spend the rest of my life in our new home with you."

After breaking away from a kiss, he grins at me. "Well, good thing we won't have too long to wait."

I lean away with a curious look on my face.

"You ready to go home, soon-to-be Mrs. Stevens?"

A huge smile forms after he calls me that. "Our house is finished? We can all go home together?"

He reaches for Gavin's hand and starts leading us off the jetty. "I'll never settle for any other way."

Walking from the beach through the entrance to our house feels brand-new, even though no construction was done there. We wanted to keep our shared deck, just removing the small railing that marked the end of my house and the beginning of his. The house still holds its charm, and I never want to remove that memory of my mom. As we walk through the sliding glass doors, we stand in awe of our now huge kitchen with state-of-the-art appliances and granite countertops. It connects to a breakfast room where a new wooden table sits that can seat twelve people.

Cole leans into me and says, "Thought it would be great for family dinners. Everyone can fit around it." I kiss his cheek to let him know that I love it.

The family room is a combination of the previous ones with my décor and his electronics. My sectional couch surrounds a dual-sided, stone-faced fireplace that houses a very large television with surround sound speakers. I giggle to myself and think about how boys never grow too old for their toys. Next to the family room is a set of French doors that walk into a huge game room. All of Gavin's old toys are in there, plus new ones like a Ping-Pong table, pinball machine, and one thing that catches my interest. I wander over to the corner next to the window that faces the ocean, and there is a two-person Mrs. Pac-Man machine, the same one my father and I would spend hours playing. I brush my fingers across the top while Cole stands behind me.

"Thought you could get back some of those lost years with him." As he renders me speechless, I pull his mouth over mine and deeply kiss him to show him how much I love him.

Gavin's screaming breaks us apart from our affection. "Oh my gosh! Hurry up!"

We run down the stairs to find Gavin standing in the hallway, pointing to his bedroom. "It's so big! I have my own surfboard room!"

Part of his bedroom remained untouched since my mom was the one who decorated it for him, but the other side of the room we decided to turn into a surfboard storage room. Carter helped us by building three different types of boards for him that are all leaning against the walls. It is the perfect addition to what my mom had already started.

He excitedly reaches for our hands to take us for a tour. "Mommy and Daddy, can you believe it? It's like the coolest room ever!" Hearing Gavin call Cole Daddy will never get old.

With a glimpse into our bedroom, I notice how much more space there is now that it has its own sitting room with a loveseat, chaise lounge, and fireplace. The rest of the downstairs is made up of two more bedrooms and an office for Cole's real estate work.

While our home is perfect in so many ways, my favorite part remains unchanged: the swing that sways on the porch. Sneaking out while Cole and Gavin are playing in the game room, I sink into it and throw my head back. I close my eyes while it swings back and forth with the gentle breeze.

I get up from the swing and walk to the porch railing. With a sigh of relief, I breathe in the salty air and glance out into the darkness, grateful for the silence of it. As I move back toward the swing, I trip, but am caught by steady arms bringing me back to that day I met him on the beach. "Sweetheart, we really have to stop meeting up like this. Or you just need walking lessons."

I nestle with him on the swing and ask, "How long have you been hiding out in the dark?"

"Hmm … well, I put Gav to bed a few minutes ago, so not too long. But long enough to admire that sweet ass of yours as you leaned against the railing." He nods toward the edge of the porch.

My cheeks flush and I fidget in my seat, embarrassed by his compliment.

He tips my chin up to him and chuckles huskily. "I love that I have this effect on you … that I can make you squirm like that." His voice lowers to a growl. "But right now, I'm thinking of a different way to make you squirm."

Completely turned on, I climb on top of him over the hardness popping up from the Velcro of his board shorts. I still can't believe that I have this type of power over him. God knows he can make me melt with just a look in my direction. Wanting my fiancé at that very second, I rip open his shorts and reach in to grasp him and gently jerk my hand up and down. His breaths shallow, he lifts the tank top over my head and unclasps the bikini top I'm still wearing. Grabbing my chest with some force, he leans in and begins licking my breasts, my nipples hardening with every sensation.

I slide off his lap and bring his shorts down with me. Shimmying out of my own shorts and bikini bottoms, I do a little stripper dance for Cole that causes a shiver to shoot through his body. I push him back on the swing and mount him, feeling every inch of him slide into me. He moans out, "Ohhh … so meant for each other. You fit perfectly around me."

I begin to rock faster on top of him, trying to feel

him through my entire body. With the sweat from our bodies rubbing against each other, I yell out louder than I intend, "Cole, I need to feel all of you … please … harder … faster."

Granting my wish, he thrust his hips with force while I endure the pain of his girth that stretches me from the inside out. Running his lips down my body, it's as if his mouth is searing my skin, and the burning sensation makes me ride him even faster. When our breaths shorten and our bodies constrict, I yank his head up and we come together, basking in the pleasure of each other.

****

After a spa day at Lila's, I walk into the aroma of a home-cooked meal. Following the sounds in the kitchen, I am met by the sight of Cole chopping vegetables, Gavin setting the table, and my dad stirring some concoction that he is spicing and tasting. The soothing sounds of The Zac Brown Band blare through our surround-house speakers while Cole sings along, and Gavin head bangs even though it's far from that type of song.

"Am I interrupting a guy's night? Or are you cooking me this feast? Which, by the way, smells delicious." I move next to Cole and whisper, "And looks delicious, too." His low growl turns me on so that I back away before I attack him.

"Well, honey, the three of us thought it was a perfect time for a family dinner … a very special one … an engagement one." My dad, decked out in a *Back off. I'm the Chef.* apron, has that goofy father-of-the-bride grin plastered across his face.

I hug him and place a kiss on his cheek. "Sounds perfect! Now what can I do?"

Cole grabs my waist and leads me to the stairs. "No way. The bride does nothing but look beautiful. So go get dressed. Our guests will be arriving any minute."

Shaking my head, I start down the stairs and yell up. "I seriously have the best men in my life."

Gavin yells back, "Don't ever forget it, Mommy." An explosion of laughter follows his comment, and I hurry to my bedroom with a skip in my step.

Lila, Carter, Heidi, and Dusty all arrive together, bearing gifts and excitement in their voices. Cole never told any of them about proposing, so when we passed on our news earlier that morning, the girls were dying to see my ring and the guys could only think about one thing, the bachelor party. Lila and Heidi push through their men and practically rip off my finger to get a glimpse of the ring.

Between the oohing and aahing, Lila spurts out, "That bastard. That's one huge fucking rock on your hand. And of course, Milena had her hand in it … literally."

I laugh at her candidness and add, "Like you actually thought death would stop my mom from controlling this part of my life. She had a plan for everything."

As Gavin pulls Lila away to see the new game room, Heidi continues to grasp my hand. As she admires my sparkling finger, a stray tear drips down her cheek. Startled by her onset of emotion, I squeeze her shoulder. "Everything okay? Did I do something wrong."

She shakes her head and explains, "No, I'm just a blubbery mess when it comes to weddings and brides. Especially when it happens to be the person that saved my brother." She wraps her arms around me tightly. "Camryn, I can't tell you how grateful we all are that you're in his life. He's alive again because of you."

Peeking over her shoulder to Cole, whose baby blues are admiring me, I blow him a kiss, which he pretends to catch in his hand. After I lean away from her embrace, I glance at her, her hand still gripping mine. "No, I can't take credit for that. We saved each other. We brought each other back to life."

She hugs me again, and my words finally sink in. All this time I had been fighting the idea of us, blaming myself for what happened, trying to protect him from me. Instead, we needed everything to happen, to feel the pain of loss, in order to breathe again, a breath that we now share together.

When she pulls away from the embrace, she gushes, "I've always wanted a sister."

I smile back and add, "Now you have one."

Everyone fits around our new table with a few empty spots to spare. Cole insists that one day those open places will be filled with more children of our own, making me smile at his want for a large family. As we all enjoy our decadent, chocolate engagement cake, I stand up to make an announcement. "Thank you for such an amazing evening. Everything was—or should I say is— perfect. As I watch our best friends and family gather around this table tonight eating, talking, celebrating, I made a decision. One that my fiancé doesn't even know yet."

I glance down to Cole who is watching me with curious eyes. "I realize that I've been searching for perfection my whole life, but instead I always fell short and focused on the negative."

Cole's hand clutches mine as I begin to express more. "Coming back home, I found out I was completely wrong. In my life, perfection is an amazing son who lights up my darkness, a fiancé who is, and always will be, my better half, a father who is willing to give me a second chance, and family and friends who support me in more ways than I could ever imagine."

I take a deep breath and continue, "What I'm trying to say is that I don't need to search any longer. Everything perfect is sitting right here around this table. And I don't want to wait any longer."

I grip Cole's face in my hands and continue. "I don't want to be your fiancé. I want to be your wife. Cole, will you marry right here on this beach—our beach—in one week?"

Cole raises up from his seat, never taking his eyes from me. "I already told you, when it comes to you, my answer is always yes." He slowly moves toward my lips and gently meets his to them.

Clanking her glass, Lila's voice brings us back to our guests, "As the self-declared maid of honor, I want to make a toast."

Everyone raises their glasses in the air.

"I once told my best friend that perfection doesn't exist. But this one time in my life I was wrong. It does exist. It's just different for everyone. It's what I call … Gavin cover your ears, please … perfucktion. So to Cam and Cole's perfucktion."

By the time dessert is eaten, our beach wedding is planned. Lila is handling bridesmaid dresses for her and Heidi, and summer suits, as she calls them, for the guys. Heidi is taking care of flowers and decorations. Dusty already has a call into a reggae band he knows, and Carter hires Jace, his employee who is also a photojournalism student, to take the pictures. Finally, my dad is in charge of the food and cake. I already know the dress I want to wear, so Lila and I make plans to handle that tomorrow.

After everyone leaves and Gavin is passed out on the couch, my father hangs around and helps us clean up. There is one more plan for the wedding that I need to take care, so I ask my dad to come out on the deck with me.

Leaning on the railing, I cuddle next to him to savor his warmth from the cool late-summer breeze that is blowing through. "Thanks for everything, Dad."

"No, sweetie, I should be thanking you for letting me back in. There's not a day that goes by that I don't regret some of the decisions I made."

Before he can go any further, I interrupt. "Stop. Don't do that to yourself. You made the decisions that were best at that time. You put yourself last so everyone else could be happy. So no more regrets, okay?"

He nods, but I can still see him wrestling with those choices in his head. "I need to ask you something, and it's totally fine if you aren't comfortable with it.

"You know you can ask me anything, Goldfish."

"Will you walk me down the aisle and give me away next week on my wedding day?"

Watching tears trickle down his face through the reflection of the light shining from inside the house, I hold him tighter against me. "It will be the greatest honor of my life."

For a moment, we stand against each other and gaze out toward the sound of crashing waves. The ocean was a place of fond memories as a child with my father, one that's become the same for my own son. And now it will be a place of unforgettable memories when he marches with me toward it to give me away to the man I love.

****

A crystal-clear sky and soft ocean breeze characterize our wedding day. Even after enjoying a late night of club music, dancing, and shows with half-naked men, I pop out of bed feeling alive. The guys slept at Dusty's while they partook in their own bachelor party festivities. From what Lila heard from Carter, there was gambling, strippers, and beer. Living thirty minutes outside of a casino town always has that effect on a guys' night out.

Lila spends the morning primping me as she does my nails, hair, and makeup while Heidi puts all the finishing touches on the decorations. She spreads rose petals from the bottom of our deck to the archway that is set up in front of the ocean, where Cole and I will stand to profess our undying love for each other. Gerbera Daisies and Calla Lilies are woven throughout the trellis and match her and Lila's bouquets. She made mine with red and white roses, which she says symbolizes the love and life Cole and I have given to each other.

After Lila and Heidi help with my dress, a knock comes to my bedroom door. I open it to see my father and Gavin on the other side, both wearing khaki-colored pants and white button-down shirts. They stare in awe of me as I stand in my wedding gown.

"Wow, Mommy, you look so pretty!"

I crouch down and plant a kiss on his nose. "Thank you. You're not too shabby yourself."

He rolls his eyes at me and replies, "I know that, already."

I laugh at his lack of modesty as he runs away upstairs to go find the snacks Lila and Heidi made for him.

My father reaches for my hand and brings it to his lips. "You look stunning. Just like your mother looked in that same dress on our wedding day."

From the day I saw this gown hanging in my mom's closet, I always knew I would wear it on my wedding day. It is a champagne-colored silk gown that flows down to my feet with a small train that follows, but it hugs each curve on my body perfectly. Its straps drape over my shoulder and hang loose, exposing most of my back. Silver appliqués wrap around my hips to separate the top of the dress from the bottom.

"I figured it could be my something old." Securing the jeweled comb Lila placed in my hair, I ask, "You remembered that she wore this on your wedding day?"

"How could I forget? She looked like an angel." His gaze becomes distant, as if he is reliving that day in his own thoughts. It's apparent that, although my mom hurt him, he never stopped loving her.

I kiss him on the cheek and hook my arm into his elbow. "You ready for this walk, Dad?"

He looks at me with adoring eyes. "Never been more ready for anything in my life."

As we make our way to the deck overlooking the array of colors from the flowers and the reflection of the sun off the gleaming water, Lila hands me a gift bag. I eye her with confusion, but she just shrugs her shoulders. "I'm only the messenger."

Pulling out a square, velvet box from the bag, I unfold the note card and begin reading it.

Beautiful Girl,
In this box is a symbol of us—our present and our future. Wear it every day as a reminder to always look ahead. When you walk down the aisle today, I'll be waiting for you at the end ... just look up.
Love always and forever,
Cole

I open the box to find a diamond eternity band. Raised between the diamonds are the birthstones of Gavin, Cole, and me. When I removed the ring, a small slip of paper falls out that says, *There is room for more birthstones. Let's plan to fill up the entire thing!*

Warmed by his love for family, I place the ring in front of my engagement ring to represent our eternal love for each other—our future.

When we hear the cue from the reggae band, Heidi, Lila, and Gavin all start to march down the stairs to the rose petals that mark the beginning of the aisle. My father and I lag behind to wait for the tempo to slow, the signal of our entrance. As we wait, my dad grips my elbow and whispers, "You're nothing short of amazing. Have no doubts that Cole found his perfect match." He takes a deep breath and leads me, a daughter he sacrificed his own time and life for, down the aisle to the man who will now take control of my heart.

Cole looks striking in tan linen pants and a white button-down shirt that is untucked at his waist. Just enough of his sleek chest pops out from the top of the shirt to make my body tingle all over. His hair, which had grown out longer in the last few weeks, is styled with each strand gelled perfectly in all different directions. It's what I consider the perfect mess. His blue eyes sparkle against the backdrop of the clear sky meeting the shimmering ocean. As my dad places me into Cole's grasp, I am met by watery eyes and the sexiest smile, which stops me dead in my tracks.

He whispers in my ear, his breath sending shivers down my spine. "You just took my breath away."

I whisper back, "Pretty sure mine still hasn't showed up." After a deep kiss, we turn our attention to the minister, who is clearing his throat, distracting us from our intimacy.

After he greets our small wedding party and introduces the two of us to the congregation, he turns his attention to us and directs, "I understand you both have written your own vows. Cole, when you're ready, you may begin."

Taking hold of my hands and staring deep into my eyes, he begins. "Camryn, when did I fall in love with you? When I was seventeen? When I found you again a few months ago? I'll never know because I don't think there was ever a time that I wasn't in love with you. The very first time you looked into my eyes, you tied me down and I was left unguarded. You are the only person who can see through my broken soul to find the parts that are complete, reach into my shattered heart and somehow make it whole again. Without you, I don't exist, my heart doesn't beat, my soul is left empty. The day you said yes was the day my life began."

The honesty in his words sends tears down his cheeks, compelling me to brush them away so I can see the joy that now lives behind his eyes. His vows trump any previous thought that I am destroying him because through these words, I can only see healing.

Bringing me back to the moment, the presider summons. "Camryn, it is now your turn to pledge your love to Cole."

Still shaky from his heartfelt pledge, I take a deep breath and wipe the tears from my own cheeks. "Cole, in you I've found my other half, the person who gives me purpose … my soul mate. Without you I'm lost, my life incomplete. You have given me a reason to stay, to believe in love, to trust in forever. You have shown me how to give a part of myself that can break, to love hard when there is love to be had, and to accept that our own perfection can exist. You found me when I was lost. You saved me when I didn't feel worthy of saving. With you, I'm finally able to breathe again."

In the moment of silence that follows, we stare in each other's eyes to see the reflection of two people that were once adrift now anchored by love and commitment. Our hands tremble from the depth of emotion we expressed as we place our wedding bands on each other. Once declared husband and wife, Cole dips me down to the rose petals beneath us and lands a kiss on my lips that weakens my knees and practically knocks me off my feet. As we walk hand-in-hand down the aisle together, followed by the ones we love, I gaze into the eyes of my husband, my lover, my other half, and know that we have finally been found.

****

Six Months Later…

RECLINING IN THE CHAIR, I SIT FROZEN, STARING INTENTLY AT THE CONTINUOUS SWIRLS ENGRAVED ON THE CEILING PANELS THAT SURROUND THE LARGE FLUORESCENT LIGHTS. I PICTURE HIM GRASPING MY HAND AND KISSING THE TOP OF MY HEAD, ASSURING ME THAT EVERYTHING WILL BE OKAY. HE USED TO ALWAYS MAKE ME FEEL SAFE AND DESIRED, LIKE I AM THE ONLY PERSON THAT EXISTS IN HIS WORLD.

Rolling my head toward the sound of the nurse's voice, I become even more aware of the loneliness that crept its way into my life with no sign of leaving. After clearing her throat and repeating my name for what was probably a fourth time, the nurse says, "Mrs. Stevens … Camryn … do you understand?"

I force a slight nod and stare as the nurse exits the room with a smile that radiates pity. With my breaths shortening and lungs constricting, I dash out of the medical building to avoid the impending panic attack.

Outside in the parking lot I can see him—just waiting. As soon as his baby-blue eyes meet mine, he begins to walk toward me. He is reaching out to me, calling me to safety in his grasp. As I inch toward him with my hands extended, he pulls me in with steady arms. Just then, he presses me close to his chest and everything goes white…

Awakened by the dream, I shift my body over in bed to face him. My fingers trace over his tattoo of the once broken heart that is now being held together by a dark-haired angel. Always awakened by my touch, his clear eyes glisten at me. "Cole, I'm okay. Go back to sleep. It was just a dream."

A comforting grin stretches across his face as he asks, "Did you finally see your happy ending?"

I reach down to feel the growing swell of my stomach and smile. "Ending? Nope. Just our happy beginning."

The End

EVERNIGHT PUBLISHING ®

www.evernightpublishing.com

Made in the USA
Lexington, KY
09 September 2018